SAD LISA | COLIN MCANDREW

SAD LISA

Colin McAndrew

Published in 2018 by Drew Gordon Publishing

Grateful thanks to Alana Hay for the cover illustration
and Fraser MacDonald for the cover design.

Publishing Services provided by Lumphanan Press
www.lumphananpress.co.uk

For Julie, Fynn and Robyn,
the reason I strive to succeed in everything I do.

For the friends who have supported me,
I learned something from all of you.

For Noah, who taught me that heartbreak can lead to inspiration.

For Buddy, who saved my life.

1

I HATE THE RAIN. I especially hate Scottish rain. It just seems so much colder and wetter than any other rain.

I'm sitting in my car, parked across the street from a block of tenement flats. I don't have the engine running or the radio playing. I look out of the window and I can see people scuttling along the street, hurriedly trying to get home to escape the torrent of water pouring from the angry sky. Black umbrellas hurry along the pavement and the occasional flash of a Waitrose bag tells me I am in a posh part of Edinburgh.

A glance at my watch tells me it's almost seven thirty p.m. I look at the tenement again. The flat on the second floor is my target. The lights are on in what looks very much like a stereotypical student domain. The curtains are half hung, barely visible through the unwashed windows.

It's dark and the rain is not letting up. Water is rushing

along the street now, almost chasing the people carrying the umbrellas.

I quickly glance in all my mirrors and wait for the street to empty. When it does, I pull my hood over my head and step out of the car. Calmly, I walk across the road to the entrance of the flat. The door has a damaged entry system, with half the buttons missing, I smile as I put the lock pick back into my pocket; too easy. I look over my shoulder, quickly scanning the road behind me, and push the door open.

As I expected, the hallway is littered with push-bikes entangled in a maze of chain locks and stacks of phone directories still in the plastic because no-one can be arsed to bend down and pick them up. Random piles of takeaway menus are scattered across the floor, chucked in because someone couldn't be bothered to post them through letterboxes. Crappy dance music thumps upstairs, possibly from where I am headed. I walk up the concrete steps and pass several more push-bikes, which are padlocked to the banister. I kick a few empty pizza boxes out of the way as I walk along the landing to the next flight of stairs. This is the second student related 'job' I've done in recent weeks; students are all the same, live like pigs.

I get to the second landing and stop in front of the target location, a solid wood door, the brown paint blistering around the brass handle. The music that I heard downstairs is much louder now; it's coming from inside the flat. I hesitate momentarily to consider my entrance and ring the doorbell. I wait thirty seconds and no-one answers. I ring the doorbell again and bang on the door three times. Another thirty seconds pass and still no answer. I press the doorbell, hold my finger on the button and in short, hard hits, bang my steel toe cap against the base of the door. The loud music stops and I hear footsteps approaching and an exclamation of "fucking hell!" I step back and prepare myself. The chain rattles and a key turns clumsily in the lock. As the door creeps open I pull my hood down. The rusty chain pulls tight and two dark-rimmed eyes peek over it with caution.

"Yeah?" a man says, in a dozy, London accent, looking at me, somewhat puzzled.

Before he can utter another word, I take a step back and with one kick burst the door open, breaking the chain and knocking the guy out cold. I step into the hallway and look around. The man is lying motionless on the floor, his dark-rimmed eyes now shut and blood trickling from his nose. His student attire of long khaki shorts and a football top barely register as I notice the cigarette he dropped starts to burn the carpet, so I step on it.

As I expected, the décor in the flat is crappy. Empty poly-styrene boxes litter the surfaces, with posters of Scarface and Che Guevara on the grimy walls. My nose wrinkles at the familiar stench of weed and I spot a huge cock drawn in permanent marker on a framed 'House rules' print.

Another guy rushes into the hall and stops dead, looking startled to see me. This one has a shaved head, a pierced eyebrow, smelly, never-been-washed jeans, and a Star Trek T-shirt. I don't think he is going to be a problem and before he has the chance to say anything, I ask:

"Is this Tim?" I point to the unconscious guy on the floor.

"No, that's Fraser. Tim's in the lounge, and who the fuck are you?" he stutters, trying to be a hard man.

Just then, a tall, skinny effort appears in the lounge door-way, holding a joint and flicking the ash into a glass ashtray. He's over six feet tall, wearing semi-fashionable clothes and sporting dark, floppy hair that covers half his face.

"So, what's your problem, mate?" His faux cockney twang fails miserably to hide the plumy undertones in his voice. He reeks of 'Daddy's got money'.

I don't answer but smile, finding his nonchalance amusing.

I walk straight up to him and look into his stone-grey eyes. He doesn't flinch at first and I don't blink, staring being a particular talent of mine. He eventually looks away and nervously flicks his spliff into the ashtray.

"Do you know Michelle Thompson?" I ask as I gently take the ashtray from his hands. He resists slightly, his eyes glancing to the left as I say her name.

"Doesn't ring a bell. Should I know her?"

I smirk at him and take a few steps back, maintaining eye contact the entire time, feeling the cold glass of the ashtray in my hands.

"Pretty petite girl, dark hair, brown eyes, met you at the Laughing Scotsman in town last week. You got a bit rough with her."

He twitches, looking a little nervous, but quickly composes himself.

"Yeah, I remember now, she's a little scrubber, a cock-tease. Stunning girl but not much up here." He taps his temple.

With a bitter smile he takes another draw and bravely blows smoke in my direction, flicking ash onto the carpet with a disdainful glare. I take a step back and empty the contents of the ashtray over his unconscious friend.

"So, forcing yourself on a woman is okay?" I growl.

"Look, mate, I don't know who you are and I really don't care. She was teasing me all night long and then she wouldn't even give me a blow job. I didn't rape her or anything; I just tried to feel her tits and that didn't get me very far; she started crying for her mummy." He sniggers immaturely, and takes another drag, smoke escaping from his nostrils this time.

"Well, dickhead, that girl happens to be a very close friend of mine and my associates. When you upset her, you upset us. The fact that you did not rape her makes you lucky to be alive, I could be splitting your head open with an axe right now."

The ashtray feels cold and hard in my hands, its red

Budweiser logo barely visible under a film of black ash. It was stolen from a pub back in the day when you could smoke in one, no doubt.

"Well, that's sweet, mate," he replies, blowing out smoke between every word and flicking ash behind him. He produces another arrogant snigger, but his hands are shaking.

"Don't say I didn't warn you." I shrug my shoulders and turn my back as if to leave, still rotating the glass ashtray in my hands.

"Can you get fuck out of here now?" asks Tim, gaining confidence at the thought of my departure "The door kicking was really scary and I'm very sorry," he mocks me.

I spin round to face him, swing my right arm back and launch the ashtray at his face, hitting him straight between the eyes with a merciless crack. I don't want to kill the guy, just teach him a lesson.

Tim lets out an ear-splitting scream, bringing his hands up to his face, blood streaming from his nose. I walk towards him and deliver a pin-point accurate kick to his nuts. It surprises even me how hard it is. He lets out another, muffled cry and drops to the floor.

His silent Star Trek pal in the corner squeaks and begins a shaky, half-arsed advance towards me, not knowing whether to have a go and try to look hard or just stay out of the way.

"Don't even think about it," I command. "You are two down, don't make it three." He lowers his head and without a sound steps backwards, stumbling against the wall. A pretty sensible decision considering the mood I am now in.

I turn and walk towards the door, leaving posh boy lying on the floor crying like a baby.

I turn to Star Trek. "I would probably phone an ambulance if I were you. When that cunt stops crying, tell him there will be no more talking because next time, he won't even see me coming."

Star Trek nods, staring down at his tatty Converse, not daring to make eye contact.

I walk out and head down the stairs. Posh Boy's sobs echo down the stairwell. I can hear Yale locks clicking behind doors in response to the commotion, and I jog towards the entrance, making a quick exit.

The rain hasn't stopped and I pull my hood up again, walking back to my car. With one press of the remote key, the doors unlock and the lights flash on and off. The immediate area is illuminated for a split second and sheets of rain bounce off the car bonnet as I open the door.

The engine starts with a growl and I drive to the end of the street, merging with the traffic on the next road. Three streets down I ask voice control to "call Callum" and pull into a space, turning the lights off.

"Aye?" answers Callum.

"It's done," I say.

"Thanks, mate. Sore one?"

I smile before I answer.

"Crying like a little girl. He won't be pretty for a while, put it that way. I'd probably question his ability to procreate because I'm pretty sure I burst one of his nuts too."

Callum laughs. "Superb, mate."

"Tell your niece he won't be bothering her again."

"You are a legend, bud. Get yourself to my house, we're doing the Friday night usual."

"No worries. See you soon."

I hang up and can hear sirens in the distance: time for me to make a move. I start the engine and take the quickest route to the Forth Road Bridge. Job successfully completed, albeit one of the easier ones compared to Callum's usual assignments. I play Eric Clapton to celebrate and as 'Layla' blasts out of the stereo the events from the previous hour fade from my memory.

2

WITHIN HALF AN HOUR I am in the Fife countryside and arrive at a secluded house, beside an area of woodland, at the foot of the Lomond hills. It's eight fifteen p.m. and although I'm still on the driveway, I can hear dance music coming from within. The party is just warming up.

This is Callum's house. He is the gaffer, the boss, the person in charge. A self-made businessman, well known across Fife and Edinburgh, whose canny investments in clubs, properties and shops made him his first million at twenty-eight. Now, at the age of forty, he is well and truly loaded.

Our paths first crossed at amateur kickboxing competitions. I moved into illegal Mixed Martial Arts fights to make a living and did pretty well, earning a decent reputation on the street. Callum had a keen interest in the sport and in knowing the local guys who could handle themselves, skills he could potentially employ to use to his advantage.

The first words he uttered to me were, "I'll pay you three times as much to paste cunts who kick off in my clubs. See you at the Vine Pit at nine p.m. on Saturday."

Admittedly his recruitment methods required some work, but it was the start of a mutually beneficial relationship for both of us.

Pretty soon the word got around that you didn't misbehave in Callum's clubs. The job was common sense really; block the hard guy troublemakers at the door, let the pretty girls in and keep an eye on the coke heads: if you caught them early enough their gear came in handy for later. Two things Callum would not tolerate were weapons – anyone with a blade was banned for life – and harassment of women in his clubs was a pet hate. Despite his occasional underground dealings, his moral compass was generally on the right setting.

Callum has done his fair share of shady dealings but then who in his position hasn't? Officially, and technically, I am on his payroll as the manager of his clubs, a job I have never actually done for him. He pays me £200k a year to represent him and his interests, basically doing the things that he can't be caught doing.

I park my car behind Callum's Range Rover and turn off the engine, grabbing my phone and a bottle of Grey Goose before I get out. I walk up the gravel driveway towards the white Georgian-style mansion, past the perfectly manicured lawn and neat flower beds surrounding it, indicating an owner with slight OCD tendencies.

I can hear music and laughter coming from the house. A light is on in every room and before I get to the door, it swings open. A dark-haired stunner smiles and throws her arms around me.

"Callum said to let you in," she murmurs in my ear.

Her sweet breath is laced with alcohol and her voice has a foreign lilt. She pulls me in by the hand and points to the direction of the lounge before sauntering into the kitchen area. I wonder how many lines she has taken. Callum's house is a lavish affair, with a warren of bedrooms, lounges and studies, perfect for entertaining and no room out of bounds.

"Good evening, brother!" shouts Callum, bringing me a beer and putting his arm around my shoulders.

"Thanks for doing that wee job, mate. I know that was ABCD but you know I appreciate it."

Above and beyond the call of duty was a daily occurrence in my job, not that I would correct him.

"No worries, captain, that's what I do," I reply, taking a swig of beer and walking with him into the kitchen.

On the marble topped island, I see a mountain of white powder on a sheet of glass. Like the beers in the fridge, it's there for the taking, no expense spared. I remove my jacket and hang it over the back of a chair.

"Fancy a dabble?" asks Callum as he prepares a couple of lines with a black Amex.

"Don't mind if I do," I reply as he bends over and snorts the white powder up his left nostril.

"Fucking hell, that's some proper shit," exclaims Callum, standing upright with a wide-eyed look on his face, massaging his nostril with his finger.

I smile as I test my left nostril; the right doesn't offer the same level of suction.

I take the rolled-up fifty from Callum and snort the line that he prepared for me. Fuck me, it's good stuff. My face immediately numbs and I double-blink, pinching my nose between my finger and thumb.

Callum laughs at my reaction and slaps me on the back. We move through to the main lounge where the party has congregated. It's a large room with a white fireplace centre-piece, a seventy-two-inch smart TV on the wall and tasteful, minimalist décor made up of creams and 'mocha'. Predictably, the men are sitting down and talking while the women are dancing around with each other to the music. On the corner couch a couple are feeling amorous and sucking the face off each other so Callum politely reminds them to get a room.

Callum's niece, Michelle, runs up and delivers a kiss onto my lips as she wraps her arms around me. "Thanks for speaking to that wanker for me," she says seriously and for a moment I could see that Posh Boy must have really scared her.

"You're welcome, just stay away from tossers like that, you can do better."

"I know, thanks." She gives me another kiss on the cheek and returns to her friends for a dance. She is half-buckled already.

I look around the room: there are many beautiful women here. Callum wouldn't have it any other way. They are not love interests as such, more for show. Perhaps this makes him shallow, but he thinks it's good for his reputation and more importantly good for business.

The dark-haired girl who opened the door drops into my mind and I scan the room looking for her. When I find her, she is looking right back at me. She really is beautiful, with a lightly tanned complexion, high cheek bones and her eyes… oh dear God. My eyes take in her tight-fitting jeans and simple vest top, a refreshing contrast to the short skirts and cleavage on display elsewhere.

I lean over to Callum and ask who she is.

"She's one of the girls who works in the club. She just started. From Eastern Europe somewhere. Tidy as fuck, eh?"

Callum's compliments were few and far between; having his pick of women made him difficult to please. This girl was obviously special.

"What's her name?" I ask casually.

"Dunno, Lisa or something," replies Callum with disinterest. He has been distracted by the uncut Blurred Lines music video on the massive TV. "I'd use her shite for toothpaste," he utters in a droll tone. The naked model in the video has attracted his full attention.

I smirk at his banter and swig some more beer then look around, noticing that Lisa has left the room. I get up from the chair and as the cocaine is kicking in my confidence levels are through the roof. I feel a sudden urge to find her but first I walk into one of Callum's many bathrooms to check that there is no white powder around my nostrils.

I give myself the once over in a mirror. Nostrils checked. Stubble at just the correct length. Blonde hair textured and looking good. Wait. What the fuck is that? A fuckin grey hair in my sideburn? Nope, not happening and I rip the hair out with my fingertips. I inspect the rest of my face. Eyes still blue, although they do give away that I have been snorting gear. Fuck it, so has everyone else.

Nothing spilled down the T-shirt, great. Rolex looking good and I have my favourite jeans on, sorted.

I leave the bathroom, turn into the hallway and almost collide with Lisa.

"Oh, I am sorry!" she exclaims, laughing and putting a hand on her heart in mock fright.

"Ah sorry, we almost bumped heads there," I say, smiling.

"You are Ronin, right?" she asks me, formally sticking a hand out.

"Yeah, that's right," I say and accept her slender hand into mine. "And you are Lisa?"

"Yes! How did you know this?" She laughs with surprise.

"I know everything," I say as I let go of her hand and continue to walk down the hallway.

She laughs again as I walk away and I hear the bathroom door close behind her.

Shit, was that too corny? I think to myself. The coke confidence is wearing off and my usual self-doubt creeping back in.

As the night goes on, we see each other frequently, exchanging shy smiles and secret glances from opposite ends of the room.

It's now two a.m., half the cocaine has gone and the party is in full swing. The thirty or so people in the house are letting loose in every public room, drinking, dancing, snorting, talking shite in that order, on repeat.

I find Davey in the kitchen, a hard nut I've known for years. A long-time associate of Callum's with a reputation akin to a Mafioso. His stories, if they are to be believed, scare the shit out of me; he's fucking mental.

"I wis oot ma nut, ken? So, ah says to the boy, don't come fucking near my wuman again or I'll break your balls wi' your own fuckin' heid! I can't be fucking arsed with thae' Kirkcaldy radges, ken why Ronin? Cos they're fucking crazy, every single one of the bastards!" For a moment he looks deadly serious. Then he throws back his head, roaring with laughter, acknowledging the irony in his statement.

I laugh too. He is fucked; foam is gathering at the corners of his mouth from the incessant talking so he takes another swig of his beer. He launches into the same story again and I look around quickly for an excuse to escape.

Cheering is coming from the lounge and I see Callum leading a crowd of revellers through the hall towards us in the kitchen. There is a look of mischief on his face.

"It's time for a challenge, Ronin," he says, beaming.

"No, no, no," I say, waving my hands in dismissal. "I'm not doing it anymore."

"Come on, mate, just one more time. It's big Disco, he fancies his chances."

Everyone is piling into the kitchen and gathering around the central island.

I give in.

"Okay, get the stuff but this is the last time."

Callum smiles and heads through to his garage via a door at the far side of his kitchen.

Disco appears from the lounge, snarling comically, telling me he is ready for me. I smile and shake my head in disbelief. Disco is over six feet tall and despite his impressive stature, it's common knowledge that he doesn't 'do' gyms; his fitness regime is limited to walking his Lhasa Apso and occasionally living it large at an old school rave on a Saturday night. Disco's partiality to ecstasy pills gave him his nickname. Generally, an all-round good guy, so I am reluctant to do this with him.

Callum comes bounding through from the garage with police body armour, acquired in return for a favour after a certain DC Fitzgerald was 'seen' frequenting a massage parlour, and dumps it on the kitchen floor. To ready himself, Disco approaches the white powder on the table and snorts a couple of big lines.

"Come on," he goads, pulling his T-shirt off to reveal an extremely hairy body, slightly protruding pot-belly and man boobs. His jaw is on autopilot and this nakedness with his gurning makes it an unpleasant sight.

Everyone cheers as he pulls on the body armour and dances around like a boxer, stopping to tense his jelly-covered muscles at me in defiance. The group erupt in laughter, clapping their hands in support.

"Come on, let's go!" shouts Callum as he leads us out through the French doors into the back garden and onto the lawn behind his kitchen. Everyone laughs again as we watch Disco trying to walk in the padded body armour, like an ice hockey goalie.

Disco and I face each other. He is psyching himself up, still tensing the little muscle he has. I grin at him. I'll let him choose.

"Okay, how hard do you want it?" I ask.

"As hard as you can, I'm ready. Come on, you poof!"

The crowd let out a pantomime "Oooooh!"

"Are you ready?" I ask Disco, as I get into position and prepare to kick him.

"Come on, while I'm young, ya fanny!" he shouts.

Thud! I deliver a sledgehammer side kick into his midsection and with a groan he crumples to the ground in a heap. Everyone cheers and laughs. Disco staggers as he gets up and throws up all over Callum's patio. When he is finished he approaches me, wiping his chin of any remaining puke.

"Jesus Christ, that was a kick and a half. Let's do it again!"

"No chance. Once is more than enough for both of us," I reply.

"Aye, I just lost the sausage supper I had for ma tea."

I pat him on the back to make sure he is okay. I don't like being the centre of attention, getting too old for it now, but it's a crowd pleaser and I get a certain buzz out of it although would never admit it. Most people go back into the house, the party games now over. Davey appears at my shoulder and hands me a joint.

"That was fucking class, man."

I smile and wave the joint away. Smoking in any form just doesn't interest me.

Callum approaches and puts his hand on my arm, still laughing from the kick. "That was fucking superb, mate. I will never get tired of seeing that."

We head back to the kitchen for more beer and the doorbell rings. Callum looks at me with a raised eyebrow and heads towards the front door. Three a.m. is a bit late for visitors.

He peers through the window and snorts "Fuck" to himself and his jaw clenches. I'm half expecting the police but get the feeling it's someone worse. With an exasperated shake of his head, Callum opens the door.

3

I WALK DOWN THE HALLWAY towards him, curious to see who has caused such a reaction.

Three men step through the doorway, exchanging insincere hand-shakes with Callum and strut down the hall like peacocks showing off their feathers.

The penny drops and I realise who they are. I fucking hate these pricks. Sandy Pratt and his two lackeys like to think they are gangsters. Sandy is a forty-something, chubby, balding little fucker whose eyes are too small for his bulbous head and clothes too tight for his expanding waistline. He comes towards me, sweat trickling down his left temple, looking wired, clearly fucked up on some kind of gear.

"Ronin, how you doing, my friend?" he shouts as he approaches me, offering his hand and a simpering smile. He's winding me up; there is no love lost between us.

I grimace inwardly and reluctantly shake his hand to keep

the peace, exchanging a few words of strained banter and nodding politely to his two flunkies, who are trying to look hard. I look behind them towards Callum, who is closing and locking the front door with a sigh. Davey has followed me down the hall and introduced himself, so I edge past them to catch Callum.

"What the fuck is that cunt doing here?" I ask.

"Fuck knows, mate. I wouldn't have him here if I had the choice."

"Well tell him to fuck off then!"

Callum raises an eyebrow and pats me on the shoulder. "Keep your friends close but your enemies closer, mate. I've been doing a bit of business with him."

He leaves me to join them and for a moment I'm taken aback that Callum would consider working with these pricks and why he hasn't told me about it.

I join them in the kitchen, where Sandy is boasting about a girl he allegedly shagged in the toilets of Callum's nightclub.

"She went like the clappers, fucking shaved fanny, plastic tits, the whole package, like."

"You've been doing too much gear, Sandy, because that's clearly a pile of shite, either that or you've got a fucking wild imagination," quips Davey, laughing.

The group snigger with him and Sandy's face darkens. He quickly composes himself and attempts a fake laugh. "There's nothing imaginary about these, my friend," replies Sandy, as he pulls a pair of black French knickers from his pocket.

"Fuckin hell, you stole them from your ma's drawer, ya cunt!" retorts Davey and everyone else bursts into laughter again.

Sandy, now clearly pissed off, smiles at Davey and puts the knickers back in his pocket. "Speaking of knickers…" he says, looking towards the living room full of scantily clad women, and heads in their direction.

The two goons scowl at Davey, who flicks his middle finger at them with a brazen grin. As they turn their backs Davey laughs out loud.

"Who invited that bell end? I fuckin hate that wee troll. He looks like fuckin Les Dawson except sweatier!"

Callum and I laugh but the others don't. The Les Dawson reference is lost on the younger crew.

"Just watch him, though, he's one to keep an eye on," utters Callum, suddenly changing the tone of the conversation. "He's a spiteful wee bastard at times, so he'll be thinking of ways to get back at you now."

Davey shrugs and takes a swig of beer. "Fuck him, he can bring it on if he wants to, he doesn't scare me."

I glance at Callum and he looks back at me. His face is still. He's clearly got something on his mind since that prick turned up.

I change the subject. "That's decent stuff you've got tonight, not like the talcum powder you had last time."

"Aye, it definitely is, mate. I went back to the other boy I know. He phoned me to say he had some dynamite stuff, so he got the business."

I nod in agreement and swig my beer as Disco launches into a story about the dynamite eccies he had at T in the Park in 2007 and the sniffer dog who wouldn't leave his balls alone. That's what happens when you tape a bag of pills to your nut sack.

4

It's much later now, taxis have been and gone and the few remaining stragglers are crashed out in various bedrooms and on couches and floors.

The music is turned off and Callum, sitting on a sofa, swigging a beer, is flicking between music channels. Other folk are in the spiral of coke-inspired conversations, saying the most random shit, and talking over each other, unable to get their words out fast enough. One guy is desperate to speak and is impatiently nodding, waiting for his turn, butting in every time there is a pause in the conversation.

I sit down next to Callum who nods to me. I nod back. We are buckled, full of drugs and beer and at this stage in the evening raised eyebrows and simple nods can say so much.

I look around the room and I notice Sandy Pratt and his goons are missing. I turn to Callum. "Has that wee arsehole left?" I ask.

Callum scans the room and replies, "I didn't notice him leaving, maybe he's upstairs. Go and check the wee cunt's not trying to unlock the safe in my bedroom."

Callum produces a dry smile and I get up to start my search.

I walk through to the kitchen where Davey is still talking, this time to a group of younger guys and girls. The storytelling has moved on to the time he bribed a local MP and council planners to build a block of flats. His guise as a builder affords him the opportunity to camouflage many of his criminal activities.

"Have you seen Sandy?" I ask him.

"Not for a while. He was bothering the Eastern European lassies earlier, then he slithered upstairs," Davey replies.

Come to think of it, I haven't seen Lisa for a while. I walk into the hallway from the kitchen, passing a couple of bathrooms and a dining room and arrive at the foot of the stairs. I hear voices and look up to the top landing; the noise is coming from one of the bedrooms.

As I get to the top of the stairs, I trip over a girl, who has passed out 'starfish' style on the floor, with a glass of wine in one hand and a white handbag in the other. I take the glass from her and place it on the window ledge. She's still breathing, so I move her into the recovery position and carry on.

Sandy's goons are standing at the end of the landing in front of a bedroom door. Hands clasped, legs apart, clearly guarding the entrance to the room. A blonde-haired girl in a short dress and bare feet is trying to push past them. They are nudging her back, laughing, as if it's a joke, but the girl is clearly distressed.

I walk over to them, and the blonde looks relieved to see me. "It's not funny anymore. Lisa is in there with that sleazy bald guy and she wants to come out. They won't let her out and they won't let me in."

"It's okay, I'll sort it," I reassure her. "Alright, boys, what's going on?"

They both smirk and one replies, "Nothing, just standing here for a rest, chief."

I smile back and move towards the door. They both move their shoulders together, blocking my path. "Can't let you disturb them, chief," one growls and puts his hand on my shoulder.

"Get your fucking hand off me," I tell him slowly.

The lad is big, but he's young and looks worried. He removes his hand and I take a step back looking the two of them up and down. The shaved heads and long overcoats don't make them gangsters, despite what they may think.

"CALLUM!" I shout, hoping that my voice will travel the distance of the landing and downstairs. I wait a moment. There's no answer, so I turn to the girl and tell her to find Callum.

"Shouting for your boyfriend?" says the red-haired one. I smile at him. If this kicks off, I'll break his nose first. I hear a muffled noise coming from inside the room and step towards the boys again.

Callum comes up the stairs behind me. "What the fuck is it?" he says, pissed off that there is drama brewing.

"That wee arsehole is in there with a girl and won't let her out," I tell him.

"For fuck's sake," utters Callum as he pushes past the two goons and tries to open the door. It's locked. He thumps on the door. "Sandy, what the fuck is going on?"

There is a commotion from inside and the door handle turns. Lisa's voice screams, "Help me!"

I move towards the door again and the two morons react. One pushes Callum and the red head takes a swing at me. I instinctively lean back and his punch misses me by a mile. I swing my arm before he regains composure and crack him on the nose with a hard punch from my right hand. He falls back against the door, his hands holding his face. The other goon turns to me and before he can react I smack him, just as hard, and he collapses next to his buddy.

"Kick the fuckin door in," shouts Callum.

I take a step back and smash the door open, breaking the lock, sending splinters of wood in multiple directions.

Sandy Pratt is standing in the middle of the room with Lisa. His shirt is open, belly hanging out and he has a fistful of Lisa's hair in one hand and a tight grip of her arm in the other. She is whimpering. Her lip is burst and bloody, face bruised and she has mascara-stained tears streaming down her cheeks.

"She's a fuckin slut, fuck her, don't get involved Ronin, it's not my fault, she deserves this." Sandy is ranting but making little sense, he's foaming at the mouth and it looks like he's on something far stronger than coke.

I move towards him slowly, keeping an eye on his movements. He is holding Lisa's hair so tightly that his knuckles are white. I signal to her to keep quiet and calm down, she nods slightly in agreement.

Callum grabs my arm and whispers, "Don't hurt him." I throw him an incredulous look but nod reluctantly.

I go straight up to Sandy and his bravado disappears as I grab his wrist. He releases Lisa's hair without a struggle and hastily pulls away from me with glazed, wide eyes. He's clearly off his fucking tits, sweating profusely with dilated pupils. I want to fucking leather him.

Lisa scrambles away from him and runs out of the room. Callum follows her and I can hear his calm tones trying to put her at ease.

"Fucking sit down," I say to Sandy, pointing to the bed.

He hesitates so I grab him by his fat chin and force him to sit. It takes all my control to resist smashing his pasty face and throw him out the window. Callum's instruction has pissed me off, but he's the boss.

"I know she wants me, she fancies me, I could tell the last

time we met. Her pals were there, they will tell you. I couldn't find her, she disappeared, but I've found her again, its destiny, it's destiny, it's meant to be." He's speaking quickly, barely coherent and eyes now rolling in his head. What the fuck is he on?

Callum walks back in and shouts, "Not fuckin good enough. Get the fuck out of here now!"

The two goons appear. I'm ready for round two if they want it but they grab Sandy by the arms, haul him to his feet and drag him into the hall. The red-haired goon mumbles something as he walks past me, so I smack him in the side of the face, channelling the unspent rage I had reserved for Sandy. My hand throbs as a consequence and he doesn't get up this time.

Callum gets on his mobile and arranges for some help to cart these pricks out of here. I can hear Sandy ranting from downstairs and I go out to the hall to find Lisa.

She is sitting on the red chaise longue at the end of the landing with the blonde. She looks up at me and I beckon her over. She's not crying any more but she is obviously shaken and walks up to me without saying a word. I lead her to another room with an en-suite and soak a cloth for her. She dabs her lip gently, grimacing with pain. Her friend follows behind her, ranting about how she is going to arrange for her cousins to 'batter' Sandy.

The doorbell rings and I look out of the bedroom window to the driveway below to see a white van in the drive and two men standing at the front door.

"They're here," I announce. "I'll be back in a minute," I say to Lisa.

I go downstairs. Callum and the two men are struggling to escort Sandy and his goons into the back of the van. Davey appears with a hammer.

"Need a hand, guys?"

"I think they've got it covered, Davey, thanks."

"Fuck sake, I miss out on all the action."

When Sandy and his crew are safely in the back of the van, the two guys shout me over and put a small plastic bag of white powder in my hand.

"Here, take this, it's good stuff. We took it off a wee radge earlier on."

"Thanks, mate," I say, passing the bag to Davey.

It's amazing what money can buy. Callum even has CID boys on the payroll and these two are as bent as they come. Davey hands the bag to Callum, who chucks the coke dismissively onto the table. He's clearly calling it a night. A bunch of stragglers are still hovering around and Davey tells them it's time to go home.

"Go and see if Lisa's okay. Tell me if she needs anything," Callum whispers to me and then retires to the sofa.

I knock gently on the bedroom door upstairs, opening it to see Lisa curled up on the bed. When she lays eyes on me, tears start rolling down her cheeks again and she tries to wipe them away with a tissue.

"Are you okay?" I ask. I sit carefully on the end of the bed.

She nods and continues to sniffle into her tissue.

"What happened back there? Why would anyone want to go into a room with that little sleaze bag?"

"I didn't want to. He tried to invite me into his room but I refused. Then he pulled me in, locked the door and wouldn't let me leave. The two guys held the door shut and pushed me back in whenever I tried to unlock it to get out. It was horrible. He started dancing around and asked me if I found him attractive. Then he hit me when I didn't answer quickly enough. I didn't know what to say to him. He wasn't like this last time I saw him."

"You know him then?" I ask, surprised.

"Yes, we met in the Vine Pit a few months ago. I was with my friends and we were dancing. He kept asking us to join him and his friends and sent champagne from the bar to us. He tried to be charming but I made it clear that I was not interested."

I gently lean over and pull her hand away from the side of her face. There's a red scrape just at the side of her cheek bone. Lisa doesn't put up a fight; she lets me inspect the wound.

"I think you'll need to clean that up. You're going to have a bruise there. Did he do anything else to you?" I ask.

"No, he kept grabbing at me and trying to hit me but I managed to dodge most of them. He was very wasted," she replied.

"Why don't you go and have a shower. I'll get you some clothes to wear. You'll feel better after it."

Lisa nods uneasily, looking at the door.

"Don't worry, he's not coming back and nobody will disturb you."

She manages a delicate smile from underneath her tear-soaked face.

I leave the room, closing the door behind me. What a fucked-up way to end what was a great evening. There's nothing like a fight to sober everyone up.

As I get downstairs, I see that most of the lights are out and only the sound of Callum's TV breaks the silence. Callum has passed out, a beer on the arm of his chair. I move the bottle on to the table next to him and check that he's still breathing: he is. I turn off the telly and leave him to sleep.

I head back upstairs and into Callum's bedroom. I open his drawers to look for some shorts and T-shirt or something loose-fitting for Lisa. He's a tall fucker, so everything is massive. I pick up a random set of shorts and T-shirt and close his drawer.

Outside Lisa's bedroom, I can hear the shower. I give the door a gentle knock and because there is no reply I slowly open the door and peer in. There's a pile of clothes on the floor next to the en-suite door. I lay the shorts and T-shirt on the bed and pick up a couple of beer bottles that are sitting, half empty, on the bedside cabinet. As I head towards the door, I hear the shower stop and slow drips of water landing on the shower tray.

The en-suite door opens and Lisa walks out, still dripping wet. I look and then look away quickly. She's completely naked.

"Sorry, I was just bringing you some clothes; I'll leave you to it."

I put my hand on the door handle and Lisa moves towards me again.

"Don't leave," she says. I still can't look at her, even when she places her hands on to mine and stands at the side of me. I'm still holding onto the door and I feel unusually embarrassed.

Then I let go of the handle and turn to face her. I look at her eyes. Without the mascara and make-up she is naturally beautiful.

Lisa leans towards me, as if she wants to kiss me, but I swerve and grab a towel from the back of the en-suite door. I wrap it round her and sit her on the bed.

"You don't need to do this, you don't owe me anything," I say.

"I want to," she says and leans towards me again.

I put my hands on her shoulders to stop her from getting too close. Her forwardness surprises me and I wonder if she is still scared and looking for comfort.

"You've been through enough tonight. Get some rest."

She looks hurt, almost as if she's going to cry again.

"Sorry, but this isn't the right time for either of us. I'll be downstairs if you need me."

She looks down and nods. She pulls the towel tightly around her and stands up, turning her back on me. I leave the room silently, closing the door behind me. I exhale loudly, heart pounding in my chest, rattled by the effect this girl has on me.

Davey is snoring face down on the kitchen table, and I spot an empty sofa in the hallway next to the front door. I lie on it, exhausted, head buzzing from the narcotics and events of the evening. I look at my watch: it's four fifty a.m. For a house that was pumping earlier on, it's now eerily silent. I need to get some sleep.

5

I HEAR THEIR VOICES GETTING louder. They've been drinking, again. The aggressive, spiteful tones and slurred speech expose the level of their intoxication. They are barely making sense as they spit out angry words in an all too familiar exchange of insults.

Their voices are so loud that I can't hear what Fred Flintstone is saying to Wilma on the telly.

I peer around the corner of the kitchen door and watch them spew out hatred to each other, pointing fingers in each other's faces; their emotions are dark, clouded and unreasonable from the cheap vodka they've been guzzling. During the vicious fight, they manage to pause, hurriedly lighting cigarettes and sucking on them like they are their only source of life for the next few seconds.

The woman chucks her empty fag packet at the man, baiting him to lash out. He takes a long, slow drag from his cigarette and blows the grey smoke into her face.

The woman hits the man in retaliation. Not a slap but a punch, to the left cheek. Then another and another. She draws blood. He's tried to restrain himself, clinging to his morals, but she goads him, drives him to breaking point, spitting in his face and screaming, "Hit me! Hit me!"

Silently I start to cry, terrified. I know it's game over. The man wipes the greasy, vodka-scented mucus from his cheek and delivers a right hook to her cheek bone. She goes down like a ton of bricks. He's not finished. With incredible, anger-fuelled strength, he tosses the kitchen table onto its side, so he can get to her. He leans over her slight frame, delivering hard, accurate strikes to her face. She is too dazed to fight back. He straightens up and delivers two final kicks to her stomach and stands back, pausing to review his handiwork.

He lights another cigarette and leans against the table, puffing on it in between panting from his exertion.

There's no shouting any more, only a barely conscious whimper coming from her, a sound that still haunts my soul. He tosses various objects from around the room on top of her. Dish towels, newspapers, teabags, anything to add to the humiliation. He grabs three apples from the fruit bowl and drops them on the floor, stamping on the pink exterior until the skin bursts and kicks the squashed pieces at her.

Ladies and gentleman, I introduce you to my parents.

My sobs are uncontrollable now, catching in my throat as I try to stay quiet. I find it difficult to breathe. Witnessing such violence at five years old is petrifying. I'm shaking all over, rooted to the spot with fear but desperately wanting to flee the horrific scene in front of me.

My father spots me from the corner of his eye. I bolt like a frightened rabbit, negotiating the short hallway, up the narrow staircase, along the short landing and into the linen cupboard. He pursues me and I barely get the louvre door shut before it is thrust open.

I put my hands up to block any blows that may be coming my way. Nothing happens and I open my eyes. My father is standing in front of me, breathing heavily and sobbing, swaying at the same time. He's drunk and looks like a tramp, all dishevelled with a week-old stubble. His hands are shaking from all the punching, his knuckles are red raw and he has my mum's blood on his fingers. He still manages to hold on to the cigarette.

"I didn't want that to happen, son, but she pushed me too far. She's always pushing me too far."

Silence, I have found through experience, is the best response in these situations.

I sit back in the linen cupboard and my muscles relax; they are no longer tensed and ready to spring into action. It hurts when you have been tensing for so long. I don't know what to say or what to do. I have given up. Nobody is right here. They are both wrong, so wrong to behave like that towards each other and absolutely despicable to behave like that with a kid in the house.

My tears are drying up and I sit in silence as I watch my father pace back and forward. He wants to go downstairs but he's scared to see the result of his handiwork.

I stare at the floor and start to cry again, not out loud. I internalise the pain. Tears stream down my face and drop onto my T-shirt like drips from a tap. I pull a towel down from the shelf and wrap it around myself. I want to be hugged and comforted. I don't want to have to think about what I just saw ever again but I already know it will haunt my dreams. I look down to see the front of my shorts are damp. I can't show him that, he'll go crazy. I spread the towel over my legs to hide the wet patch.

I hear someone whisper my name. A voice that is familiar but I just can't place it. It's like an echo. I look around and my father is gone. It feels strange and I can't see anything, like I am in a room full of fog. Someone touches my arm.

"Shit, what the fuck!" I exclaim as I roll off the couch in Callum's hallway. Sitting on the floor I realise that I have had yet another bad dream.

I wipe the sweat from my face and look up to see Lisa standing in front of me.

"Did I frighten you?" she asks.

"I was dreaming, you probably woke me up at the right time, it wasn't the best dream."

She nods and sits down on the floor next to me. I look at my watch, it's seven a.m. I've only had a couple of hours sleep.

I look around: the whole house is in silence. Only the ticking noise coming from the radiators can be heard as the timer for the heating clicks on.

"Are you okay?" I ask.

"Will you come upstairs and lie beside me?" she asks.

I let out a frustrated sigh and put my face into my hands. I'm too tired for this shit.

"I thought we discussed this?"

"No, I don't want any jiggy, jiggy, I just want to know you are there. Come and talk to me."

I laugh at the use of the phrase 'jiggy, jiggy' and I look at her. She looks so beautiful, despite the bruises. She smiles and holds out her hand to me, beckoning me to go with her.

I sigh again and stand up, take her hand and follow her upstairs.

"Stop sighing," she scolds. I laugh to myself and shake my head.

She leads me into the room and lies on the bed, patting the space beside her, inviting me to join her. I crawl onto the bed and kick off my boots. She lies on her side, staring at me. I stare back. She has a strange, almost contented smile on her face.

"Talk," she says.

"What about?"

"Anything. Tell me what you were dreaming about."

"I don't want to talk about that."

She frowns and almost asks why. She hesitates, sensing she shouldn't persist and suggests something else.

"Tell me what you love."

"Love?" I ask.

"Yes, who, what, where. Anything you love. Nice things that warm your heart."

I sigh.

"There goes the sighing again," she exclaims, with a cheeky smile on her face.

I lie back on the pillow and stare at the ceiling. I think about everyone and everything I love.

"Love isn't a word I use often but I do love some things and some people."

Lisa listens, her eyes wide with genuine interest.

"I love my Aunty Jean more than anyone. She raised me when my parents left. I love Callum and a few other close friends. I love cars and I love music. I love the feeling you get when you see a great movie or read a great book. I love simple things like a roaring fire on a cold day. It's the simple things that make me happy."

I look back at Lisa and she smiles.

"What do you love?" I ask her.

"Hmm, that's easy," she exclaims as she rolls onto her back and looks at the ceiling, almost mimicking what I did. She stays silent for a moment, then rolls back onto her side and stares at me again. "I love life and whatever it has to throw at me!"

I roll onto my side and stare into her eyes. There's something different about this girl, something engaging, inspiring.

I like her. I really, really like her.

I smile and nod in agreement. "Well said."

"Tell me about your Aunty Jane," she says.

"Aunty Jean," I correct her.

"Yes, tell me about her."

I sigh and stare at the ceiling again.

"More sighing?" she scolds.

I smile but continue to stare at the roof. My Aunty Jean tells me off for the same thing, the sighing. I'm not even aware that I do it. My thoughts just seem to exhale sometimes.

"I call her Jeannie, not Aunty Jean. She is actually my mother's Aunty but has taken care of me since I was a little boy. She is the kindest, most generous person you could ever meet."

"Why do you sigh when you think of her?"

She's got me there.

"I don't know. Maybe it's because I think about why she had to raise me instead of my parents, not that I would have it any other way"

Lisa looks at me intently, waiting for me to continue.

"My parents left me when I was a little boy. They went out one night when I was asleep and never came back."

Lisa has tears in her eyes. "This is terrible," she says gently.

"They had locked me in the house, so I couldn't get out. I was alone for two days, scared, hungry and cold. My Auntie Jean found me and took care of me."

"Where did your parents go?"

"I heard various stories over the years. They are dead, at least I think they are anyway. They were always into bad things and I heard they got involved with a bad crowd and did something that pissed off the wrong people." An unexpected, single tear escapes from my left eye. "I don't like talking about them."

Lisa reaches out to wipe away my tear and smiles.

"So, there is a real person behind the bad-boy reputation."

I raise an eyebrow and roll onto my back, staring at the ceiling again. Lisa stretches out her hand and lays it on my stomach. I don't react, I lie still for a few minutes. When I glance at her, her eyes are closed. She feels safe and she's going to sleep.

I reach over to the bedside lamp and turn it off. The sound of her light breathing soothes me and I take the gamble to go back to sleep again.

Fuck me, what a night.

6

I OPEN MY EYES AND try to focus properly. The sunlight shining through the window blinds has woken me up and by the looks of things, Lisa has been awake for a while. She isn't next to me, so I sit up and glance around the room.

I look at my watch. It's just after nine thirty a.m.

Voices can be heard from outside somewhere, so I go over to the window to investigate. This bedroom is at the front of the house and the voices seem to be coming from the back garden.

The en-suite door is open, so I go in to use the toilet. I wash my face and glance into the mirror. I've looked better but I'll do. It's not the first time I have slept in my clothes and I'm sure it won't be the last.

I head downstairs to the kitchen, carefully negotiating empty bottles of beer and high heels scattered randomly along the landing. I can hear headboards rattling as some guests get rid of their horny hangovers.

As I get downstairs, chill out music is playing and the French doors leading from the kitchen to the back garden are open. I spot a fresh pile of gear on the island. Shall I? Ah fuck it, why not. I snort a line and take a can of diet Coke from the American-style fridge. Still following the voices, I walk into to the garden and find Callum in the hot tub with Lisa and two of her friends, drinking champagne.

"Morning, son!" shouts Callum as he beckons me towards the hot tub.

I laugh and ask how long they have been in there.

"Just been here half an hour. Thought it was a great way to start the day. Other than the half a Snickers and pint of Coke I had"

I laugh again, shaking my head. The line I took has kicked in and has really helped to clear the haze.

Lisa and the girls are whispering to each other and laughing. I approach the side of the hot tub and Lisa leans over and plants a flirtatious kiss on my cheek. "Good morning, sleepyhead," she jokes, sipping on a glass of chilled champagne.

In the absence of bikinis, they are all sporting their underwear, leaving nothing to the imagination.

"Are you coming in?" enquires Callum.

I think about it, but not for long and head back to the kitchen. I grab a cold beer from the fridge and take everything off except for my Calvin's. I jump into the hot tub beside the others. The warm water feels great and Callum clinks his champagne glass on my bottle of beer. I can think of worse ways to deal with a hangover.

Lisa slides through the bubbles towards me and points to the horrible bruise on her face. Fuck me. What a mess.

"Does it hurt?" I ask.

"Not any more," she replies, waving the champagne glass in

the air with a smile. I roll my eyes and laugh. I can't help but think about how distressed she was last night. She's obviously being brave by acting like it was nothing.

The bubbles are fizzing both in the hot tub and in the champagne glasses. It's so warm and the sun is starting to creep round the garden. It looks like it will be a nice day.

"What's on today, son? Just want to hang about here?" Callum enquires with a relaxed tone, indicating he is in 'could not give a fuck' mode.

"Sounds good to me," I quickly reply. A cold shiver goes down my back, that feeling when you know you have forgotten something important. "Oh wait, fuck, I totally forgot, I'm supposed to be taking Jeannie for her shopping."

I throw an apologetic look at Lisa and jump out of the hot tub, grabbing a towel from the pile on the table. "Sorry, guys. I can't let Jeannie down. I'll be back later, though." Lisa looks at me quizzically, "She's my Aunt Jean, you know, the love of my life?" I joke, grinning, reminding her of our little heart to heart last night.

Callum laughs and gives me a thumbs up. He knows how I feel about Jeannie, so he doesn't even force the issue. "Go and sort out Jeannie and give me a shout. We are going to Italian John's club tonight so I'm sending Nancy for a shopping trip again. It goes without saying I'll need you there. I've got a bit of business to attend to. The girls need dresses and I'm guessing you'll be needing some new work attire?"

"Sounds good, tell Nancy that I don't want a Boss shirt again, I don't like the fit. Tell her to get me D&G."

Callum laughs. "Okay, bud. Gimme a shout when you are done and we will head off from here."

Nancy is Callum's long-suffering personal assistant, housekeeper and part-time mother. He pays her an absolute fortune to do everything for him. She cooks, cleans up after him, arranges his dry cleaning, manages all the gardens and maintenance of the house. She even buys clothes for Callum and us cronies when we all go out. She has impeccable taste. She gets special treatment at Harvey Nicholls in Edinburgh, the staff know her by name and she spends a fortune, on behalf of Callum. She genuinely cares for Callum and he trusts her implicitly.

The girls are well on their way now, so they wave goodbye and blow kisses as I quickly dry myself and throw on my clothes. They let out screams and whistles as I drop my towel and shamelessly bare my backside accidentally on purpose.

I grab my jacket from the coat hooks in the kitchen and check both pockets for my car keys. I help myself to an energy drink from the fridge to straighten the head, but spy the pile of powder on the table. It's impossible to resist so I snort a quick line before dashing out the front door.

Before I get to my car I hear a commotion in the garage, followed by loud expletives. Davey appears out the side door holding his head, looking confused.

"Alright, Davey?" I shout over.

"Fuck me, Ronin, I just woke up in a fuckin' canoe, my back is in bits!"

I laugh. "How did you end up in the canoe?"

"Fuck knows, the last thing I remember is pissing in the sink."

Laughing, I get into my car. I fuckin' love my car. It's beautiful. Sixty-seven grands' worth of pure BMW muscle, my absolute pride and joy. If anything happened to it, woe betide the person responsible. No-one messes with my car.

The engine starts with the push of a button and the growl from the exhausts makes me smile. A quickly reverse and I'm out onto the country lane, on the road heading towards Kirk-caldy to go and meet Jeannie.

I tap the volume button on my steering wheel and Back in Black by AC/DC starts to pump out of the Harmon Kardon stereo. The head is bobbing, the hand is tapping, the sun is shining. What a perfect morning.

Within fifteen minutes I am in the east side of Kirkcaldy and I pull up outside Jeannie's house. It's nothing special, a one-bedroom sheltered house with a door entry system that never fuckin' works. The outside walls are grey and she has a small patch of grass outside her living room that can be accessed via a patio door.

The house is in a built-up council estate full of old people and lazy bastards on the dole. There are a few dickheads in the area, as there tends to be in any housing estate. I tried to buy her a house near me but she wouldn't hear of it. She has lived in this part of town her entire life.

I can see Jeannie standing at her kitchen window and waving. She's waiting for me. Probably been at that window for twenty minutes. I wave to her and walk quickly to her front door, negotiating the numerous plant pots on the path; Jeannie loves her flowers. She has already opened the door, so I don't even have to ring her bell.

"Hello, my son!" she shouts and lands a big kiss on my cheek.

"Hi, Jean," I say back in a cheeky tone.

"It's good for the kitchen," she replies with a wheezy chuckle.

Same hygiene joke, said the same way every time we see each other.

"I'll just get my coat. Hold on two ticks."

I watch Jeannie toddle off through to her bedroom. It's always her best coat when she is out with her favourite boy, or so she keeps telling me. She's a small woman, just over five feet and with a set perm and gold, round glasses with fake rubies in the legs. She dresses well and smells of imperial leather soap. She has never worn make-up; her natural complexion and rosy cheeks are endearing. My heart warms every time I see her.

While I wait for her, I glance out of the kitchen window to admire my car.

"What the fuck?"

I watch a wee boy with a shaved head and an earring crouched down at my wheels. The wee bastard is stealing the valve caps.

I run out the house and towards the car. The lad looks round to see me coming and bolts. Shit he's fast. I've got no chance of catching him. He darts through a hole in a neighbour's hedge and starts jumping fences along the row of back gardens.

"Wee bastard!" I exclaim and I give up, turning to walk back towards Jeannie's house.

"Where did you go?" asks Jeannie as I go back in her house, out of breath.

"A wee shite was stealing the valve caps off my car."

"What did he look like?"

"A wee tink with a shaved head and an earring"

"Aye, that's Shaun. He's always in trouble. His mother likes the drink, so he wanders the streets. He's always getting a chase from someone. Poor wee lad"

I don't say anything. I feel bad now it's not the wee fuckers fault although he was the one stealing my fucking valve caps at thirty pounds a set.

"Okay, are you ready?" I ask as I pick up Jeannie's shopping bag for her.

We walk out of the house and down the path to my car. The low profile of my car isn't ideal for a woman in her seventies but Jeannie is surprisingly fit and manages to get in without a problem.

"Where are we going then?" I enquire.

"Asda, the butchers and then the post office."

I start the car and the exhausts growl again. Music booms out from the stereo at the same volume I had it set at when I turned the engine off.

"Good life!" exclaims Jeannie as she hears the lyrics of Stan by Eminem blasting out of the speakers.

"Sorry," I say, hitting the mute button.

Asda is only a short trip away and I park as close to the entrance as I can get. I open the door for Jeannie and collect a trolley. As we walk in, Jeannie bumps into a couple of her old pals and I automatically roll my eyes. Here we fuckin' go. I love her to bits but past experience tells me she will talk to every person she meets whether she knows them or not. We will be here for two hours and by the time we are done, there will be three items at the checkout, bread, milk and tea bags. Shopping with Jeannie is an absolute riot.

"Hi, Jean. How's yer leg?"

"Hello, Margaret. It's not too bad the day, thanks."

"That's good hen, you need to look after yersel."

"Aye, I'll stop playing the football maybe."

They all laugh. I smirk to myself. Jeannie's patter is superb.

"Who is this strapping lad with you?"

"This is my laddie. That's right, you'll no have seen him for years. Takes me shopping every week. He's as good as gold."

The old pals look me up and down nodding their heads in approval.

"Well, I better get on. He's a busy lad. He's got better things to do than walk aboot here with me."

"See ye later, Jean. Take care, hen."

I smile politely and watch them walk away, clutching their shopping bags then fixing their head scarves before going outside.

Jeannie rolls her eyes at me. "I cannae be bothered wi those two. The first one with the red jacket, her laddie is intae the drugs and he's in and oot of jail. The other one with the duff perm, she is that one whose daughter married a black man."

I cough and look around, hoping no one heard her. I

continue to push the trolley while Jeannie looks in every bargain basket on the way into the store. She picks up a packet of hot cross buns and puts them down. She picks them up again and gently places them in the trolley.

"That's a good price for them."

We walk at Jeannie's pace and the stopping and starting continues for an hour and thirty-seven minutes. By the end of the full tour of Asda, I am carrying one bag of shopping. The contents are: milk, a loaf of bread, tea bags, ginger snaps and a bar of Imperial Leather soap. She put the hot cross buns back.

I never complain because this woman saved my life. She raised me as her own son and even refers to me as her 'laddie'. I never argue with her, because the way I see it, I am and always will be her boy.

We push the trolley through the automatic doors to the carpark. I lift her small bag of shopping and put it into the boot. I clash the trolley back into the scattered variety of different sized carts and look around for someone to come to tidy the mess up. There are no attendants to be seen so I leave it.

"Okay, to the butchers now?" I ask Jeannie.

"Yes, ma son. Is that okay? Are you not too busy?"

I smile at her.

"Of course not. Let's go."

I drive to the other side of Kirkcaldy to Jeannie's favourite butcher. She is a true creature of habit, according to her they do the best steak pie in Fife. As we make our way there, Jeanie rants about how the mince in supermarkets is all gristle and the only place we should ever buy meat is the local butchers. I don't say much, just make the odd sound in agreement. I let her get it out of her system.

I park outside the shop window and Jeannie waves to Tam, who is proudly arranging trays of meat in his window display cabinet. Jeannie has known Tam for thirty years. He is a semi-retired butcher and only works on Saturdays. I jump out of the car and walk round to open Jeannie's door. I park with her door at the curbside, so she can get out safely. It would be easier if I popped in to get her meat for her but I know Jeannie wants to speak to Tam to say the same thing she said to him last week and every week before that.

"Hello, Jean," shouts Tam from over the counter. "How are you today?"

"Hello, Tam, I'm fine but this leg is giving me terrible jip just now."

I raise my eyebrows at this, her leg wasn't too bad apparently, when she spoke to the two old dears in Asda.

I look over at Tam in amusement, Jeannie loves to get attention, especially from him. He's a portly old chap, with a red face and a cheery disposition. He arrives in his shop very early to ensure he is prepared; sleeves rolled up and always immaculate. He wears his butchers hat and uniform with pride. I think Jeannie has a wee fancy for him.

"Hello, son. How are you doing?" he asks me, smiling politely.

"I'm fine, Tam, thanks." I give him a thumbs up as I stare at the variety of burger creations they have on offer. "A haggis and broccoli burger?" I ask Tam in disbelief.

"Aye, that's the apprentice trying to make his mark." Tam shakes his head in disapproval. "We'll never sell those."

Jeannie is in deep thought looking over the mince and sausages section. It's a serious decision for her.

Tam stands at the counter opposite her, patiently waiting for her to decide what she wants. He doesn't sigh, he doesn't roll his eyes. He waits with a smile on his face and I admire him, he's a professional.

"I'll take a pound of the best mince please, Tam, and four sausages."

No change from last week then. Tam jumps into action and quickly picks up a heap of the mince with his hand. He drops it into the scales and he's bang on. A pound exactly.

"Have you got the good steak pies in, Tam?" Jeannie enquires.

He knows exactly what she is talking about. "No, Jean, I'm afraid we only made the steak and potato this week. I'll put one of the good ones with the pastry aside for you next Saturday, for when you come in."

"That's grand," exclaims Jeannie, smiling gratefully.

Tam finishes wrapping up her sausages and mince and hands it to her in a plastic bag. I try to pay him but he waves me away.

"No, no, don't be daft."

He winks and I know he is looking for a favour in exchange.

"That's very decent of you, Tam. Thank you and I'll see you next week," shouts Jeannie as she makes her way out of the shop.

I nod to Tam that I'll be back in a minute.

I help Jeannie into the car and add the plastic bag from the butchers to her shopping in the boot.

"I'll just be a minute" I tell her as I close the car door and go back into the shop.

"Jeanie is looking well, Ronin," Tam says.

"Aye, she's a trooper. So, what can I do for you?"

"I'm needing a door kicked in, son. Can you help me out?"

"Give me the details" I reply.

"The laddie down the stairs from my flat is causing an awful trouble. He's always got the music blaring and has all sorts going in and out of there at all hours of the night. Could you have a word with him because all I get is a mouthful of bad language when I try to broach the subject. He's a nightmare."

Tam has known me since I was a child because I have been in and out of that shop with Jeannie for as long as I can remember. His eyes well up with tears of frustration and I can see that he has had enough.

"Okay, leave it with me. I'll boot his door in and give him a slap. He won't know it's anything to do with you. Okay?"

"That's magic, son, thanks very much." He wipes his nose with a hanky and immediately goes to wash his hands.

"No worries. Don't wait so long to tell me you need help next time, though."

Tam nods and I leave him to it.

I get back in the car and start the engine.

"What's he wanting you to do?" asks Jeannie.

She doesn't miss a trick.

"Nothing for you to worry about," I respond, forcing a smile.

"Well as long as it doesn't get you the jail, son."

I laugh, she's as sharp as a tac.

"Don't worry Jeannie, honestly."

My phone pings, it's a text message from Callum.

"The boy is here. How many?"

Translation:

The drug dealer we use frequently has arrived at my house. How many grams of class A drugs do you think we will need to enhance our evening?

"5 plenty. Still leftovers" I text back.

He responds with a thumbs-up emoji.

The final stop is the Post Office, close to where Jeannie lives. We stop outside and Jeannie is staring at me blankly.

"What?" I ask her.

"I'm trying to think what I needed from here."

"Stamps?"

No.

"Writing paper?"

No.

"Envelopes?"

No.

She's looking at me as if that is going to help her remember. We sit in silence for almost two minutes, looking at each other. All the while, she is racking her brain.

"Oh well, doesn't matter, son," she finally says. "I'll just go home"

I sigh inwardly, this isn't the first time this has happened. I do a U-turn in the road and within a minute I am back at her front door.

Jeannie undoes her seatbelt and tries to open the heavy door. I jump out and run around to help her out. I open the boot and pick up her bag of messages.

"That car is a smasher," she offers randomly.

"It certainly is," I reply as we walk up the path towards the security door at the front of her building. I push it open and hold it as she walks past me and unlocks her front door. She has three locks, all which are used every time she leaves or enters the house.

My phone pings again and I take it out of my pocket for a quick look. The message is from Callum again: "bring drink from club"

I reply back with the same 'thumbs up' emoji.

Callum has a contact in town who organises booze in bulk. Occasionally, I have to pick it up from the back door of a nightclub. A totally dodgy arrangement but I know we are not the only people who benefit.

As Jeannie opens the door, I walk past her and lay the messages out on the kitchen table. She goes to put her good coat away and as she does so I spy two handwritten envelopes on the table, both without stamps. They are addressed to Anne and Mhari, her two old pals she met years ago when she worked in the linoleum factory. She likes to keep in touch with them the old fashioned way. I quickly put the envelopes in my pocket, mentally adding another job to my 'to do' list.

"Are you staying for a cup of tea, my son?", Jeannie asks as she joins me in the kitchen.

"I'd love to, Jeannie, but I have loads to do."

Jeannie looks disappointed. "Okay. Well, come and visit during the week. I'll make your dinner for you."

"It's a date!" I say then reach out and give her a kiss on the cheek, trying to cheer her up.

"Be good and if you can't be good, be careful," she calls after me as I open her front door.

"Lock this door now," I command affectionately, as I leave her house.

I feel suddenly tired, as though I am starting to fade. My list isn't getting any shorter and I still have a shitload of things to do. I get back into my car then glance over to Jeannie's kitchen window to see her standing looking out, waving me off.

I head straight out onto the main road and access the phonebook with the controls on my steering wheel. I scroll through the names until I find Dinky. He's the manager at the BMW garage. We're not exactly friends but we know each other well. I have spent a fortune buying cars from him over the years, so he tends to give me preferential treatment.

I dial his number and he answers almost instantly.

"How you doin'?" I ask.

"Fine. Want a new car already?" he jokes

"Nope. Some little shite stole my valve caps, so I need a new set. I'm heading to your garage now."

"Okay, I'll get some and have them ready"

"Cheers, see you in two minutes."

Okay, job one complete, don't have to think about that now.

Next item on the list, I have to kick that guy's door in for Tam, and after that, home and changed for the gym.

After a good hour in the gym, I'll shower and pick up the booze for Callum.

Fuck me, no rest for the wicked. To think I could have

spent the day sitting in a hot tub with half-naked women and drinking champagne. My priorities need reviewing.

Jeannie is the exception of course. She'll always be at the top of the list.

7

I ARRIVE AT THE BMW garage and park in the 'Customers Only' space at the front door. I can see Dinky in the showroom, sipping a coffee, looking at his mobile. The entire showroom is made of large glass panes and he sees me coming.

"Ronin," he exclaims as he extends his hand out to shake mine.

"Can't stay long, mate, got a million things to do," I inform him politely.

"Your valve caps are in my office, come up here just now."

I follow Dinky upstairs to his office, which overlooks the entire showroom. He closes the door behind me and tilts the blinds.

"You've got to try this shit," he urges as he passes me a silver bullet full of cocaine. I do the necessary tapping and twisting with the bullet and take a deep sniff from the top. That's brightened me up.

"Fuck me, that's alright. Where did you get that?"

"One of the salesmen in the Glasgow office," smiles Dinky as he helps himself to a couple of sniffs.

I sit back on the leather couch at the far wall of his office and watch as Dinky peeks out of the blinds to check that nobody has caught us in the act.

"Fuck me, look at the tits on that" exclaims Dinky, waving me over to look at the girl working at the service desk.

"Nice, mate. How long before you bang her?" I joke.

"Depends on how quick she wants a promotion."

We laugh and Dinky offers me a coffee.

"Nah, mate, I'm in a hurry. Where's my valve caps?"

Dinky walks over to his desk, opens his drawer and tosses a cardboard box with the valve caps inside.

"I've put these on my account," he informs me.

"Did you see me reaching for my fuckin' wallet?" I respond with a smile.

Dinky laughs and tells me to go and fuck myself. We walk out of his office and one of the salesmen is reversing a brand new M4 into the showroom. We both stop to admire it.

"Special edition, first one in the UK," Dinky tells me, clearly trying to tempt me. I give him a knowing glance and, unable to resist, I quickly walk down the stairs to look at the car.

Fuck. It's stunning. Beautiful colour, special edition interior, competition package. Shit. He's got me.

"You're a fuckin' wanker," I tell him. "Do the deal for me. I want it ASAP."

Dinky laughs and tells the salesman that the car is sold. The salesman looks surprised, like he can't believe his luck.

As I walk out of the showroom and get into my car, Dinky waves cheekily through the glass. My lack of restraint has just earned him another great fucking bonus. I give him the finger with a smile, speeding out of the car park. I hadn't intended to buy a car today but fuck it, why not?

I head over to Beatty Crescent to the flat where this little prick is causing problems with old Tam. I check my watch. This shouldn't take more than ten minutes.

Tam lives in a row of tenement houses, which have been converted into flats, and his garden stands out amongst the rest in the middle of the street. He has clearly spent years making it look immaculate: large sections of his garden are filled with impressive rose bushes and his grass is perfectly landscaped.

Despite this, I can see very clearly that Tam's hard work has been ruined by the dickhead in the flat underneath him. His section of shared garden is overgrown and littered with cigarette butts and empty lager cans. A couple of mangled deck chairs lie on their sides next to the front door and the rubbish in the wheelie bin is spilling over the top. This is the place.

I park my car on the opposite side of the street and glance over. I can hear the sound of utterly shite techno music booming out the front windows, which are open, with shabby curtains flapping about in the breeze. It's always beige curtains hanging in these shitholes.

I get out of the car and stride across the road with purpose. The front gate is broken and I can either head straight upstairs to Tam's flat or turn left to the techno flat. I turn left and walk around the corner to the front door. This little shit has allowed people to piss on his front doorstep. The stench is overpowering. This guy is disgusting.

I need to get this done quickly, so I take a step back and boot the front door in. One kick is all it takes and the door swings open to reveal a house mostly in darkness, with very loud music playing. Nobody has heard me, so I walk through the hall, following the source of the music, and come to the doorway of a lounge. The room is a complete mess, empty lager and cider cans, glass bottles, takeaway boxes and CDs strewn across the living room floor. A couple of younger lads, probably in their mid-twenties are dancing about with their council estate style moves. They have their tops off, revealing pale, skinny bodies and crappy tattoos that must have cost a fiver. The fake Burberry baseball caps complete the stereotype.

It seems they have dancing partners too. A couple of skinny middens, with matted hair cuts and lashings of cheap make-up dance between the boys, as if they are at a rave in a club. They are also topless, apart from their bras and are wearing skinny jeans that are loose on their junky physique.

It's a standard druggy party. The other guests are spaced out, slumped in half-broken chairs and staring at the Xbox, which has been on pause for hours.

None of them even notice I am in the room.

I walk over to the stereo and kick it over. The music stops.

They all look at me and start to mumble some drug-slurred abuse. I rip the curtains off the wall and the curtain pole falls to the ground. The room is filled with light and they continue to stare at me, blinking as their eyes adjust to the daylight.

One of the more sober guests, who can still focus, approaches me with a very coherent, "Whit ye daein tae ma hoose, man?"

I push him down on his seat, and he looks at me blankly, making no protest, then I pick up the CD player. I walk through to the most disgusting kitchen I have ever seen and I throw it in the sink on top of a month's worth of dishes. Just to be a bad bastard, I turn on the taps and head back through to the lounge.

"You've got an hour to get the fuck out of here. Starting now," I tell everyone in the room.

"Who the fuck are you like, gadge?" enquires one of the guests.

"If you knew who I was, you would do as your told. Let's put it that way," I snap.

The flat owner comes at me with a blunt knife. The weapon of choice for any ned.

"Fuckin come on then, cunt!" he shouts and does a kind of river dance spliced with the walk someone would have done if they were part of the Manc scene in the nineties.

I laugh at him as he lunges for me. Taking the knife from him is easy but I need to make sure he knows that I mean business. I hit him hard in the face and he goes down, as I expected him to.

"That's bad, like," said one of the half-naked girls, scratching one of the many scabs covering veins on her arm.

I slam the knife into the door and snap the blade.

"You've got an hour to get the fuck out of here, or I'll be coming back with four or five pals, got it?"

"Aye mate, dinnae work yersel', he wis gonnae get kicked oot anyway fur no payin' his rent."

I look at the scabby effort who spoke and remind him once again. "One hour."

Before I turn around to leave, I see the skinny girls gather the items of clothing they think belong to them and stumble out of the front door. They look even worse when the daylight hits them.

I walk out the house and head back to my car. I sniff my shirt: hopefully I won't need to go back there. It was stinking.

Once again, I hit the start button and the car starts with a beautiful tone from the exhausts.

The faint sound of 'Itch' by Nothing But Thieves can be heard playing on my stereo, so I crank up the volume. Now there's a tune. The cocaine I got from Dinky has helped with my energy levels and I feel good about the car I just bought. I quickly get on to the dual carriageway along the top end of Kirkcaldy and head home.

8

IT DOESN'T TAKE LONG FOR me to get out of the town and into the country, I am pleased that there is nothing but rolling fields and green trees to look at, the peace and quiet calms me. It is why I purposely chose to build a house in the countryside ensuring I'm close enough to civilization when I need to get there.

I stop the car in the driveway and unlock the front door.

My house is a custom-built villa with a view over the hills. The front wall of the house is all glass, so that the scenery can be appreciated from most rooms. I love the real fireplace and stone chimney, which cost me an arm and a leg but it's worth it. There are four bedrooms and just as many reception rooms, which is more space than I need, but comes in handy when I host the odd get together. Despite the size and views it's never really felt like home in the five years I've lived there.

I also have a cottage in the highlands, left to me by a

great-aunt some years back. It's my bolt hole, a perfect hide-away that no-one knows about, not even Callum. Every now and then I go off-grid and escape up there to recharge and switch off; no wi-fi or phone reception, just peace and quiet.

I close the door behind me and toss my keys onto the wooden table in the hallway. The cleaner, Agnes, has been, so everything is tidy and polished. I run upstairs and throw on my gym gear. Pulling a trackie top over my head I run back downstairs and grab an energy drink from the fridge before jumping back into the car.

I really cannot be fucked with the gym today but the quicker I get there, the quicker it will be over with. That place is full of the dickheads on a Saturday afternoon who are pumped up on 'roids and can't hold a conversation without telling me how hard they are twenty times.

The gym is basic, nothing special. It has free weights, some resistance machines and a cardio section. It's owned by a decent local guy, who likes to lift weights and make money from his gym. We have a simple arrangement: I don't pay because of my connection to Callum.

The gym is an old refurbished warehouse and sits on the edge of an industrial estate in Kirkcaldy. It has been painted white outside and has the word 'GYM' in bright green letters on the wall.

I pull up and return a few waves to the ladies who have just finished one of the exercise classes. My gaze lingers on the leggings and sports bras as they pass the car and I think of Lisa and wonder what she would look like in gym wear. I walk in the front door, passing the girls at reception, saying hello and exchanging pleasantries. I hand my car keys to one of them: they look after them for me. I recognise a few faces, as I approach the weights section. The first person to say hello is Ugh. He is a big fucker, is very strong and can lift the heaviest weights in the gym; unfortunately he smells like a fuckin' donkey.

We call him Ugh for two reasons. The last three letters on his car registration are UGH and he looks like a cave man with messy hair, a dodgy beard and huge shovel-like hands that could hold a club of some kind. He's a good guy, despite the terrible body odour.

Tony is also here. This guy is the poser's poser. He is in his mid-forties and has a haircut like an action man. He's a good-looking guy, takes care of his appearance and trains hard but he loves himself. I'm fairly sure he can't walk past a mirror without kissing it. He's always stinking of aftershave and wearing the trendiest gym gear. Despite his narcissism, he's a decent guy.

The last person to acknowledge my arrival is Jasper. Now this guy is a deviant. He cannot help but bang any woman that shows the slightest hint of interest in him. His sordid stories keep us entertained every week at the gym and range from banging his best friend's mum to being caught hiding behind a Christmas tree when an unsuspecting husband arrived home early.

Today's story has already started but it doesn't take me long to catch up. Jasper stops half way through a sentence to give me a quick "A'right son?" before continuing.

"So, I get this fuckin' dirty tart back with me during the week. I was staying in a hotel in Newcastle because I was down at head office. Me and some of the other boys from the team went hunting for fanny and stumbled upon these slack hoors who were just gagging for it."

I cringe at his courses but know the punchline will be worth it.

"So, I take this young thing back to my hotel room and she is up for anything. I mean anything. I was putting it in her arse, spitting on her face, everything. I started to panic that I had run out of dirty things to do when it turned to rimming. She started to lick my arse and I was loving it. Just to be funny,

I thought I would squeeze out a wee fart and see how she reacted."

Jasper pauses for a reaction. We all burst into laughter. Jasper is laughing too and then his face changes.

"The only thing is, I followed through."

"You what?" we ask in shocked chorus, followed by an uneasy silence. We look at him, poised for confirmation.

"I fuckin' sharted on this poor girl. Honestly, I thought it was going to be a cheesy air biscuit but instead she got a face of oxtail soup."

We fall about laughing, hands over our faces, tears streaming down our cheeks. That is the best Jasper story yet.

"What happened?" asks Ugh, in between bouts of laughter.

Jasper has a smug smile on his face, the storyteller in him pauses for effect, everyone in the gym is looking at us to see what is going on.

"She went fuckin mental. She screamed and ran into the bathroom. She spent about twenty minutes in the shower. I couldn't kiss her after that, I had to tell her to brush her teeth. I kind of felt bad about it afterwards."

I stare at Jasper in disbelief. Not because I don't believe him but because of the way he describes how he felt 'bad'.

Once the hilarity and pleasantries are over I get on with my workout . I am still feeling jaded and can only perform at about sixty per cent. The lack of sleep and reliance on narcotics with energy drinks has affected my motivation. I do a half-arsed circuit mixing free weights and machines using the very little energy I have left. Some young athlete type with tussled hair and a tight-fitting T-shirt has started to run on the treadmill across from me and he's making me feel bad. Fuck him. I can be as fit as him, just need to stay off the hard stuff.

On the way out of the gym, the lads are talking to a group of ladies at the front door. I collect my keys from the girls at reception and I head out. Jasper has his phone out taking all the numbers that he can get and Tony is flexing every muscle.

"Your crew going out tonight, Ronin?" asks Jasper.

"I'm sure we will be. Won't be going anywhere until ten p.m. at least though."

The lads all nod in agreement as if to say, "We'll see you out and about."

I head home and straight for the shower. It's a high pressure bad boy that makes you clean as a whistle. I follow the same routine of using the expensive shampoo and face wash, body scrub and finally body wash. Agnes, my cleaner, regularly comments that I have more products in my bathroom than she does in her entire house.

As I come out of the shower, I ask Alexa to play Chandelier by Sia to get me in the mood for going out. I glance at my mobile, lying on the bed and see a couple of missed calls from Callum. I sit on on top of the blue duvet rubbing my head with a towel and phone him back.

"Aye?" I hear him say as the sound of splashing and women's voices fill the background.

"You still in that fucking hot tub?" I ask him

"Of course, why would I go anywhere else?" He chuckles at the same time as me. "It's getting cold now, so heading in to get ready. Just checking you're on your way."

"Just out the shower, so will be there soon. Need to go and pick up the booze, too."

"A'right son, see you when I see you."

"No bother," I reply.

"Hurry up, Ronin!" Lisa's sweet voice sings down the phone. There's all the motivation I need right there.

"Lisa is pished, so you better come and look after her again," suggests Callum sarcastically.

"Aye, fine," I reply flippantly and hang up.

I toss my phone on the bed again and lie back, staring at the ceiling. I'd love to fall asleep right now. I listen to the music playing in the background and close my eyes. A few minutes won't make a difference.

I feel myself drifting into a comfy slumber and my leg twitches like a personal alarm from my body reminding me not to fall asleep.

"Fuck," I exclaim in the form of a sigh as I sit upright and walk over to my oak wardrobe.

Nancy has hung all of my clothes in the most efficient order you could ever imagine. A row of T-shirts, a row of jeans, then my shirts, jackets and accessories like scarves and hats. I grab a pair of dark jeans and a horrendously expensive T-shirt with a £250 price tag hanging from the sleeve.

I walk over to my matching chest of drawers and pull out a pair of neatly folded socks. Then I walk over to my shoe rack and select a pair of brown boots to put on.

I ensure I am happy with my hair and splash on a favourite aftershave.

By now, Alexa is playing some Justin Bieber crap, so I command her to shut down.

I pick up my phone and put it in the pocket of my jeans. I walk over to the wardrobe with the safe: it's bolted to the floor. I enter the password and pull out a wad of fifty pound notes. I don't check how much but it looks like about a grand. It should be enough. I lock the safe and fold the money, putting it in my other pocket in my jeans. I open the watch case on top of my chest of drawers. I pull out my favourite Rolex and quickly clip it on.

Time is pressing on and I need to get moving. I snatch my keys from the table in the hall, quickly glance around the house and then I leave, locking the door behind me.

It takes ten minutes to drive from the house back into Kirkcaldy and I park my car at the back entrance of Italian John's nightclub.

There are massive bins filled separately with empty bottles and rubbish. Takeaway cartons lie scattered across the yard, complemented by the odd pile of lumpy puke, random single high heels and used condoms. It seems that CCTV doesn't scare people into decency any more.

I take a set of stairs from the yard up to a fire exit and bang on the door. After a minute or so, I hear someone struggling with a lock and falling over something behind the door. I smirk to myself. It sounds like John, the owner of the night-club. He's a little Italian guy with a real Italian name but calls himself John to sound more Scottish. His accent is mixed with Scottish slang and Italian lingo that we all find amusing, especially when it confuses new customers.

After a fight with the door, he pushes it open and greets me with a big smile.

"Ronin. How's it agoin'? he asks in his cheerful way, holding out his hand.

He's wearing tight jeans; a white shirt unbuttoned half way down to display his hairy chest and three gold chains. The outfit is finished off with a blazer and a pair of loafers, no socks. His black hair is thinning to reveal a bald patch, despite the fact he has it swept back. He is pushing fifty if not older but he thinks and acts as though he is still thirty.

I smile and shake his hand. I like him. He may be a dodgy wee fucker but he's good to us and always makes a fuss when we go into his club.

"Callum said you've got some booze to be picked up?" I ask him.

"Aye, it'sa here by the door. Go and opena yer boot and one o' the boys will take it doon for ye."

"Superb," I say and walk down the stairs towards my car.

"You gonna come here the night?" he calls after me.

"I'd think we will. Probably after ten sometime."

"Nae bother. I'll geta the VIP area for you, okay?"

"That'll do nicely," I tell him with a thumbs up.

"Aye, yer pal Sandy, he'lla be there an' aw."

I frown wondering who he means so when the penny drops I do a double take, he's talking about Sandy Pratt. My previous enthusiasm for going out is dampened at the mention of that wanker's name but I make no comment.

I continue down the stairs to the yard and press the button on my remote to open the boot of my car.

A seagull is pecking at a pool of puke in the corner of the yard. I turn away and watch for whoever is bringing down the booze.

Two young lads appear at the fire exit, carrying crates of beer. They bring it down and gently load it into my car, nodding to me acknowledging that I am friends with their boss and therefore, in their eyes, I must be important.

The next time they come down with a box of Veuve Clique champagne and a box of Grey Goose vodka.

I thank the boys and tip them with fifties. They give me an appreciative nod and disappear back up the stairs, closing the fire exit behind them.

I close the boot lid and get back in the car. I text Callum: Booze collected, on my way. I finish the message with a winky emoji.

Bohemian Rhapsody by Queen has just come on my play-list in the car and I crank it up as the sleek, polished body of my Beemer flashes past all the other cars on the road and I speed towards Callum's house. I don't care what anyone says, everyone sings along to that song. I do too. As loud as I can and with plenty steering wheel slapping and head bobbing.

This is the start of the Saturday session. I'll need to try to keep my head reasonably straight because Callum mentioned business later. I hope it's nothing too serious because I'm in the mood for a blow-out.

9

I ARRIVE AT CALLUM'S AND I can hear music playing. I get out of the car and approach the front door. Before I can stretch my hand out to ring the bell, the door is whisked open and Lisa is standing there with a playful smile on her face. It's déjà vu.

"Hello!" she exclaims as she pulls me in the door by the hand.

She's looking fantastic in a beautiful dress tonight. Lisa has managed to do a good job at covering up the bruise on her cheek: I can barely see it. Her hair is tied up in a loose fashion with wisps falling from the clasp, framing her face. The black dress and black heels match perfectly, complementing her tanned skin and long, toned legs.

"Where have you been? You left me alone with these guys to drink champagne and now I am drunk!"

She laughs and continues to drag me through the hallway

by the hand and into the kitchen where the party is beginning again.

"Put him down, Lisa. Firfucksake, he's only in the door, let him take a line and get a beer!" shouts Callum as he opens the fridge and chucks a bottle of beer across the kitchen to me.

Lisa laughs and lets go of my hand as I catch the bottle of beer and put it on the table.

"I'll get the drink from the car," I say and head back the way I came in. As I approach the front door, Nancy comes down the stairs and greets me.

"Hi, sunshine, how are you?" she asks and lands a kiss on my cheek.

"Good to see you, Nancy. I'm looking forward to seeing what shirt you got for me today."

"Oh, you'll love it, Ronin. The gay guy in Harvey Nicks kept it aside for me. He said he hasn't sold any of them yet as it's next season but he did me a favour."

"Nice," I exclaim as I continue out of the front door towards my car. I open the boot with the remote on my car keys and pick up the cases of champagne and Grey Goose. They are fairly heavy but I have started to lift them now, so I can't put them down. I use my legs to lift them out of the boot and conscious that Lisa might be watching I try my best to walk into the house like the weight is no problem for me. I put the boxes down on the kitchen table, the guests cheer, and Callum opens the box of champagne.

"He's some boy, that wee Italian fucker. Never lets me down," he comments with a grin.

He puts the bottles of champagne into the fridge as other people unload bottles of vodka and arrange them as a showcase on the bar at the other side of the kitchen.

"I'll get the rest of the beer from the car," I say as I turn to leave the room.

"Fuck that, take a line and chill out. You've been running

around all day. Eric will get the beers. Eric, make yourself useful, go and get the beers from Ronin's car."

I laugh as Eric scuttles from his seat and runs out the door. Eric is a dweeb who wants to be cool but is basically a fud. He's a suck-up and does anything that Callum asks, which is mainly shit that nobody else wants to do. I'm fairly sure that he would wipe Callum's arse if he asked him.

Lisa walks up to me and takes my hand in a flirty fashion, leading me to the freshly delivered pile of cocaine on the bar. She has this amazing way of saying things with her big beautiful eyes. She doesn't say a word when she looks at me and I feel like she can see my soul.

She hands me a rolled-up fifty and I snort two lines from the sheet of glass on the bar.

"Wow!" I exclaim as the powder burns the inside of my nostrils.

Lisa smiles and takes the note from me, snorting a couple of lines quickly. She does a follow up sniff and asks me to check for any residue around her nostrils.

I point to her chin. I'm joking and I tell her so while she panics and wipes at nothing. She laughs and gives me a playful punch on the arm.

"You better get changed. I saw the shirt that the lady bought for you."

"Nancy," I inform her.

"Yes, I saw the shirt, it's really nice. I would have chosen the same."

"Good. The last one she bought me was a fuckin' monstrosity. What about you? Are you happy with your purchases?" I ask Lisa as I admire her dress and entire outfit.

"Yes, I love it all. I gave her my size and she bought me two dresses, jeans and a top for tomorrow, new underwear and lots of beautiful Chanel make-up."

I laugh as she describes the experience with excitement.

"Yes, Callum is good to all of us."

"Yes, very good. He's a good boss, I like him." She looks over the room to where he is standing. I start to feel a little jealous, which is unlike me.

"Oh, do you?" I ask, trying to be playful.

"Yes, but I like you better," she answers and delivers a gentle kiss on my cheek and touches my face softly.

She smells amazing. If I didn't know myself better I would say I was falling for her but in my line of work, it's best to keep women at arm's length and not get too close. The risk to them is too great. I won't be doing this forever, though. When the time is right I'll stop, I'll settle down. Stranger things have happened.

Lisa walks away and joins the other girls at the other side of the kitchen. I can't stop looking at her. She catches my eye and winks. I respond by sticking my tongue out at her cheekily. She smiles and turns back to her conversation with the girls.

Callum approaches me with my beer that I left on the table and hands it to me.

"So, are you going to bang her or not?" he asks.

I laugh and shake my head.

He lowers his voice, "Listen, a word of advice mate, don't get too close to that one."

"Eh?" I say, looking at him suspiciously.

"Just listen to me about this."

There is an uncomfortable silence and he changes the subject.

"Anyway, what the fuck have you been doing all day?"

I pause for a second, trying to process what he has just said, before telling him about Jeannie and the gym.

"Who was at the gym?"

"Just a few of the usual boys. Jasper was there and he was telling us about a girl he shat on."

Callum splutters as he laughs with a mouthful of beer.

"Fuck me, it doesn't surprise me that he's taken things that far. He's a deviant bastard."

"No, I'll give him some credit. He didn't hover above her and shit on her chest or anything. She was licking his arse and he sharted."

We both laugh and some people in the kitchen look around to see what the hilarity is all about.

"Well, if there is anyone who could do that to a girl, then he's the one."

I agree and swig back more of my beer.

Eric comes scuttling over to us, to gain approval for having brought in the beers and stacking them in the fridge. I thank him and ask how he is doing. I always feel bad for him. He is one of those poor souls who wants to be clever and popular. I think Callum keeps him around out of pity.

"Want me to clean your car, Ronin? It's stunning," Eric asks me in a subservient manner. He is trying his best to impress us.

"No, you don't need to do that, Eric. Just have a beer and chill the fuck out," I tell him.

He nods nervously and looks to Callum for approval.

"Go and clean his fuckin' car. The valet guy has left his stuff in the shed," orders Callum with authority. I look at him in surprise, with a 'What the fuck?' expression on my face. "If he doesn't do it, he will be twitching all night. Just let him get on with it and he'll be happy."

I nod reluctantly as Eric scuttles off again to go and wash my car. I am not entirely comfortable with it but I have no doubt he will make a good job.

"You better go and get changed, son; the rest of the team will be here soon and we don't want you looking like a fuckin' IT support engineer," mocks Callum and he points upstairs to where Nancy will have ironed and hung my new shirt.

I laugh then give him the finger as I leave the kitchen and

head upstairs to the dressing room. A huge room filled with Callum's clothes and every toiletry you can possibly think of. As I make it upstairs, Nancy comes out of the room, humming a tune to herself in her usual merry mood.

"It's hanging up for you darlin'" she says as she skips past me and points into the room with her thumb.

"Thanks, gorgeous," I say in response. She loves a bit of flirty banter.

I get into the room and as I expected, the new shirt is hanging up. It's perfectly ironed, with the D&G tag still on it and with another hand-written tag hanging on it, saying 'Ronin'.

The room smells great as Nancy is trying out some new incense and candles. She always manages to get the combination exactly right, never overpowering or smelling like an old woman at the pantomime. I put down my bottle of beer on the dresser and look into the huge mirror on the wall above it. I'm looking a bit tired. Not that I'm surprised. I have kicked the arse out of it for the past twenty-four hours.

A large sigh escapes from my lips as I pull off my T-shirt.

"More sighing?"

I hear Lisa's voice from outside the door and she walks into the room with a smile.

"What are you doing up here?" I ask with a smile and I chuck my T-shirt at her playfully. She catches and smells it.

"Mmm, it smells like you," she says seductively.

There is a moment of silence between us as we look each other up and down. Her eyes are amazing; I can't stop looking into them. She starts to move towards me slowly and I stand still as I watch her approach.

She lightly touches my chest and walks round the back of me, almost tickling my back with the tips of her fingers. I can feel goose bumps appear all over my body. Thank fuck I went to the gym today: I'm looking decent in the right places.

I inhale and appreciate her scent. She walks back round to the front of me and stops with her face centimetres from my face, her lips almost touching mine. I lift my hands and gently run them down her back. Her dress is backless and I can feel how smooth her skin is. She puts her hands on my sides and gently runs her fingertips up and down, caressing my skin.

I tense my muscles. Partly out of excitement and partly to try to impress her. Fuck, Callum's warning resounds in my head.

We kiss. A full on passionate kiss.

She softly trails her hand from the side of my body and down to the front of my jeans. She rubs me through my jeans and smiles when she feels a hard bulge down there. I grab her ass and squeeze it as we kiss some more. She lets out a moan of pleasure as I do it.

She steps back and delicately wipes her lips.

"You better get dressed," she teases as she leaves the room.

"Oh, come on!" I shout after her. I'm standing with a raging hard-on that has pitched a tent in the front of my jeans.

I laugh to myself in disbelief. She's a nightmare. I wanted to take her to bed there and then. She knows that but I am hopeful we can pick up where we left off later; otherwise, I will have blue balls from hell.

"Fuxake," I whisper under my breath as I try to recover from the moment and put on my shirt. I rip off the tags and toss them into the bin under the dressing table. One last check in the mirror and I'm happy with what I see. The shirt is slim fit, black, with a very subtle but stylish logo stitched onto the left breast. Exactly what I wanted, subtle but well made with expensive fabric. I pick up my beer and down the contents of the bottle. I might as well get myself in the mood: the coke has given me a buzz.

I leave the dressing room and check the front of my jeans. The lump of wood has settled down now and I can at least walk normally again. I head downstairs and find that a few more guests have arrived. The kitchen is busy and the bar is heavily laden with booze in various forms. Somebody has placed a bag of blue pills next to the pile of coke. Pill's aren't Callum's thing, so I wonder where they have come from.

There is a young lad in the corner. I haven't seen him before but I can hear him boasting about having Spice and offering it to some of the guests. I don't care who he is but he's not selling that shit at this party. I quickly nod to Davey, who knows immediately that's something's up and comes over to my side. I nod in the direction of the dealer and without saying a word, we go over and grab him. He shouts in protest as we drag him outside through the French doors into the back garden.

"What the fuck is your problem?" he exclaims.

I search his pockets and pull a bag of Spice from his jacket.

"Who gave you permission to sell this shit here?"

"Sandy gave it to me and told me to dish it out."

"That fucker's not in charge here, I am. So, get the fuck out of here before I break your neck."

The lad pauses for a moment and then starts to move as Davey takes a step towards him.

Davey takes the bag and holds it up to the light. "Fuck me, this shit is lethal, I took it once and was fucked for a week." He throws it into the wheelie bin.

Davey checks the side of the house to make sure the lad has left and we go back inside and act like nothing has happened.

Lisa throws me a puzzled look. "Don't ask," I say, shaking my head.

Someone turns the music up and the beat becomes addictive. Everyone in the room is moving to the rhythm of the music. Despite the earlier altercation, I get the feeling it is going to be a decent night. The beer is flowing and maybe, just maybe, I will get to take things further with Lisa.

10

I'M GETTING INTO A ROUTINE now. A couple of beers, a couple of lines and repeat when necessary. A few guests are obviously following different ratios and are mangled. Jaws are wobbling, shite is talked and some people are dancing in a way that should never be acceptable in society. Drugs make people do crazy things.

Just like Mickey the liar.

If you have a car, he has two. If you have fifty pounds, he has a hundred. You can see where I'm going with this. Mickey is one of the boys. He has been part of the crowd for a long time but we can only tolerate him in small doses. He talks utter pish and thinks that people believe him. He's currently talking to a young lady about the Lamborghini that he used to have but sold it because he wasn't using it, allegedly.

His phone rings and he answers it loudly, so everyone can hear.

"Mick's machines," he bellows, so that everyone is looking at him. He owns a second-hand car lot and thinks that the business name is cool. Nobody else does.

"Yes, my man, I can sort that out for you, just give me a call on Monday, no problem. Yes, yes, cash is fine. If you call it twenty grand, I'll give it to you for that."

Davey's back and looks across from the bar where he was snorting a couple of lines. He approaches me with a wink and shakes my hand, listening intently to Mick's phone call. He rolls his eyes and walks over to Mick while he is on the phone. He starts impersonating Mickey, standing behind him, to everyone's amusement.

Mickey finishes his phone call and turns around to see Davey mimicking holding a phone with his hand.

"Fuck off, Davey, I can't help it if I need to take constant business calls. It's just as annoying for me too."

"We will soon sort that," exclaims Davey.

He grabs the phone from Mickey and drops it into his pint glass, which is full to the brim of beer.

"No more calls for you, Mickey."

Everyone erupts in laughter as Davey parades the room with the pint glass held high, showing Mickey's phone bobbing up and down in the amber liquid.

Mickey is raging and looks like he is going to cry. He pulls it back though with a loud announcement that he 'was due for a new phone anyway'. I feel bad for him. Just for a second though. He really is full of shit, so Davey has put him in his place for a while.

The doorbell goes and before anyone can even approach the door, it swings open and Bungalow Bill bounds in. He's holding a Tesco bag filled with his carry-out and has clearly been energized with some type of illegal substance before he came here.

Bungalow Bill got his name because people say he has

nothing upstairs. That seems to be true. Every time I meet him, he seems to be nothing other than clinically insane. He's not a violent guy; in fact, he is quite the opposite. He just does whatever he can to make people laugh. He makes his living by falling over in an amazingly convincing way. Usually he falls in large supermarket chains. He looks out for floors that have just been cleaned. His biggest pay out to date was when he slipped on a grape in large supermarket and broke his leg in two places. How the grape got on the floor remains an unanswered question but we all know what happened. He doesn't just fall over either. He has to do some kind of acrobatics so that when he does eventually land, the damage is more serious.

He is walking fine at the moment, so he must be due for a fall soon.

When he walks into the kitchen, the place gets loud almost immediately. He has such a presence. Everyone knows he is hilarious and they gravitate to him in droves. He does the rounds of saying hello to everyone and bows down to Callum, pretending to worship him. He gets up and shakes my hand… quickly followed by a lick to my face. By the time I have reacted and wiped the dampness from my cheek, he has moved on to feeling up people inappropriately. He gets the odd slap from women for his cupping of their breasts or squeezing of their arse but he takes it all in his stride.

The whole room is watching Bungalow Bill now.

He spots Lisa and her friends at the other side of the room. He drops his carrier bag and approaches what is clearly a group of beautiful women.

"Oh now. Who are you?" he asks Lisa as he walks round her, assessing her measurements with his eyes.

Lisa laughs with embarrassment and looks over at me, eyes wide in disbelief. She watches me as Bungalow pretends to cuddle her, his tongue hanging out in jest.

"Will you marry me?" he asks as Lisa tries to edge away from his nonsense.

"Hmm, I think you will have to ask my bodyguard," Lisa replies, still laughing at his animated patter.

She looks over to me and Bungalow stops in his tracks. He spends a few seconds looking back and forth between Lisa and me. Then he bounds over and shouts, "You lucky bastard!" before slapping me on the backside and running off into the other room.

Everyone laughs, except Callum, and the noise levels increase in the other room as he causes havoc with the others in there.

The main guests have arrived now and the party is picking up momentum. A combination of chilled dance music and chatter contributes to the relaxed atmosphere and mood.

Callum turns to me and suggests, "Taxis at ten?"

I agree with a nod and pick up my phone to indicate that I will make the phone call.

The taxi company we use know Callum's house, they know me, they know what we get up to and they also know, more importantly, that we tip very well. I order two minibuses for Callum, me and the main guests. Then I tell them to send another half dozen cars for the remaining people in the house.

Callum looks over the room to me for a progress update. I nod to him again to indicate it has all been taken care of. He nods back and then does a side nod, beckoning me to follow him out to the garage through the door in the kitchen.

A lot is said between us via head nodding but that only comes from being friends for so long.

I follow Callum out into the garage and he points to a glass sheet with some lines of white powder chopped out in great precision.

"Try this stuff. It's fuckin' dynamite," he directs me with an excited tone.

He hands me a rolled-up note and I snort a line up each nostril. "Woooo!" I shout, as I rub my nose and hand the note back to Callum.

"Amazing, isn't it?"

"Definitely. That's instant."

"Aye, it's straight off the boat."

"Nice."

"Just keep this for our team, don't let any of the fannies know that it's here."

I nod in agreement. This is too good to share with the masses.

"Listen, all that carry on with Sandy last night, I need you to turn a blind eye."

I don't respond, just look at him and wait for an explanation.

"I'm involved in some business with him which will earn us good coin, that's all I can tell you right now. I'm seeing him later for an update, he wasn't too impressed about his method of transport home last night, trying to keep on his good side now you know?"

I shrug my shoulders. "Now I know why I couldn't smash him last night." I've known Callum a long time and this is the first time I have felt uneasy about his choice of business partner.

We walk back out to the kitchen and I start to feel the hit. Confidence levels are through the roof and the prospect of a good night stops me thinking about that dickhead Sandy Pratt. Lisa approaches and whispers, "Follow me." Everyone watches as we leave together. It's clear that Lisa wants people to know that we are interested in each other.

We don't speak, I just stare at her legs and perfect bum moving up the stairs in front of me while her perfume delicately wafts in my face.

We go into one of the spare bedrooms that hasn't been

claimed by anyone yet. She still hasn't said anything, but she gives me a look with those beautiful eyes that tells me she wants me.

We kiss again, passionately and attentively. She gently nibbles my earlobe and whispers, "I want you to be with me tonight. All night. In the club, I want you by my side. After that I want to lie naked with you in this bed."

I smile and respond with, "Sounds good to me," defying Callum's earlier warning.

Another kiss and she wipes the lipstick from my face and winks at me. She walks out of the room knowing she's got me wrapped around her little finger.

"Ronin, the cars are here!"

Callum shouts from downstairs and comes bounding up to meet me on the landing. He hands me a wad of fifty-pound notes. "This is for the ABCD last night."

There is no point in arguing with him when it comes to cash bonuses. It's a lot easier to take it and thank him.

He hands me a silver bullet.

"It's loaded with the gear from the garage."

I smile and he gives me a coke-induced hug and again I'm suspicious: he's not a hugger.

We head downstairs and Callum barks various orders to Eric; lock the doors, stock the fridge for the after party, make sure everyone gets in a taxi. Eric obeys without question and runs around in a panic.

We all pile into the first minibus. The driver knows us, so we say the usual hello and exchange some idle banter. As the driver slides the door open, I see Lisa sitting on the seat in front of me. Her legs are crossed and her smooth, toned thighs invite me in with the help of a smile. She pats the seat next to her and I sit down without hesitation.

Callum decides to sit in the front with the driver. He catches my eye in the driver's mirror, frowning slightly. As the vehicle starts to move, I feel Lisa's hand gently clasp mine. I look at her and again she says nothing, just looks at me with those amazing eyes and I wonder what the fuck Callum's problem is with her.

I lean forward and look over Callum's shoulder to see he is texting Sandy Pratt. *Package secured, get everything ready... .C.*

11

THE DRIVER STOPS THE VEHICLE at the front entrance of the club and accepts a fifty-pound note from Callum as a tip. Kirkcaldy taxi drivers love him because he tips so well.

All the way to the club my mind was going over and over the words in Callum's cryptic text to Sandy, trying to think of an explanation. What is the package? What needs to be ready?

As the thoughts are spinning in my head, I have to give myself a shake. The combination of drugs, alcohol and serious lack of sleep is giving me the come down from hell. It's paranoia, that's all it is. I know enough about Callum's previous shady deals to know that a 'package' could mean anything and I've no logical reason to doubt him; he's one of my best mates who I would trust with my life. Despite rationalising all this, I still feel uneasy.

I pull the bullet out from my pocket and administer it into

my nostril, taking a quick sniff. Callum does the same with his and Lisa leans over to take a hit too. Now adequately intoxicated, we are ready to go inside and see what the night brings.

We spill out of the minibus as a crowd and are faced with a massive queue of people waiting to get in the front door. Bright pink neon lights spell out 'Danza' and the muffled tones of dance music can be heard from within, occasionally escaping in loud bursts every time the door is opened to let people inside.

I walk past the queue and go straight to the front door. The bouncers know us well and after shaking hands and exchanging some banter, they ask how many. I say there are six of us, with the rest not too far behind. They wave us in, ahead of everybody waiting, sparking an unhappy chorus of protest and abusive language from punters in the queue.

As soon as we get through the door, Italian John skips enthusiastically up to us. He makes a fuss of the ladies in our party and follows with some eager hand-shaking and back-patting of the lads.

"Look ata dis eh? All-a the beautiful people have come-a to my-a wee club. Ladies, you look-a magnifico! I have-a the champagne on ice up-a-stairs."

Callum and I smirk to each other. His patter is murder but he's a great host.

The short Italian strides ahead and leads us upstairs to the VIP lounge, where the entire area is cordoned off for us to use at our disposal. Three staff stand behind the bar, dressed immaculately with 'Danza' emblazoned in pink across the front of their black T-shirts, waiting to serve us drinks.

The VIP lounge is a classy venue, with mood lighting, expensive and tasteful seating and well dressed, polite bar staff who smile when they speak to you. The girls go straight for the champagne and the sound of popping corks signifies the official beginning of the evening, like the starting pistol for a race. Whoops and cheers accompany the eruption of bubbles; the excitement is palpable, which makes me smile.

John sits beside Callum at the bar delivering half-Scottish and half-Italian rants about business, a particular favourite being his annoyance with cleaning crews and how they steal drink, thinking he doesn't know about it. Callum listens politely, sipping his drink with occasional glances in my direction and rolling of the eyes.

I scan the area as I always do. Despite being Callum's friend, I am also his employee and when I am with him I am on duty. I need to make sure I know what's going on around me because something always kicks off in a nightclub. There are too many phony hard men fuelled by alcohol and designer drugs who want to settle a beef with their fists, and the women are even worse.

Sandy Pratt is already in the area and I see him with two of his fake gangsters sitting at the other side of the room. He's bursting out of a three-piece suit, sweating profusely and offering sleazy chat-up lines to girls half his age. His accomplices are sporting freshly applied plasters to the grazes from where I left my mark last night. I'll be keeping an eye on them tonight.

I can see the dancefloor from the VIP lounge and I look over the balcony with mild interest. It's busy as usual and among a sea of bodies moving to the music, I see a large crowd clustered together in the middle of the floor. It's a mix of posers, wannabe body builders and women in tiny clothes: legs and tits everywhere. Nothing new to see but the more I watch, the more it seems like people are gravitating towards one guy, who has definitely read the 'how to be a complete fud' handbook. I feel instant dislike towards him. He is over-confident and brash, which rings alarm bells. His whole appearance irritates me; his white polo shirt has the collar pulled up and he has a pencil-line beard with a pair of sunglasses balanced on his head. "You're in a nightclub, where's the sun, you fanny?" I mutter to myself.

Nothing seems to be happening with the group, so I quickly scan the rest of the dancefloor and I am satisfied that we can relax and be comfortable. The rest of Callum's crowd have arrived from the house and are being escorted into the VIP lounge by the head bouncer, Mac, a good guy who we have known for years.

I catch Mac's eye and tap the side of my nose, nodding my head in the direction of the toilets. He smiles and heads off towards them. I follow him and hand him my bullet. He knows what to do, so I leave him to it while I assess my hair and clothes in the mirror.

"Fuckin' hell!" he cries as he takes a hit from the shiny device.

"I know. Decent, isn't it?"

"Where did you get that shit?" His face is instantly red as he enthusiastically sniffs another dose of powder up his nostril.

"It's straight off the boat."

"It certainly is." He rubs his nose, inspecting his face and black suit for any incriminating white residue.

"Stick around and you can get some more later," I offer.

"Thanks, mate, but if I have any more of that I'll be on that dancefloor myself!" He laughs and heads out of the toilet, back down to the main floor, with a slight spring in his step. I walk back into the VIP lounge, and the party has moved up a notch: everyone has accelerated into full party mode.

Someone is missing. Davey.

Shit the bed. That usually means trouble. I'm not worried about him, just worried about what he is capable of.

I walk over to the balcony again and look down to the main floor. Carefully and slowly, I try to identify Davey from the moving shapes and silhouettes in the area.

I spy him but what the fuck is he doing? He's standing near the entrance on his own, watching people come in. Something isn't right, so I catch the attention of Callum, signalling to let him know that I am going downstairs. He responds with a simple nod and goes back to entertaining the harem of model-like beauties which has surrounded him.

Mac is standing at the bottom of the stairs which leads up to the VIP area. He sees me coming down and jumps to attention, overcompensating for the fact that the gear I gave him is working very well.

"I need you for a second," I say in his ear.

He nods and follows me obediently, full of Columbian stimulated keenness.

I approach Davey, shaking his hand as I ask him what he is doing. He is fairly drunk and is very wound up about something.

"My lassie and fuckface have split up, I always knew he was a wanker, ken? Didn't like him from the first time I met him." He spits the words out angrily.

"What's he done now?" I ask, knowing this is not the first drama between them.

"Ah, he's fuckin' done it this time, the wee cunt has sent photos of Marie to all his mates, gone right roond the houses, every fuckin' cunt in Kirkcaldy's probably seen her minge by now." His eyes are red and wild, he's wanting blood, I can see it, oh dear.

"What are you going to do?" I ask gently, keen not to exacerbate the situation.

"I'm gonna give him a permanent injury," he says matter-of-factly.

"Let me sort it out, Davey. Don't get your hands dirty on a wee shit like that."

"He'll be here soon enough. Thanks for the offer but I have it sorted."

Davey smiles and steps into the shadows. I watch as he reaches into his trouser pocket and pulls out a long, shiny, metal object, just enough to show me what it is.

A fuckin' sword. He has cut a hole in his pocket and the blade stretches the length of his leg.

"Fuckin' hell, Davey, don't use that," I urge him quietly.

"Why not?" he asks me with genuine surprise.

"Well, I don't think attacking your daughter's ex with a sword is going to bring many good things your way. How about we go and get a drink, do a few lines and I'll ask the bouncers to boot fuck out of him later?"

Davey shakes his head at me with defiance. I put my hands on his shoulders and look at him sternly in a way that tells him I am not fucking around.

"Come on, big guy, let's put the sword somewhere safe and have some fun."

It takes a second or two. Davey looks at the floor, then the entrance and then me.

"Ah, okay. Maybe I'm overreacting a bit."

"Good man, Davey," I say and I nod to Mac to get him to join us. "Don't get me wrong, the boy needs a kicking but using a sword is just going to get messy. I'll make sure he gets what he deserves."

Davey momentarily looks emotional and thanks me, the red mist disappearing from his eyes. We walk into the disabled toilets at the far end of the club and Davey pulls out the sword. The dents and scratches indicate that it's well used, and not from carving the Sunday roast. I take it from him, surprised at its weight, and hand it to Mac.

"Do something with it. Keep it safe somewhere and we will pick it up next week."

The bouncer looks at me expectantly.

I sigh and exhale a 'Fuckin hell' with exasperation as I hand him my bullet again. He quickly supplies each nostril, thanks me and, attempting to hide the sword under his black blazer, takes it to the office behind the main bar.

I figure Davey needs to straighten himself out a bit too, so I hand him my bullet. He takes what he wants and then checks his appearance in the mirror.

We leave the disabled toilet and Davey heads straight up to the VIP lounge. I am just about to join him but the fanny with the sunglasses catches my eye again. He is getting a lot of attention from various people and I suspect he is a small-time dealer or has some cash to splash.

Fuck it, I'll leave it. My instincts are out of control tonight. I'm over suspicious and paranoid. I need to cut loose a bit.

I start to walk upstairs towards the VIP lounge. When I'm halfway up, the door opens and a crowd of excited ladies with a few men all herd en masse down towards the dancefloor. I pull myself to the side, up against the banister as I let them pass.

As I turn forward again I see Lisa, slowly walking down the stairs towards me. The beautiful eyes, the stunning figure and the dress that makes every movement a work of art.

No matter how cool I try to be, there's nothing I can do but smile. She smiles back at me and as she arrives on the same step, she pushes her body up against mine and delivers a kiss so sensual I never want it to end. She pulls back and gently drags her fingers across my chest.

"I'm going for a dance, want to join me?" she asks.

"Tempting, but I need to check in with the boys upstairs."

She smiles as if she knew I was going to say that, "Okay, I won't be long."

She gives me a little kiss on the cheek and heads down to the dancefloor where the group are waving to her to join them. All the men stare and step up their embarrassing Dad dancing as they look at her, hoping to be noticed. I don't blame them; she is special. She's a head-turner, the kind of woman that walks into a bar and wives start hitting their husbands because their eyes have popped out of their heads and jaws have hit the floor.

When I get back into the VIP lounge, Davey is laughing and joking with Callum and the other lads. It seems like the sword situation has been diffused… for the time being. My check in takes the form of a few nods and raised eyebrows from the boys. I let out a sigh and wonder why I have to sort out everyone else's shit. But it's all I know and what I'm good at.

I lean up against the bar and listen to the exchange of stories. Callum has some crackers, stories of every rule in the book being broken, tales about unattainable women and furious husbands, dodgy business deals gone wrong and legendary 'business trips' with the boys.

I feel the coke wearing off a little, so I casually stroll into the toilet and chop a couple of substantial lines on the back of the toilet seat. That's me sorted for a while and I walk back to the bar to order a beer. I feel my heart flutter as the gear courses through my veins and feel the urge to contribute enthusiastically to the conversation. After a while, I get itchy feet and scan the area again, looking down to the dancefloor, watching everyone bounce to the tunes.

I see Lisa and the girls, all dancing around and having a great time. I'm not a dancer, never have been, but there's always a first time for everything.

Callum approaches on my left side, scanning the dancefloor with me. He's checking out his options for company later; I can read him like a book. There's only one lady on my mind though and I am keeping it that way.

As I take a swig of beer, Callum nudges me and points downstairs, making two fingers walk across an imaginary table. "Let's talk a walk."

We head downstairs and into the area next to the dancefloor. A variety of people approach us to say hello and do the obligatory ass-kissing. Callum's power and influence are like a magnet and it's embarrassing how obvious, even desperate people become when they try to gain his favour and be his 'friend'. He sees them coming and has become skilled at batting them off with cutting one-liners.

As we reach the edge of the dancefloor, Lisa spots us and dances her way over to where we are standing. Two of her friends follow and they try to lure us to go with them and spank the planks. It's not happening. They knew that before they approached us but it is an excuse for Lisa and me to have another kiss before she disappears back into the pulsating throng of bodies.

"She's keen, eh?" Callum comments as we stand watching the movers and shakers strut their stuff on the dance floor.

"So am I," I reply with a smile.

Callum shakes his head and sighs. "You need to listen to me about her, she's got trouble written all over her."

I raise an eyebrow and there is an awkward silence between us. Callum looks like he's about to say something but decides against it, shaking his head in disapproval again. He turns away stiffly, pretending to check out the ladies on the dancefloor but he is rattled, I can tell. I just don't understand why.

My bladder is telling me I need to break the seal and use the toilet. Taking my chance to escape, I signal to Callum that I'm heading in that direction as Davey and Bungalow Bill join us. Their appearance is a welcome relief from the growing tension between us. I leave his side, still confused as to why he wanted to take a walk. Usually that means he wants to show me a tidy girl or talk business. Clearly, this was neither.

As I walk towards the toilet, I glance behind me and I am astounded to see Callum shaking hands with the fud in the white polo shirt and dodgy facial hair. They are talking earnestly into each other's ears over the booming music. I almost walk back to find out what the hell is going on but I check myself for being paranoid again. It remains in the back of my mind though, niggling like a trapped penny in a money bank.

As I walk through the toilet door, Trevor, the black toilet attendant appears. He's just starting his shift and laying out an extensive selection of fake aftershaves beside a hand basin. He pops some small change into a silver tip tray to make it look like he's having a shit night. He holds out his hand to me with enthusiasm. He's another one who adopts a British name despite being from Nigeria.

"Have you washed your hands?" I joke with him before shaking his hand.

Trevor laughs. "How are you doing, mate?"

After exchanging pleasantries, I head to the long, steel urinal fixed to the wall. I stare down as I start to pee on the blue cakes and watch as they crumble. Chewing gum and oddly, some empty pint glasses have a place within the steel basin and some dirty bastard has had a go at trying to fill one of the glasses with bright yellow piss.

When I finish, Trevor is waiting with the handwash and a pile of paper towels. He makes sure that I get plenty of time to wash my hands thoroughly, pressing the tops of the taps for me. I award him a tenner and he thanks me wholeheartedly. I smile as he sticks the money in his pocket and leaves the coins in his tip tray untouched.

A couple of intoxicated younger lads barge in and tell Trevor to go and fuck himself when he offers them aftershave. I take a small step towards them and they quickly change their minds. People are always so unnecessarily rude to toilet attendants; they are just trying to make a living.

I head back out into the club and see Callum standing at the top of the stairs, now deep in conversation with Sandy Pratt. As I make my way towards them, Callum catches my eye and ends the conversation abruptly before I get the chance to hear what they are discussing. This irritates me, to say the least. It's also unnerving. Callum is never usually secretive about any of his activities, especially with me.

Sandy hurriedly pushes past me on the stairs, nodding and mumbling some kind of half-arsed pleasantry, which I ignore. Callum turns his back on me and heads towards the VIP Lounge. He takes a seat away from the rest of the group and I march up to him, fully intending to challenge him about what going on. He nods his head to the seat next to him, clearly wanting a discreet chat.

12

I TAKE A SEAT BESIDE him and he can tell by the look on my face that I am suspicious about his conversation with Sandy. I don't say anything, I just swig my beer and maintain eye contact as I wait for him to start talking. He looks uncomfortable and even a little jumpy.

"I know you hate that cunt… so do I but he's going to make us some decent money."

"By doing what exactly?" I ask. "The only thing that fat little sleazeball can make is microwave kebabs and crisp sandwiches."

Callum looks taken aback at my response but continues.

"He's involved with people who need our help. I've told him that you will represent our company and help these people. It will be fantastic coin for all of us."

I stare at him, unimpressed at his bullshit: in other words he's offering my services to that loser.

"What will I be doing? Was I going to have a say in any of this?"

"It's nothing messy, don't worry, just a bit of client management."

"Client management?" I say sceptically.

"Look, there are high-profile customers flying into Edinburgh Airport to visit a…" He pauses, trying to find the right word. "Entertainment establishment. And before you say it, it's not a brothel, it's a classy joint that caters to the client needs, bespoke packages, you know? There are some wealthy fuckers who pay a lot of money for special services. All I'm asking you to do is to greet them at the airport and take them to an address in Edinburgh. You pick them up afterwards and either take them to their hotel or back to the airport. That's it."

He's talking quickly now because the look on my face says it all.

"It all has to be top secret. Some of these customers are high flyers, people who can't be seen attending certain type of places if you know what I mean?"

I glare at him in a way I have never done before, aghast at the proposal he has just put to me.

"You have got to be fucking kidding me," I mutter, trying not to draw attention to us but at the same time I'm so furious I can't hold back. "I don't want any involvement in that kind of shit, it's not my bag and I'm amazed that you are even entertaining it."

Callum puts a calming hand on my shoulder.

"Look, this isn't my usual thing but honestly all you need to be is a glorified bodyguard. I have a blacked-out Range Rover ready, you pick up the customers and drop them off. That's it, nothing else involved. We will make good cash, you will be handsomely rewarded and I am asking you this favour because you are the person I trust the most."

"I don't like where I am taking them and I don't like being involved."

"You're not fucking involved. You're fucking driving people there and picking them up. That's it. I'm starting to get a bit ratty about this now, and anyway I've asked you to do worse."

Callum is angry. I have never seen him like this with me before. I get the feeling he doesn't have much choice in it either.

"So, what if I refuse?" I ask him, defiantly.

"You can't refuse. You work for me and I'm telling you to do it. Not asking, telling. There are bigger people than me involved in this and they will not take kindly to you refusing to do your part."

I'm furious, so furious that for the first time ever, I feel like Callum's employee and not his friend.

"Why are you speaking to me like this?" I ask him, looking straight into his eyes.

Callum twitches and for a moment looks upset. He leans forward, puts both hands on my shoulders and exhales with frustration.

"Look, you know how much I think of you and appreciate all the work you do and the friendship we have. But I need you to do this for me. If you don't there will serious repercussions. These people are the real deal and are using Sandy to get me involved." He's pleading with me now. "If I don't play my part I'll need to go into hiding, I've already committed to the job. It's that serious, bud."

I feel pity for him now but I'm still angry because he has been so completely fucking stupid. It's the same old Callum though; he sees the pound signs, agrees to do stuff and leaves me to do all the dirty work.

The tension subsides a little and I turn away from him, thinking through his request. I can't believe I am going to agree to this.

"Okay, when does all this start?" I ask reluctantly.

"Soon, mate. Thanks, I couldn't make this work without you."

I give a half-hearted nod and stand up. I need a whisky. Callum doesn't stop me – he knows me well enough by now and he knows he is pushing my boundaries to the limit. I need to be away from him for a while.

As I walk up to the bar, Lisa and the girls come back into the VIP room waving empty champagne glasses. I look over to them and watch as Lisa glides around, almost floating. Her vibrancy and beauty puts me in a trance, so I can't help but stare at her.

She catches me looking and drifts towards me with a huge smile, planting a kiss on my lips, throwing her arms around me. I pause for a second to take in her sweet face. She looks back at me with those big, beautiful green eyes and we have a moment where we don't even need to say anything.

"Are you okay?" I ask her.

"I'm great, how are you?" she replies softly.

"I've been better." I waver slightly, reluctant to say any more and attempt a weak smile.

"What's wrong?" she asks, sensing my apprehension.

"I'm fine, don't worry, yeah, totally fine," I convince myself and give her another kiss. "Go and join the girls, I'm going to get a dram."

She smiles, squeezes my hand and returns to her friends.

At the bar I order a large twenty-year-old Macallan. I am feeling so deflated after the chat with Callum that I know even a malt won't perk me up.

In the mirror behind the bar I see Sandy coming into the lounge, laughing and joking with the guy wearing the polo shirt and sunglasses. "Fucking brilliant," I swear to myself and down the whisky in one gulp. Sandy disappears into the loo and I keep an eye on the polo shirt prick. I watch as he picks up the champagne and takes a swig straight from the bottle. Wanker.

Callum comes out of the toilets and talks quietly in my ear.

"I need you to take care of something for me."

"What's happened now?" I say, instantly alert and back in work mode.

"A friend of mine is in a bit of a state. She's had one too many and she needs to go home."

"Put her in a fuckin' taxi then," I snap with disbelief.

"No, she's somebody that needs to be looked after. Her ex man is a friend of ours."

He means someone who we do business with.

"Fuxake," I sigh. "Where is she?"

"Sandy is away to get her. He saw her staggering around downstairs. She can't be seen like that, she needs to go home and we need to make sure that happens."

"Where does she live?"

"Markinch. Just get her in a taxi, take her home, close the door behind you and come back to my place."

"Okay."

"You're a star. Thanks, bud."

I look behind him to see Sandy holding up a gorgeous woman by the arms. She is dressed immaculately and is stunning even by my standards. The downside is that she is barely able to stand and I hate seeing any woman in that kind of state. My protective instincts kick in, so I go over to Sandy and help to hold her up. I know who she is: Catrina Spencer, I now understand why Callum wants her taken home. Her ex-husband, Mitch Spencer, is a proper gangster who is very protective of his ex-wife, despite causing the break-up of their marriage with his own infidelity.

Sandy lets go and I sit her down. I shout to the barman to get me some water as I gently push her back on the sofa. After I pull her brown hair back from her face, I can see she has had more than just alcohol. Her eyes are glazed and her fine features spoiled by smudged make-up.

I take the water from the barman and try to make her drink

it. This woman has clearly lived a life of luxury; she's beautiful, tanned and toned. Despite this, Catrina's drunken demeanour indicates to me that she is deeply unhappy.

I ask her who she is with, where they are, what she has taken but she has lost the power of speech completely and her eyes keep closing. She needs to go home now and I'm concerned we may even need to go via the hospital.

I get up, lean out the door of the lounge and shout to Mac.

"Can you get a taxi organised, mate? Going to Markinch."

"Nae bother, give me two minutes," Mac replies as he turns and heads out of the club exit. There's always a queue of taxis waiting at the rank outside.

As I go back in to check on Catrina, I notice the polo shirt guy trying to edge his way into the crowd of girls. Callum is talking to Davey and I interrupt him to ask who the guy is.

"He's a pal of Sandy's. Polish boy, Pavel or something like that."

I don't even respond to Callum, as just at that moment I see Pavel trying his best moves on Lisa. I march over to them.

"Don't even think about it," I snarl as I square up to him. "This lady is with me, understand?" I tell him while I gently take Lisa's hand.

Her hand tightens on mine and she stands behind me. This buffoon has made her nervous.

Pavel looks me in the eye and grins smugly.

"Do you understand?" I repeat, this time slowly and staring through his eyes.

He doesn't answer me, he pulls his sunglasses down over his eyes and walks away.

Lisa puts her hand on my chest, still holding onto my hand tightly.

"I don't like him, he was very sleazy, asking me if I was interested in being a model, offering to set up a photo shoot."

"Stay away from him, whatever you do. I have to go and do

a bit of work for Callum but I will see you back at the house, okay?"

"What do you have to do?"

"See that lady over there, the one falling asleep on the couch?"

"Yes."

"I need to take her home, she's had too much and we know her ex, he's one of us."

"Why you?" she asks.

It's a fair question and I feel a little embarrassed.

"It's my job to take care of things," I tell her.

"I don't want you to go," she says, tightening the grip on my hand.

"Don't worry, the girls are all here and Callum will look after you."

She doesn't say anything, she just looks at me pleadingly. I give her a heartfelt kiss and ease my hand out of her grip.

"I'll see you back at Callum's," I reassure her and she offers a little wave to me.

The head doorman signals to me that there is a taxi waiting and helps me escort Catrina out of the club. A nod from Callum is the last thing I see before I leave.

13

CATRINA IS SO SMASHED THAT her legs don't work properly so getting her to the taxi and into it is not easy. Between the doorman and I, we somehow manage it.

The taxi driver asks where we are headed and all I know is that her home is in Markinch. I give the driver this instruction with a guarantee that I will have the exact address by the time we get there.

Catrina is asleep, passed out and slumped against me. I try to straighten her up but she flops onto my shoulder again.

"Had a good night?" the driver asks, attempting to break the silence.

"Not the best, mate. I seem to be looking after everyone else."

"There's nothing worse, son."

"Agreed."

I need to try to get a few words out of Catrina to find out

where exactly she lives. I nudge her and try to prop her head up.

"Hey, I'm taking you home now but I need to know your address."

She mumbles something incomprehensible.

"Try again, what's the street?"

"Mmmmmmmmmac.... dnnnnn.... lld....... place."

"Okay, what number?"

No response.

I give her another nudge and a little jiggle to try to grasp the last essential piece of information.

"Twenty."

That's it. I have everything I need from her and now I will let her sleep.

"Did you hear that, driver?"

"Aye, son – twenty MacDonald Place, nae bother, I'll get you there."

The rest of the journey is silent. I'm tired, so I close my eyes for a while. The last thing I see is the street lights flashing by the window as we head from the town centre and onto the dual carriageway towards Catrina's home.

I must have dozed off for about ten minutes but it felt a lot longer. The driver wakens me with the noise of his door opening and then opening mine. Taking an arm each, we manage to get Catrina to the front door then I hand him a fifty-pound note. He scrambles about for change but I tell him to keep it.

It's a struggle trying to hold up Catrina while I search through her handbag for house keys. Eventually I find them and open the door.

It's a beautiful home, decorated tastefully probably with the help of an interior designer.

Catrina seems to straighten up a bit now once she realises that she is home. I help her up the stairs and take her into the room that seems to be her bedroom, going by the décor, rejected dresses thrown on the bed, and high heels in the corner. In a clumsy manoeuvre, I manage to land her in the bed and throw the covers over her. I turn on the bedside lamp and her eyes pop open, as if she has just realised where she is.

She seems to recognise me and asks, "What are you doing here?"

"I brought you home. You had one too many tonight, so we wanted to make sure you got home safely."

She smiles and pulls me towards her, kissing me and tugging me towards her bed.

I let the kiss happen briefly but pull away. Any other time, I might have entertained a kiss from her but she is in no fit state to make that decision. Above all else, there is only one girl on my mind.

I pull away from her and turn off the light.

"Don't go," she slurs as she closes her eyes again.

I run downstairs to her kitchen to pour her a glass of water. By the time I get back to the side of her bed to place it on the cabinet, she is fast asleep.

I leave her house, lock the front door and post her keys through the letter box.

The taxi driver is waiting for me, I stride up the driveway and get into the passenger side. I give him Callum's address and take a final glance at Catrina's house. I smile to myself, relieved that she is home and feeling kind of glad that I helped her. The kiss meant nothing; she was probably just lonely. Should I tell Lisa about it? Nah, why muddy the waters? It's not relevant.

I text Callum to tell him that Catrina Spencer is tucked up in bed and ask him if he is back at his house.

Ten minutes later and there is no reply. I try to phone and there is no answer, which is strange. His phone is always on him. His behaviour right now is so out of character I feel I no longer know him or even trust him.

I think about seeing Lisa again and start to plan out Sunday afternoon. When we get up, we are going on a date, a proper date, with food, laughs and fun. I want to know everything there is to know about her. I want to get to know her properly.

They say that you always know when you meet the right one. I always thought that was a pile of crap but it's true. I am convinced beyond a shadow of a doubt she is the one for me.

I exchange some general banter with the taxi driver and close my eyes again. It will take half an hour to get to Callum's, I may as well take a power nap.

Ronin

/rəʊnɪn/

noun, *historical*

noun: **ronin**; plural noun: **ronin**;

plural noun: **ronins**

(in feudal Japan) a wandering samurai
who had no lord or master.

"masterless man, outcast, outlaw,"
1871, from Japanese, from ro "wave"
+ nin "man."

14

MY NAME IS NOT A spelling mistake. I
trained in martial arts for years but the fights didn't pay
enough. When Callum presented the much younger me with
an opportunity, I just couldn't say no. Moving into this line of
work meant I had to scale down my training. My sensei was a
dedicated and honourable man. Unfortunately when he heard
the rumours about who I was involved with and what I did for
them, he was highly offended. In his eyes I had disrespected
him and his culture; it was an unforgivable offence.

As punishment, he expelled me from his dojo. I can still
hear the disappointment in his voice when he told me. He
said that there was nothing but trouble ahead now that I had
chosen the path of a Ronin. Sensei was the closest thing I had
to a father figure in my life and I'd let him down. I'd let myself
down. I decided to adopt Ronin as my identity because that's
exactly what I had become. From that point on I moved into

a world where no-one knew my real name. I'd left my old life behind and anyone who knew me from before was shut out. I've managed to keep it that way.

I'm not really sleeping, I'm dozing, as my mind is recounting the past. I can hear an occasional disturbance from the taxi driver's radio and indicators ticking as he turns corners. Closing my eyes is enough to relax me at least and all I am thinking about is lying next to Lisa. I want to feel her head on my chest, feel the warmth of her body. The urge to see her is overwhelming so I want the taxi to hurry up and get me there.

Going back to Callum's is usually fun, but I have had enough of it already this weekend, I don't want to stay there. I want to go home to my house with Lisa, show her my home, spend time with her there and relax. I want to make breakfast for her. I want to talk to her normally without being fucked up on drugs and alcohol. I can visualise her sleepy face, feel her dishevelled hair as we lie together peacefully until we both wake up properly. These thoughts are all-consuming, it's all I can think about.

The crunch of gravel jolts me out of my dreamlike state as the taxi turns off the main road and heads up the driveway to Callum's house. My eyes ping open and I see the house is illuminated inside, telling me everyone is back. I stretch and rub my eyes. "Ah, shit," I groan at the thought of going back to the party.

The taxi driver smiles as I hand him another fifty-pound note. "Thanks, son. Take it easy."

My response is barely coherent as I get out of the car and head towards Callum's house. My only motivation for going in, is Lisa.

15

FUCK, I'M SO TIRED. I have put my body through the wringer over the past forty-eight hours and the drugs have worn off. There is no longer a buzz which means it takes all my strength to ring the doorbell.

Eric answers the door with his standard subservient manner and ushers me through to the kitchen. Everybody is fucked up once again so my entrance goes unnoticed. I help myself to a beer and I look around the kitchen. There are a couple of groups of people deep in conversation. Not all the guests have returned to Callum's after the club: the numbers have definitely reduced. I glance over to the island to see the large pane of glass is still there with the usual heap of white powder on it. The thought of taking a line makes my stomach turn, forcing me to look away.

Something's not right. As I take in my surroundings I realise that I barely recognise any of the people in the kitchen.

It's also too quiet. Where are the dancing girls and where is Lisa?

I walk through to the lounge and see Callum sitting in his usual seat, flicking through TV channels. He looks up at me and gives me a strangely lifeless nod. I look out through the back windows to see that the hot tub is empty. Only a couple of joint smokers are out there, staring back at me as I peer out. Callum is clearly not in the mood to chat so I step back out into the hall and collide with Davey who is stepping out of the toilet, fastening his belt with his buttons undone.

"Where the fuck is everybody?"

"Szzzzz ssssst, fffffp d a styp."

Fuckin' hell, Davey is completely shit faced. He's making no sense and I doubt that I will get any out of him tonight.

I push past him to run upstairs, taking them two at a time. Nobody here, the bedrooms are in darkness and they haven't been disturbed. Back downstairs, I push past Davey again, still trying to fasten his jeans. He attempts to say something but his bleary eyes and incoherent slurs are wasting my time.

Callum looks up at me as I stride into the lounge again.

"Where's Lisa?" I ask with urgency.

Callum shrugs.

"What do you mean? I left her with all of you in the club"

"Fuck knows where she is. Hardly anybody came back after the club. I wasn't up for it."

He looks at me with indifference and eventually resumes his position, staring at the TV, while stragglers party around him.

What the fuck is going on? I ask myself as I march back through to the kitchen.

There's no point in trying to interrogate Davey: he's lying face down now beside the hall table, hasn't quite made it to the kitchen. I find Eric and ask him where my car keys are. He looks at me with surprise and then scuttles off to get them.

"Here they are, Ronin. Is everything okay?"

"The girl I was with, Lisa, where is she? Where are her friends? They were all supposed to be back here."

"What girl?"

"Don't try my fuckin patience you fuckin' dipshit, the girl I was with all night, dark hair, black dress, Eastern European."

"I never noticed her."

I look at Eric with disbelief. For a moment I start to wonder whether he is lying to me or if he really hasn't noticed because he has spent all night kissing Callum's ass. I shake my head at him in disgust and frustration. Quickly, I turn and head out of the kitchen, down the hallway and towards the front door.

The fucking rain has started again, so I quickly unlock my car and get in. As I hurriedly start the engine and shift into reverse, I see lights coming up the driveway behind me. A minibus appears behind my car, so I stop the engine and watch as Sandy Pratt and a group of girls run inside the house to avoid the rain.

I quickly turn off the engine and follow the group into the house. There's a bit more noise and activity now as the group disperse to different rooms, some straight to the toilet, others head for the gear on the table and the guys take bottles out of the fridge.

It takes a moment for me to calibrate and try to establish who everyone is. They all seem to be here, except Lisa. One of her friends appears, staggering slightly, heading towards the bathroom. I approach her before she gets there. She smiles as she greets me.

"Hey, Sarah, where's Lisa?" I ask, trying to disguise my panic.

"She was with us until the end, we couldn't all fit in one minibus, so we had to order two. She will be here in the next one."

"Okay, thanks."

I feel some relief at this news and decide to take another beer from the fridge to calm myself down. I'm still uneasy about something but I can't quite put my finger on it.

The beer is cold and refreshing, helping me quickly cool down and keep to myself, exchanging idle banter with a few of the other guests. I go over to where Davey is lying and give him a gentle kick in the ribs to make sure he is still alive. He reacts with a sleepy groan and a loud fart. Yep, he's okay.

For ten minutes I wait. Eventually I hear the front door opening again and more girls spill into the house, the wind blowing in some of the heavy rain that's pouring outside. It feels like slow motion as I watch each lady walk into the kitchen. One by one they come in, scattering in different directions until there is nobody else coming in.

Lisa isn't there.

I grab one of the other girls by the arm and pull her aside. She looks at me with concern as I tighten my grip.

"Where is Lisa?" I ask through gritted teeth. "The other girl said she was coming back with you lot."

The girl screws her face up and pulls her arm away from me. "She was going to come here in the first minibus."

"She's not here. I have been looking for her."

The girl looks through to the lounge and shouts on the girl I spoke to earlier. "Sarah, did Lisa come back with you?"

"No, I thought she was getting here in the second bus."

They both look at each other and then to me with puzzled, sozzled looks on their faces. They are so drunk they don't know their arse from their elbow.

"Can one of you phone her?" I ask with urgency.

Sarah has joined the other girl and me, then clumsily pulls her phone out of her bag.

"I've no battery," she exclaims.

"Fuck me!" I shout with frustration as I turn to the other girl expectantly.

"I'll use mine," she offers and takes two attempts at using her thumbprint to unlock her phone.

I watch impatiently as the girl calls Lisa's number. I hear the ringing but she isn't answering. Eventually the ringing stops and I hear a voicemail message.

"Try again," I order but she is already ahead of me. Yet again there is no answer.

I watch as the girl sends a text to Lisa, with a simple message, "Where are you? Text me X."

"For fuck's sake!" I shout as I kick the cupboard door with frustration. "Where was the last place you saw her?" The girls look at each other and both give vague and indecisive recollections of when they think they last saw Lisa. "Give me your phone, I need to get her number," I demand, mad at myself for not getting her number before now.

At this point Callum wanders through for a beer and notices the commotion. He looks at me with curiosity. "No' found her yet?"

"She's not here and nobody seems to know where she is."

"You looking for that girl, Ronin?"

I turn around to see Sandy Pratt approaching me, with one of his sidekicks. He has a revengeful, smug look on his face and is sporting his usual messy clothing, stretched beyond recognition by his mass.

"Where is she?" I ask as I walk up to him.

"Ooh, look at you being all wound up," he chirps, goading me.

"I'm not fucking about here, where is she?"

I give him a look that shows how serious I am and he twitches uncomfortably without making eye contact.

"Look, it's bad news, buddy, but she left with Pavel."

"What?" I exclaim, with a loud cry of disbelief.

"Sorry, my friend, but she went home with Pavel. They got a separate taxi from us and went to his."

"Fucking bullshit, there is no way that she went home with him."

"She did, honestly. I'm not messing with you, my friend."

"I'm not your fucking friend and you are a lying bastard. She did not leave with him."

I can feel the rage building up in me. He's lying to me and the smug look on his face tells me he is enjoying every moment of this.

The two girls interrupt us. Sarah challenges Sandy: "She wasn't leaving with him when we spoke to her."

Sandy shrugs and turns away from me. His sidekick looking me up and down, trying to act hard.

"We're not finished here. Phone that cunt Pavel and tell him I am coming to get her, if you are so convinced that she is with him."

"There's no way I am doing that," Sandy quips and continues to walk away from me.

I put my hand out to grab him and his sidekick pushes me backwards. He's stronger than he looks and I stumble but quickly correct myself to avoid embarrassment.

Before I can react, I hear Callum interjecting, "I told you she was trouble, son."

I give him a look of combined hurt and disbelief. He knows that we were becoming an item, he knows I was keen: why is he saying this? And why isn't he coming to my defence?

My rage is all consuming and I lunge for Sandy. I spin him round and grab him by his fat throat as he drops his beer onto the floor. His sidekick tries to pull me off but I swiftly take his knee out with a crunch. He drops to the floor as I tighten my grip on Sandy's throat.

"Tell me where that fucker lives, right now," I snarl as Sandy starts to go red, choking in response to my grip.

I feel a dull thud on the back of my head followed by intense pain. The room spins and I feel dizzy. My grip starts to loosen on Sandy's throat, I try to tighten it again. I hear another thump and this time I feel myself stumbling to the ground. There is buzzing in my ears and I can't hear anything, all I can see is the black and white squares of the kitchen floor get larger as they rise up to meet my face, then bang, I'm out.

Darkness.

16

My mouth is so fucking dry and I am desperate for a piss. I open my eyes and the room is black, apart from the red standby light coming from my TV on the wall. I'm fully clothed and as far as I can tell, I am in my own bed. I lift my head and put it back down on the pillow just as quickly. I have the headache from hell and I can hear my pulse.

I take a second to wake up properly and gather my thoughts.

Fuck: Lisa, last night, the whole carry on. It's all coming back to me. I sit up again and the pain floods my eyes, heavy and unforgiving. I feel the back of my head and run my fingers over a lump the size of a golf ball. Whatever the fuck they used, it did the trick and knocked me down like a ton of bricks.

I'll find out who it was and believe me, they don't know who the fuck they are messing with.

Gently, I ease myself out of bed and shuffle across to the

window, stumbling over my boots on the floor. Fuck, my head is pounding.

I pull the cord to open the blinds and let some light into the room. The rays from the sun are blinding and I squint, looking away. I catch the reflection in the mirror of a pale, puffy and exhausted face. Somehow, I manage to shuffle to the bathroom and wash my face with cold water. Brushing my teeth while I pee seemed like a good idea but I don't have the energy or co-ordination to do a good job. I give up brushing to concentrate on my aim. Draining my bladder gives me one less area of discomfort.

My aching head is making it difficult for me to think straight, but I know I need to find out what happened last night. How did I get back here? Who put me to bed? I look desperately around the bedroom for my phone but can't see it. I am still wearing my jeans from the night before. I pat the pockets but there is nothing to be found except a wad of notes. At least I wasn't robbed.

I pull my clothes off to quickly throw on a fresh pair of jeans and a T-shirt. I pause for a second to catch my breath, holding my head: any movement inflicts pain so I need a second to recover. Taking a deep breath, I finish tying my trainers and put the wad of notes in my pocket.

My bedroom door is slightly ajar and I pull it open gently, to make sure there is nobody else in the house. I hear the TV on in the kitchen, so head downstairs to investigate. As I pass the front door, I can see that my car is in the driveway and the keys are sitting on the table in the hall. Did I drive home? No chance, the last thing I remember is hitting the deck.

In the kitchen I see a figure, with his back to me, drinking a cup of coffee while reading the Sunday papers. The TV is on, showing an old rerun of Keith Floyd flambéing a steak in France while drinking Rioja. I take a few more cautious steps before he stirs and twists his head in my direction.

I breathe a sigh of relief: it's Fred the Nurse. He's the guy we use when any of us get injured and in my line of work. I have required his expertise a few times. Despite his slightly shabby, boho appearance, he is a highly qualified nurse who, thankfully, knows his stuff. Before I can say anything, he shouts over.

"Hiya pal, you got a bit of a bash on the head last night and they called me. I brought you home after I looked at your injury. Don't worry, I drove your car very carefully. You're gonna have that sore lump on your head for a while but the headache won't last. Here, take these."

Fred pops two soluble tablets into a glass of water then swirls them around to form a cloudy mixture.

"The codeine in those will sort you right out, mate."

I have no reason to doubt Fred, therefore I pick up the glass and down the contents in two gulps. The chalky taste is awful but I'll take whatever helps this headache.

"Who called you?" I ask him as I put the glass back down on the table.

"Callum. He said you had been in a scuffle and that I needed to take a look at you."

"Any idea what I was hit with?"

"I think it was a club of some kind, just wooden but enough to take you down."

"Who hit me?" I ask.

"No idea, pal, there was only a few people in the house when I got there. Callum will tell you."

I manage a slight nod, satisfied that he is telling the truth but frustrated that I am still none the wiser. My caffeine craving is kicking in. Wearily, I go to pick up the kettle and see my phone on the worktop behind it.

"Callum asked me to stay here until you woke up, just to keep an eye on you."

I don't answer him but hastily press the buttons on the smartphone. The battery is dead so I plug it into the charger.

"How are you getting home? Do you want me to get a taxi for you?" I ask him.

"Nah, the wife is coming to get me, she wants to go for a shopping spree with the money I got paid for the call out last night."

"Fair enough. Give her a call, I'll be fine."

"Right you are, pal."

Fred pulls out an old mobile phone and taps on the large, silver buttons to contact his wife.

Waiting for my phone to have enough charge to turn on takes forever. My thinking is clearer now and I can feel anger building up as I recall the events from last night. Thank fuck the pain killers are starting to kick in.

As I wait, I pull a bottle of water from the fridge then down it in one go. I'm out of breath but I grab another and handle it in the same way.

The light on my phone appears then I watch impatiently as all the signal indicators pop up. WIFI, 4G, 4 bars, buzz, beep, beep, buzz as all the missed calls and messages come through.

I join the dots to unlock my phone and study the missed calls list. Davey, Davey, Davey, Callum. All within the last two hours.

I swipe to my messages and see a message from Callum. 'Phone me.'

That's it, nothing else. Not, 'how's the head?' or anything. He can fucking count on me phoning him because I need some answers. I dial his number and wait on the ring tone. The ringing continues until his voicemail comes on. Fuck this, I'm going to his house.

"I need to go, Fred. Just let yourself out when your wife arrives."

"Ok, pal. You take it easy."

I hand him four fifty-pound notes and tell him to have a nice time in Edinburgh. He tries to argue but I grab my coat and close the front door before he can finish his sentence.

My car wheels spin as my foot goes down on the accelerator and I roar onto the main road. I dial Davey on the hands free while I speed along the road in the direction of Callum's house.

"Morning, sir, how are you?" asks Davey in a jovial tone.

"Not the best, Davey. Where are you?"

"I'm in the pub, mate, on pint number four and shot number three, just waiting on a Columbian takeaway to arrive."

"Is Callum with you?"

"Nope, I woke up in his hallway this morning and he wasn't there. I was fucking raging I didn't make it to bed but at least I wasn't in a fucking canoe!" Davey snorted. "I headed straight to the pub down the road just to clear the head, you know?"

"I've tried to call him but he didn't answer. I need to find out what happened last night."

"What's happened, like? You needing some help?"

"It's a long story but I had a fall out with Sandy again. Then some dirty cunt knocked me clean out from behind, sneaky bastard. I blacked out and don't remember a thing until I woke up in my own house this morning, Fred the nurse was watching over me, so I knew it must have been a sore one."

"Fuck me, Ronin, I didn't have a clue any of that happened. Sandy is one dodgy bastard, cannae stand him, he's like a woman with a yeast infection – an irritating cunt."

I manage a tight smile as I overtake three cars on the country road towards Callum's. I can see flashing headlights in my rear-view mirror as they flick their full beam at me in protest.

"Okay, I have to go. I'll call you later."

"Nae bother, Ronin. Phone me if you need me."

I speed past the Iron Plough where Davey is drinking and Callum's house is only minutes away. I feel slightly comforted to know Davey is on hand. When there is trouble on the horizon he is one handy guy to have around.

The gravel on Callum's driveway scatters when I stop the car abruptly. I stride into the house. It appears empty but after a moment I hear movement upstairs. Hoping to find Callum I take the stairs two at a time and nearly collide with Nancy on the top landing. She is laden with a pile of fresh bedsheets and yelps in surprise at the sight of me.

"Goodness, hello sweetheart, are you okay?" she asks.

"Where is Callum?" I ask her abruptly.

She pauses for a second, hurt at my sharpness. "He's away through to Edinburgh for business. Said he'll be back later. Is everything okay?"

"Nope," I snap as I turn and head back downstairs.

I try Callum's mobile again and he answers this time.

"Aye?"

"Where are you?" I ask

"Sair heid son?"

"Where are you?" I ask again, ignoring his quip.

"Mirrors."

"I'm coming through now."

"Listen, son, if you think you're going to come through here and cause bother, you've got the wrong idea. Calm the fuck down and come and speak to me later."

"I need to know what the fuck happened last night and I need to know where Lisa is."

I hear Callum sigh. "Sandy told you last night, she fucked off with that Pavel. She was all over him after you left."

I know he's lying. He's actually fucking lying to me. Where is his loyalty? Does he think I am this stupid?

"Where is that fuckwit Sandy?"

"He's with me. Remember what I said to you yesterday? You can't touch him and you stepped way over the mark last night. He was telling you the truth and you lost it. You need to get your head sorted out, bud, that temper is getting you into no end of bother."

I can't listen to this bullshit.

"I'll see you soon," I snap and hang up. My hands are shaking. It's the first heated exchange I've ever had with Callum. It's rattled me and I don't like it.

In the car I push the start button, put my foot down and speed out towards the main road. I can be at Mirrors, Callum's most exclusive club, in twenty minutes. I reach into the fridge in the glove compartment and grab an energy drink. I gulp it down then in one furious crunch squash the can on the steering wheel.

I break the speed limit on every part of the journey and I am thinking about only one thing. Lisa.

Sandy has the answers to all my questions. Did she really go back with Pavel? Surely not, she didn't seem to like him. But how well do I really know her? How drunk did she get that night? Was she just another girl with an agenda? Like how much money does this guy have kinda girl?

The nagging doubt is creeping in and I start to question myself. Maybe I was stupid and got attached too quickly. It was drink and drug induced euphoria, just a figment of my imagination. I'm getting soft in my old age... was there even a connection?

Nothing makes sense, I can't get it to add up and my head is just one sore mess.

17

THE FORTH ROAD BRIDGE IS almost at a standstill, congested with Sunday afternoon drivers. The sight of the snake-like row of cars ahead catapults my rage into orbit. I punch the horn, scream profanities and deliver dozens of 'fuck you' fingers at the idiots on the road. I've had to slow down from one-twenty to a sluggish forty miles per hour, as a result my road rage makes me feel like I'm jumping out of my skin. My blood is boiling, I am irrational and out of control. The quicker I get to Mirrors, the quicker I will get some answers and the quicker I can calm the fuck down.

I clear the bridge traffic then speed towards Edinburgh, passing a number of cars, flashing my lights at anyone on the outside lane who is holding me back.

I take every shortcut I know and arrive outside Mirrors in record time. My eyes flick to the dashboard and the digital clock tells me that it's two thirty p.m. I think for a moment, put the car into reverse and move my car backwards so I can see the back entrance. The green Range Rover belonging to Callum is neatly parked in the Manager space. I put the car into first and drive up beside it. I take a deep breath: I can't storm the front entrance to create a scene. The place will be heaving with people having lunch and drinking hangover cocktails. I don't want it to get messy if I can help it.

The chef is standing at the back door having a cigarette break. He sees me approaching and smiles in recognition, about to say hello. I storm past him into the building, heading straight through the kitchen into the management area. There is a private bar with leather couches along with industrial-looking wood tables. The office door in the far corner is closed. The metal sign swinging on a nail says: 'Keep calm and wait your fucking turn!'

A few hangers-on recognise me as I walk in. They get up from the couches to speak, but I blank them and go straight to the bar.

"Is Callum in there?" I ask Rory, Callum's longest serving barman, pointing in the direction of the far door.

"Aye, Ronin, he's in the office, busy with a few people." His slight roll of the eyes tells me nothing good is ever discussed in there.

I nod to the fridge and he hands me a bottle of beer. It's freezing, just right. I down it in seconds then slide the bottle back over the bar towards him. As I turn to head towards the office door, the barman calls after me, "I don't think they want to be disturbed, mate."

I throw him a stony look before turning the handle and opening the door. My entrance is clearly anticipated and Callum stops talking to look at me blankly from behind his large wooden desk. There are two men sitting on armchairs in front of him, so I move sideways to sit on the couch beside the window, making myself comfortable. One of the men gets up to close the door I left open, clearly irritated.

Callum carries on as if nothing has happened, continuing his conversation with the men in front of him, who I don't recognise. They are both wearing black suits with identical tattoos on the nape of their necks, an oval shape with a cross like symbol in the middle. The guy closest to me is broader than the other: he has a sallow complexion and his thick curly hair hides eyes that are already too small for his face. The thinner guy is wiry like a whippet, with a shaved head. As he talks to Callum he moves a gold band back and forth across the middle knuckle on his left hand.

It takes a minute before I spot Sandy across the room, sitting on a chair beside the door I came through. He is staring at me, smirking, a fag lolling from the corner of his mouth. We lock eyes and I glare at him furiously. My stare is unwavering. I look into his hard, grey cannonball eyes and think how I fucking hate him, he blinks, snorts and looks away.

I catch the end of the conversation. The men are making satisfied noises, clearly happy with the work that Callum has done so far. I catch an accent and it's not Scottish: Middle Eastern perhaps or maybe even Russian. Callum leans over to shake both hands before reassuring them that, "There is more where that came from."

The men get up in one synchronised movement. The skinhead looks at me disapprovingly on his way out, clearly narked at me for providing an early conclusion to their little soiree. I eyeball him back. I'm not in the fucking mood for dirty looks.

As the door closes, I take a deep breath then look at Callum with frustration. My earlier rage has evaporated and is replaced with disappointment. He looks back with a similar expression and for a moment, there is silence.

"You calmed down yet?"

"Calmed down? Are you fucking kidding me? After all that shit last night?"

"What shit? The only person who caused shit last night was you."

"Let me get this straight: you are siding with that fuckin' muppet over me?"

Sandy twitches and shouts over to me, "You forgetting I'm still here, Ronin?"

"You shut the fuck up, I'm nowhere near finished with you."

Sandy sits upright in the chair, looking like he is about to challenge me. He hesitates then shuffles uneasily, not a hundred per cent sure yet that Callum will fight his corner. Before he can speak Callum starts a rant and gives it to me both barrels.

"Right, listen, Ronin, I'm fuckin sick of this. You need to get a grip. You met this bird, what two nights ago and now you can't believe she has fucked off with someone else? Are you serious? Well, bud, I have news for you: she did and you need get over it. I tried to tell you, she's just a slapper. She was in here last week with her pals, bleeding Sandy dry for champagne, only interested in the money. Aye, she's a pretty face and I'm sorry that you fell for her shit but she's not the first and certainly won't be the last. She's no good, okay?"

Fuck, his words sting, they ring true, it's so obvious now. Why should I doubt him? He's never given me any reason to question him before, ever.

Callum stands up and moves carefully around his desk towards me, seeing that I'm hurt. "This is me talking, not some random. It's me. You have to believe me. You're like my brother, I've never once lied to you."

I sit in silence as his words start to resonate with me. He's right. I barely know her and I have known him for a very long time. Why am I so sure that she hasn't gone away with someone else? I'm not.

"Look, you've been busy all week and you kicked the arse out of it all weekend. Your head is playing tricks on you. Go home to rest. Chill out. I need you at your best because our first airport run is on Tuesday afternoon."

"That soon?" I ask, awkwardly trying to change the subject.

"Aye, that's what these boys were doing when you came in. They organise the customers and we organise the transport."

I don't say anything. I feel woozy and the embarrassing realisation that I have been a fanny has kicked in. I hold my hands up to my face then lean into them, breathing out deeply. My eyes are closed and I start to connect everything that Callum has said. He's right, Lisa was just out to get what she could and if she wasn't getting it from me, she was going to get it from someone else with a larger wallet. Fuck. I've been an idiot.

It's clear as day in my head now. I open my eyes. I peer through the spaces in my fingers and see Sandy Pratt, sitting on the edge of his seat.

Callum almost had me convinced. Almost.

I see him through my hands, signalling to Sandy Pratt, giving him a thumbs up and putting his index finger up to his lips in a shhh motion. Basically implying, "I've got this under control, just let me handle it."

Sandy nods to him with a smile and Callum smiles back.

I close my eyes again. What the fuck have I just seen? I can't believe it; my head starts spinning. I need to pull my shit together. I need to make sure he thinks I believe him.

My expression goes blank, my hands drop from my face and I stand up.

"Sorry, I've been a fud," I say as I reach out my hand to Callum.

Looking relieved he catches my hand with both of his and tells me, "Don't be stupid, your passion is why I keep you so close. Just listen to me next time."

He grabs my arm and pulls me into a hug. I can almost feel the weight dropping from his shoulders.

I turn to Sandy, who is already on his feet.

"Sorry, Sandy. I hope the throat is okay."

Sandy looks surprised and shakes my hand with forced enthusiasm. He's so bad at this but I need to make sure he thinks I am over it.

"Go home and sort yourself out. I'll give you a call on Monday." Callum pats me on the back then guides me towards the door.

I leave the room feeling like a scolded puppy with my tail between my legs. The problem is, I'm not that fucking stupid. They have underestimated me and knowing that makes me more determined.

As I walk out into the management area I see that more folk have arrived and the bar is crowded with beautiful people, ready to start a Sunday session. I glance over to the bar to nod farewell to Rory and see a reflection in the mirror, inverted from another reflection on the window. Callum and Sandy are leaning towards each other, speaking in hushed tones, both watching the door in case I return.

They think they have convinced me, got me off the scent. I feel sick at the thought of Callum's betrayal but frustrated that I've ended up once again with more questions than answers. I'm no cash cow and money seems to be the only thing he loves or respects. My face flushes as the realisation dawns on me that my relationship with Callum has been merely a one-sided acquaintance all along.

Just before I exit the building I remember that one of the girls in Lisa's crowd works here. I take the door through to the main bar and restaurant, where John the General Manager is standing at the desk.

"A'right Ronin, you okay? You're looking a bit peely wally."

"I'm fine, mate, just a rough night."

"What can I do for you, big man?"

"Does that girl Sarah work here? The blonde one with great legs and too much fake tan?"

"She does, mate, but she's not in until tomorrow though."

"What time does she start?"

"She'll be here by two p.m. and then she's on until ten p.m. Do you want me to pass on a message?"

"No, it's okay, I'll catch up with her tomorrow."

"No worries, catch you later."

He shakes my hand before going back to reading the appointment diary.

I walk away but quickly turn back to him. "Actually, I'm trying to get a hold of a number for one of her friends. Any chance you could text her and ask her for me?"

"Which one. mate?" he asks.

"Lisa, the dark-haired one, from Eastern Europe."

"I have her number, mate, she has done a few shifts here. Beautiful girl. Let me get it for you."

Shit, I forgot Callum told me she worked in his club. The cloudy haze is starting to lift and I wait patiently for John to come back from his office behind the bar. There is hope yet.

"Here it is, mate. She wasn't always available so she only worked now and again. I kept her number just in case."

I copy the number from John's screen and save it quickly on my phone.

"Thanks, mate, and do me a favour?"

"What's that?"

"Don't tell anyone that you gave me her number or that I asked for it."

John looks at me, puzzled and quickly locks his phone.

"Seriously, there's a bit of shit going on with this girl and I don't want anyone to know I'm involved."

"Whatever you like, Ronin, just keep me out of it."

I nod in appreciation and hand him a fifty. John and I go

way back, I have helped him out on a number of occasions so he owes me a favour or two. I think I can trust him.

I leave the club through the back entrance, making sure that Callum or Sandy don't notice me. I slump into the seat of my car and exhale loudly. I feel emotional but manage to hold it together. I feel so angry but completely helpless at the same time. Callum and Sandy are playing me like a fool. They know more than they are letting on and are hell-bent on creating diversions to hide the truth from me.

I unlock my phone to dial the number that John gave me. It rings. That's a start. It keeps ringing until the voicemail kicks in.

"Lisa, it's Ronin, give me a call to let me know you are okay. I'm worried about you."

As I hang up, I immediately start a text to the same number.

"Lisa, it's Ronin, call me ASAP."

I plug my phone into the car charger and turn up the ring volume, I don't want to miss her call. I drive slowly all the way back to my house, keeping to the speed limit and with the radio off, needing the silence to reorder my thoughts. As I turn into my drive, the phone beeps. I grab at the phone clumsily and swipe to open the message. It's from Lisa.

"I'm fine. Don't call me again."

I feel like I've been punched in the stomach. For a moment, I can't catch my breath. I just sit and stare at the message. Brief, blunt and without so much as an intimation that she wants to see me again. Who the fuck is this person that I met? Callum was right all along. He may be up to something, but it looks like he had her sussed from the beginning after all.

I start writing responses, four or five different versions before deleting them all, throwing my phone on the car floor in bitter disappointment.

I'm not going to lie, I'm so fucking hurt by her response that I feel ridiculous. I'm exhausted and the painkillers are wearing off. Like Jeannie always tells me, things always look different in the morning. I head into the house and up to bed, turning everything off. No alarms, no phones and with a heavy heart I close my eyes. I'll wake up when I'm ready.

18

I HEAR BUZZING. BLACK AND white checked squares rotate round and round, forming a fast spinning spiral. I feel like I am falling into a vortex but it forces me backwards. It's so dark, everything is black and I can't see or hear anything. Pulses of sound echo in the distance, pushing red and green shock waves vibrating towards me. I look to the left and an old man in a brown suit is sitting next to me. I don't know who he is and I don't talk to him. He stares straight ahead, making a slight wheezing noise as he breathes through his narrow mouth. I look down and see I'm in a car. It's old and I have no idea the make or model but can see it is white with silver finishings. I peer through the windscreen and can see that we are driving up an old railway track. The track bends and becomes a rollercoaster, a very fucking high rollercoaster. I feel my stomach lurch as we approach the top and the track turns. The old man says nothing and continues to stare in front of him. The car follows the track, which starts to curve downwards, gathering momentum. I look down and each metal slat blurs into one smooth path as the car plunges forward. We move faster and faster until the car detaches from the rail and for a second I feel a sense of weightlessness as we are free-falling. I scream but no sound comes out. I go to grab the old man beside me who vanishes as soon as I touch him. I'm on my own, hurtling through the air towards the cold, hard ground.

I wake up in the dark, soaked in sweat and breathing heavily. The blackout blinds make the night infinite so I have no sense of time. I know it's a dream. I knew it was a dream before I woke up. It is the same events over and over except each time the ground gets closer and collision is imminent. The old man made it to the top of the rollercoaster this time. I wish I knew who he was. I need to stop the fucking drugs. My sleep has become traumatic instead of relaxing, with dreams so real they haunt me when I am awake.

Reluctantly, I step out of bed and feel my way towards the window to pull the blinds open and survey the grey, overcast sky. My mouth feels like the bottom of a budgie's cage, I'm so thirsty. I walk downstairs. My legs are tired so each step is an effort. I pour a pint of water from the dispenser on my fridge: it's freezing and hurts my throat as I gulp it down.

For a moment, I am convinced that the last few days must have been part of my dream. It's going round and round in my head. I catch my blurry reflection in the fridge door. All I can see are deep dark circles and pale skin: I look like shit.

I can't face turning on my phone so to distract myself I head upstairs to run a bath. I pour stress-relieving salts Nancy bought for me into the running water and inhale the musky aroma from the steam as they dissolve. Events start replaying in my mind but I block them out. It's too early to think and I need to clear my head first.

Before the water reaches the top of the bath, I turn off the tap. There are fresh cotton towels on the heating rail, ready to be used, so I gently lower myself into the water, close my eyes and relax.

I pick up the book I have been working my way through. The Art of War by Sun Tzu. It's not the easiest read but I do enjoy how much sense it all makes. I read a few pages but lose interest, I'm not in the mood so I put it back on the shelf. Reading chapters about aspects of warfare won't help to relax me.

For a moment, I enjoy being immersed in the water as it warms my tired body. I grab my cloth and start to wash down my limbs with soap. It's eerily quiet and thoughts I don't want start to invade my mind. I shout out to Alexa, "Cat Stevens mix."

Alexa, always compliant, repeats my command. The sound of gentle strumming of an acoustic guitar flows through the house, playing the familiar chords of Father and Son. I feel myself slump deeper into the bath and watch the steam rise up from the water. My muscles slacken, I can feel my body relax and drift off, allowing Cat Stevens' soothing tones to transport me to another place. His lyrics are pure genius.

I'm in Jeannie's house; she's trying to clean the living room windows because I've put my ice-cream fingers all over them. Her vinyl record of Tea for the Tillerman plays quietly in the background. It's her favourite album and she plays it over and over. I come to slightly and wonder what she is doing today. I'll drop in on her later.

I reach for the shampoo and gently massage my scalp, wincing as I touch the egg-like lump above my neck which I had almost forgotten was there. I lean most of my head back into the water to rinse the lather out of my hair, as my ears fill up with water the music becomes muffled and I can't hear the words.

I lift my head up and smooth the water away with my

hands then shove my fingers in my ears to unblock them. The haunting piano solo from the next song on the playlist begins and I know the melody but can't remember the name of it. I listen to the lyrics dreamily and the tension in my body disappears.

I sit bolt upright in the bath. What did he say? No fucking way.

"Alexa! Stop! Repeat!"

I listen to the lyrics again, more attentively this time. Sad Lisa? Cat Stevens sings about Lisa who is crying, hurt and lost. Someone is fucking with me. I'm never superstitious and I don't believe in the sky fairy, but every inch of my being tells me that it's a sign from her.

Leaping from the bath, I grab a towel from the rail and quickly wrap it around myself, using another to dry my hair and upper body as I head to the bedroom. My phone had been charging all night and now I turn it on. I pull on a clean T-shirt and a pair of dark blue jeans while I wait for my screen to light up then come alive with beeps and vibrations of missed calls and messages.

I'm going to call Lisa again. I need to hear her voice because something doesn't feel right. The message came from her phone but that doesn't mean it was from her. If I can hear her say those words to me I will be satisfied – hurt, yes, but at least I would know for sure she is okay.

I dial the number and it doesn't ring this time. It goes straight to the answer machine. That sick feeling is back again and I toss the phone on the bed, sighing heavily. The kind of sigh Lisa would notice.

I think back to each encounter with Lisa, from when I met her, to saving her from Sandy, to kissing her. Everything is crystal clear, all of it. She was vulnerable, she needed me. I opened up to her and I let my guard down like I've never done before.

I'm worn out. I leave the house to head out to Jeannie's and take my mind off it all. Monday mornings mean she will be engrossed in This Morning and hanging off Philip and Holly's every word: it's her favourite show. She will have been up since five thirty a.m. She's always been an early riser. I will take her out for a scone and a cup of tea.

When I get to her house we go through the same rigmarole of knocking four times and waiting for her to unlock the three bolts and Yale lock on the other side.

"Hello, my son," she says, welcoming me with a warm hug and a kiss on the cheek.

"Hi, Jean," I say as I walk through to her lounge.

"It's good for the kitchen," she utters while closing the door.

"What are you doing here at this time on a Monday morning?" she asks, slightly suspicious at my appearance: she saw me only on Saturday.

"I just thought you might like a cuppa and a scone from the tea shop down the road?"

"Aye, that would be nice, son. Are you sure you have time?"

"Of course, get your coat."

I watch her hobble through to fetch her good coat and feel a lump in my throat. I love her so much and I just want to tell her everything that has happened in the last few days, but she would never understand. Being in her company makes me feel at home again, and normal, if I ever was such a thing. She is my comfort blanket, she makes me feel safe.

The tea room is only a mile down the road towards the town centre and it has been there as long as I can remember. One elderly lady behind the counter is a long-time friend of Jeannie's.

"Is this your Ronin?" a plump, full-bosomed lady squawks over the counter as we sit down at a table next to the window.

"Aye, this is him, Caroline. My big laddie," Jeannie replies with pride.

"What a handsome young gentleman," Caroline remarks as she stares at me through the upper part of her glasses.

I flash a warm smile at her and look at the menu. I don't feel hungry but I know Jeanie will badger me into taking something.

"I'll have the scone with clotted cream and jam," Jeannie offers as the rather old waitress approaches our table. The woman scribbles down the order just in time to catch the follow up order of, "An' a pot of tea, hen."

"Just a green tea for me," I ask politely.

"You'll waste away to nothing, son, all that fitness is no good for you if you don't eat," Jeannie scolds me affectionately.

"Aye, son, you no wanting a bacon roll?" the waitress asks.

"I'm fine, thanks, honestly."

Jeannie tuts, rolls her eyes.

"Ah, okay then, go on I'll have a bacon buttie."

Jeanie beams and shouts over to Caroline. "Brown sauce mind, none of that so-called ketchup you have in here, he's allergic to thon cheap red stuff you know."

The small tea room has seen better days. The floral wallpaper is peeling at the edges and every chair wobbles when you sit on it. It's Jeanie's kind of place, with traditional red gingham tablecloths and silver cutlery, neatly arranged on each table. It also serves real tea in proper china cups and saucers. It attracts an older clientele. Two other tables are occupied with older couples chatting quietly, occasionally rustling their newspapers.

I look out of the window onto the street and see the rain has started again. It hasn't rained since Friday night. Shit, was it only Friday that I knocked 'Tim Nice but Dim' out with the ashtray? Feels like an eternity now.

The waitress comes back to the table with our drinks, Jeannie's scone and my bacon roll. I take one look at it but know I can't eat it. I like my bacon cremated but the fat on this one is still soft and slimy, spilling out from the sides of the roll, with the excess grease dripping onto the plate.

"You enjoy that now," she commands and I know I'll feel her wrath if I don't eat it. Silently, I watch as Jeannie cuts open her scone, applying the cream and jam with precision.

"Are you okay, son? You haven't said much. Are you tired? You are working too hard!" Jeannie says before I get a chance to respond.

I feel like telling her all about the shit weekend I had, the amazing girl I met, the hassle with Sandy and the knock on the head. I look into her kind eyes as she takes a bite of her scone and I smile, knowing there is no way on earth I could tell her anything.

"I'm fine. You're right, I'm just a bit tired," I say as I pour tea from a blue polka dot teapot into a matching cup for her.

"Well, make sure you get your rest, son, there's no point in running yourself ragged."

"Don't worry about me, Jeanie, of course I will," I reply, reassuringly.

My phone vibrates in my pocket so I pull it out. A message from Callum: 'Hope you got your head down last night and got some rest, remember we start with the airport tomorrow. Range Rover is being delivered to your house now. Treat it as your own but keep it clean for the clients. C'

Usually if Callum has something to say in more than one sentence he would phone me. Call me suspicious, but it looks like he's avoiding any direct chat with me. I lock the phone and return it to my pocket without replying.

Jeannie can sense that something is not right, because I've hardly said a word and my roll remains untouched.

"Come on, son, I think you need your bed, you really need to cut the hours you work at weekends. Late nights aren't good for you."

I couldn't agree with her more; this entire weekend wasn't

good for me. Poor Jeanie thinks I am the doorman in Mirrors, earning a bit of extra cash: if only she knew. I help her get her coat on and drop a fifty on the table. I point to it on the way out of the door and Caroline beams in surprise before winking at me.

I smile back and give her a thumbs up.

Outside her home, Jeanie hesitates before asking again, "Are you alright, son? You're awfully pale looking, are you eating properly?"

Everything comes back to eating with Jeannie, I know she didn't have much growing up.

"I'm fine, honestly, thanks." I kiss her on the cheek and I feel her eyes on me as I get into the car. On the way home, I dial Lisa's number again, using hands-free.

Straight to voicemail.

The loud club anthem on the radio is annoying me, so I turn off the stereo. A silent journey back home again, nowhere near the usual speed I usually drive at. Shit, this is all getting me down.

I turn into my driveway to see a brand-new Range Rover parked in my usual spot. I tut as I pull up in the space in front of my garage.

The Range Rover is a top of the line model. It's very classy, with blacked-out windows, looking more like a vehicle that would transport the President of the United States rather than one for dodgy runs around Edinburgh. The keys are in an envelope on the driver's seat. I scoop them up and head into the house.

It's only early afternoon, I've time to chill out, so I lie down on the kitchen couch, staring up at the ceiling. A feeling of foreboding consumes me and I can't shake a feeling that something terrible is on the horizon; either that or this come-down is the worst I've ever had.

19

LYING ON THE COUCH WOULD normally make me feel lazy but today I don't have any energy. I haven't eaten properly in days but it's more than that. I have no motivation to do anything other than lie here, feeling dejected and drowning in my own self-pity.

My phone buzzes. I glance at it wearily. It's one of those notification texts telling me that I have a missed call from an unknown number. I check my voicemail and there is a message from last night. I listen to silence for a moment but just as I am about to hang up I hear a faint intake of breath, a pause and exhale. Then click, the line goes dead. It was left at almost midnight last night when I was sleeping. My phone was off.

I rub my temple with my free hand, puzzled. Why didn't whoever it was speak? Number was withheld too.

I toss my phone away in frustration and it bounces on the wooden floor, making a cracking sound as it hits the deck.

I groan at the thought of a cracked screen which would lead to a hundred-pound visit to Ravi's phone shop, so pick it up to survey the damage. The cover has split but the screen is thankfully intact.

A plan is beginning to form in my head. A thought is nagging me at the back of my mind. The person who is the key to this is Sarah, from the bar. She knows more than she is letting on, I'm sure of it. I'll go back to Mirrors to see her: it's my only real option right now. I honestly don't have anyone else I can talk to and the person I thought was my best friend is in cahoots with a dodgy little gremlin who is about as trustworthy as a dog with a roast beef sandwich.

I think about Davey. He's a good guy but he's never sober enough to have a serious conversation about anything. I am starting to realise that I am surrounded by sycophants and hangers-on. Why couldn't I see this before? This sobering revelation has ignited a sense of purpose in me and now I need answers.

Once I am ready I head out to the car. I hesitate before opening the door as my eye catches sight of the great big, fuck off Range Rover in my drive. Shit, I'd forgotten Callum had dropped it off, it's a beast. I think I'll need to give it a test drive, ensure it is fit for purpose and all that.

I slide into the leather driver's seat and am immediately impressed by the money spent on this vehicle. It is absolutely stunning. It has the complete package with every extra you could imagine, no expense spared. I adjust the seat with the electric buttons and push the start button beside the wheel. I smile as the engine produces a gentle and refined purr, like a great big panther waking up after a snooze in the sun. Gently, I ease the large vehicle out of the driveway and onto the road. It is smooth and effortless so thankfully the pleasure of driving it distracts my overthinking mind.

My mobile rings and I glance over to see who it is. Callum.

"Oh, you're not too busy to phone me now?" I snap as I answer.

"Eh? What are you on about? You need to snap out of this, son," he scolds me angrily.

I say nothing and there is an awkward silence.

"Did you get the Range Rover?" he asks after a moment.

"I'm in it now, taking it for a run."

"Nice machine, eh?"

"It's exceptional, very nice to drive indeed."

"Shacunt, that must be the first time you and I have had a conversation without using swear words!."

For a moment, I forget how pissed off I am with him and let out a laugh. Callum laughs too and then there's a silence again.

"Are you a'right, Ronin?"

I don't answer.

"Honestly, bud, you're making me feel on edge and that's no good."

"I'm fine, just a bit confused about that Lisa girl."

"Firfucksake, you need to get a grip. That's your biggest weakness, you know that?"

"What is?"

"You've got a big heart and people take the piss. It's the only flaw you've got. I've seen you fight three people at once with the ferocity of a starved wolf but as soon as you hear a sob story and a pretty girl flutters her eye lashes, you go all gooey inside."

"Fuck you!" I shout. "Doesn't make me a bad person."

"No, it doesn't make you a bad person. It just lets the bad people take advantage of you."

"Noted. I'll try to thicken my skin."

Silence again for what seems like an age until Callum eventually speaks.

"Where are you anyway?" He's making an attempt to lighten the conversation.

"Just heading along the coast road up to Anstruther, thought I would see what this thing can do," I lie. I can't tell him where I'm headed.

"Aye, okay, just make sure it's clean when you take it to the airport tomorrow."

I don't answer, still smarting over his pervious comment.

"You'll get a phone call from a guy, Joe, tomorrow morning. He will tell you who you are picking up and all the other details."

"Okay, I'll look forward to that. What am I making out of this?" I ask sarcastically.

"You'll get a grand cash for your work."

It's a decent lump of coin, so I don't say anything.

"That okay?"

"That's fine. I'll be there tomorrow and let you know how it goes."

I hang up before Callum can respond.

I am only ten miles from Mirrors and it dawns on me that I have overlooked a fairly obvious detail. What if Callum is in his office when I get there? I go through his normal weekly routine, trying to work out where he would be. I relax after a moment when I remember he doesn't go to any place two days in a row. He'll be at another one of his clubs or doing something he shouldn't be doing. Erring on the side of caution I park a couple of streets away and walk to the club. I'll avoid his private lounge if I take the punters entrance.

I glance at my watch. It's eight minutes past two.

John the General Manager sees me coming and rushes to meet me before I make it to the bar.

"What are you doing back here, Ronin?" He glances around nervously before lowering his voice. "I've heard there is some really dodgy shit going down, mate."

"Like what?" I ask, noting a complete change in his demeanour since we spoke yesterday. This is interesting.

He leans into me, looks around again and whispers. "That Lisa girl, the one you are looking for, has hooked up with a Polish hood." He swallows anxiously. "You know, Ronin, he is not one who will take kindly to you sniffing around her."

For a moment, I stare at him, my eyes telling him everything he needs to know. He twitches, tries to maintain eye contact and looks towards the door.

"Of course, maybe that's just the rumours, that's all I've heard."

"Who told you that?" I say, and John knows I'm pissed off.

"I'd rather not say."

"Okay, come here a second and I'll tell you what's going on," I say, nodding towards the admin office behind reception.

I follow him into the office and I close the door behind us.

As John is about to speak, I pin him to the wall by the throat and grab a sharp pencil from the desk. I shove the point up his nostril, just enough to make sure he doesn't move.

"You seem to forget who I am, John. Don't mistake friend-liness for weakness, I'll shove this pencil so far up your nose, you'll be sneezing lead for months."

John gasps in a panic and nods, indicating he understands. He brings his hands up to shoulder height, palms facing me, in surrender. He's not going to fight back.

Slowly, I remove the pencil but keep it close enough to his nostril that he dares not move.

"Now, who told you Lisa's hooked up with some Polish guy?"

John splutters, he can't get the words out quick enough.

"One of the waitresses. Sarah. She was trying to get hold of Lisa. She went to her flat and all her things are there. She said the people in their crowd had heard she hooked up with a Polish hood, he has loads of cash and they are holed up some-where, having a time of it."

His words cut through me and my heart sinks. How can

this be true? She was not interested in this Polish fucker. If she was she deserves a fucking Oscar because I didn't see it.

My hand drops to my side and I ease my grip on John's throat.

"Get. Sarah. Here. Now," I demand quietly.

John looks at me as he adjusts his shirt and wipes beads of sweat from his brow. "Don't cause a scene, Ronin. It's not you who will get fired, it's me."

"Just get her," I snarl, snapping the pencil in half above his nose. "There won't be a scene if you don't tell anyone I'm here. Bring her here calmly and quietly, so I can talk to her, and then I will leave. Okay?"

John nods as he backs out of the room.

The few minutes he is away gives me time to think. Why is John involved in this mess all of a sudden? Yesterday he knew nothing and was happy to help, something or someone has got to him.

After a couple of minutes, the office door opens and John ushers Sarah into the room. She looks startled to see me and glares at John furiously: clearly he didn't tell her I was here. She looks at me boldly and folds her arms. John scurries away, closing the door quickly behind him.

"I know what this is about," she says, just before I begin talking.

This surprises me.

"I phoned you last night. I just got your answer machine and I almost left a message."

"You did leave a message, why didn't you speak? What was that all about?"

"I thought you were looking for Lisa."

"I am. Do you know where she is?"

"She's with the Polish guy. Listen, I know what you are going to say, and I couldn't believe it myself but that's the God's honest truth."

I raise my eyebrows sceptically.

"Honestly, you're a nice guy, Ronin, so that's why I was phoning you. This guy is minted, and he has whisked her away, they are living it up in some expensive hotel."

Her words twist like a screwdriver into my stomach and I swallow hard.

"How do you know for sure?"

"I spoke to her. She has turned her phone off because she knew you would call her. She's trying to make it easier for you."

"Easier for me? I was fucking worried about her."

"That's just the way she is, Ronin. You aren't the first guy she's dropped like a hot potato. You just have to forget about her." She smiles sympathetically, a smile that doesn't quite reach her eyes, and leaves the room.

I pull a chair over to the desk and slump into it. That's it then. I have pissed my friends off and embarrassed myself, all because I thought I had some kind of special connection with a girl, who has turned out to be everything I thought she wasn't. Standing up, I kick the chair across the room, wheels spinning as it slams into the wall. I've behaved like a right dick. I need to try and make amends, especially with Callum. Sandy can go and fuck himself though, I still hate that cunt.

I walk back into the bar and John is hovering by the front entrance, waiting for me to leave.

"Everything okay, Ronin? Sorry, I wasn't being difficult before, I just don't want to get involved in any trouble."

"That's the first sensible thing you have said today, John. Stay out of it. Thanks for letting me use the office. I've spoken to Sarah, so I know the truth."

"I'm sorry, Ronin. Women, eh? Fucking nightmares, all of them."

I nod and shove a couple of fifties into his shirt pocket.

"Sorry about your nose."

I get back to the Range Rover and a traffic warden is hovering by the passenger door. That's all I need, I tell him to fuck off and I'm in the car, foot down and away before he can get the ticket out of his machine.

20

I'M GOING HOME TO GET my shit together. I have behaved like a demented, lovesick teenager over the past couple of days and the fog is finally lifting. I have behaved like a complete fud.

I need cheering up. Davey.

I need to get a hold of Davey. A nutcase yes, but actually a great conversationalist, surprisingly. He always has time for me; he will sort me out.

I dial Davey's number and a female voice answers.

"Davey's phone."

She laughs, and I hear giggles from other women in the background.

"Is Davey there?" I ask, slightly irked by their childishness.

"Whooooo's calling?" she asks in a dramatic, high pitched tone.

"Tell him it's Ronin."

I listen as she shouts on him.

"Davey… Davey… Davey… Daaaaaaaavey!"

"Whaaaaaaaat?" Davey shouts from somewhere in the background.

"There's some grumpy cunt called Ronin on the phone for you!"

"Give me the phone you skanky bitch," Davey orders and I hear the muffled scraping sounds as he grabs his mobile from her.

"Aye, Ronin son. How you doin'?"

"Good, Davey. Are you behaving?"

"Aye, bud. Just sitting out the back in the summer house."

"Okay if I pop down? Could do with a chat."

"Oh fuck, what have I done now?" he says drolly.

I smile.

"Nothing big man, just need to run something by you."

"Course, son. I'll be here, just pop in."

"Thanks, Davey, see you soon."

"Aye, bring beer for me and wine for these hoors."

I laugh at the chorus of 'Fuck off' coming from the gaggle of women in his company.

The Range Rover slips through gears as smoothly as my own car. Same gearbox. It's not as fast but it can still shift. I'm over the Forth Road Bridge on my way to Kirkcaldy. I need to get to Davey and talk to him before he gets too blootered.

I stop at the Co-op to get booze for Davey. He appreciates a good beer, so I buy him some organic ales and some reduced-price wine for the ladies he has in his company. Even reduced-price stuff seems too good by the sounds of them.

I'm out of the Co-op and back in the car quickly then it is just a matter of minutes to Davey's house. He lives in a fairly rough part of town, but his house sticks out like a sore thumb. It's painted on the outside, he has remodelled the interior and has a back garden with a hot tub and summer house converted into a bar. The 5 series BMW in the driveway is also a fairly good indication that he has more money than most of his neighbours.

Normally I would be reluctant about leaving a brand-new Range Rover parked in this area, but people know not to mess with Davey, so I'm confident it will be safe. I walk round the side of his house and head into his back garden through a wooden gate. There's a chimenea burning, a large sound box pumping out 80s rock music and Davey shouts to me from the hot tub.

"Ronin, in you come, son. The water's lovely!"

His face is red and his eyes bloodshot and glazed from a bender which has clearly lasted several days.

I wave to him then head towards the hot tub, where the bubbles are churning, and two rather rough looking women are sitting at either side of him. Both are covered in smeared fake tan, gold jewelry decorating their tattooed bodies, and with eyes half closed they looked just as smashed as Davey.

"Here's the beer and wine, Davey. How you doing?"

"Thanks, son. I'm just chilling with these bints before I start work again tomorrow."

The two women come to slightly and stand up, staggering, holding on to each other. They try to give Davey the evils and storm out of the hot tub, grabbing the bag full of wine from me and dishing Davey a "fuck you." They are both topless and wearing cheap G-strings. Just as classy as I expected them to be.

"You coming in?" Davey asks me as he swigs from a bottle of beer, carefully balancing a cigarette on the edge of the hot tub.

"Nah, I'm good, mate. Just fancied a beer."

"Fair enough, the water will probably be radioactive after those two have had their fannies in here."

He laughs even before I get the chance to react. That's exactly what I wanted, inappropriate banter and a few chuckles. The two ladies return from the kitchen with pint glasses filled with cheap wine.

"Nice stuff this, young man," one of them comments as they both jump back in the hot tub.

"Never seen you here before, whit's your name?" asks the one with the black eyeliner shaping a cheap Amy Winehouse look.

Davey interrupts before I can answer.

"That's Ronin ye daft hoor, ye never heard of Ronin? He's one of Callum's crowd, Head of Security, batters everyone and then feels bad aboot it."

He laughs again, and the two women look me up and down, impressed now that they know I have a reputation as well as a title.

"You wanting a line sweetheart?" the other woman asks me in between giant gulps of her pint of wine. She nods over to the table where there are half a dozen white lines chopped out in preparation for a coke binge.

I look at the lines then back at the women. Nope, this is not what I came for. I should have known this wouldn't help me. "I'm sorry, Davey, but I'm not up for this. I thought I would be but I'm not. I need to go."

I don't even wait to see Davey's reaction, I head straight through the garden and out the side gate towards the Range Rover. I'm almost there but Davey comes running behind me. I turn and smile as I see him hobbling towards me, bare feet, bright blue speedo and with all of his faded tattoos exposed for the world to see.

"What's wrong, bud? You okay?"

"Sorry, Davey, I'm fine. I just kicked the arse out of it at the weekend and I'm still a bit tired."

"Aw, come on, if an old cunt like me can keep going all weekend, then a young buck like you can handle it."

I smile and shake my head.

"Thanks Davey but I've got to go. I'll see you later in the week."

"Okay, son." Davey gives me a thumbs up and watches me drive away.

What the fuck is wrong with me? I'm all over the place. Maybe I'm depressed again. Nah, Jeannie's right, I'm not looking after myself properly. I need to take all this stuff seriously, I have a job at the end of the day and I get paid very well for it. I can't lose it every time a pretty girl smiles at me.

Home, bed, episode or two of the Sopranos and I'll be asleep. That's my plan.

Tomorrow is a new day with a new set of duties. Let's not forget I'm getting paid big money for it. Screw the head, Ronin. Stick to what you know, and it will all come good.

That's exactly what I do.

I lay in bed and wonder if the mind is a marvelous or heinous thing. I thought that a song from a playlist was a sign. I thought that I had something special with a girl who was drunk on champagne and high on drugs. What an idiot.

Lisa? Lisa who? That Polish fucker can keep her.

21

I SLEEP LIKE A BABY. I wake naturally at eight twenty-three a.m., which is unusually late for me. As Jeannie would say, "You must have needed it, son."

I go through the usual routine: shower, shave, clothes, hair. Actually, I feel different today, I feel like having breakfast, I feel good. Finding out the truth about Lisa is a weight off my shoulders. I can get back to my usual self and hopefully regain favour with Callum. If he wants a driver for high-profile clients, I'll be the best fucking driver he has.

Just as I finish hosing down the Range Rover, my phone rings. It's a withheld number, so I'm guessing it's the call that Callum told me to expect. When I answer, I don't say anything. The man, Joe I presume, on the other end has already started talking.

"BA flight from London, gets in at twelve twenty. A Mr MacRoy, he will be carrying a small suitcase and will look for a vehicle with your registration in the arrivals zone. Stand by the car and wait for him. When he gets into the car, do not speak unless he speaks first. You will receive a text with an address and post code. Drop off at the destination and return one hour later, do not be late."

The phone goes dead.

Okay, I have my instructions, so I better get ready to go. A nice leisurely drive to the airport is no task at all. I'm uncomfortable about the destination, although I have no information. I can only imagine what goes on, but then who am I to judge? If it is what I think it is then it's a universal problem that is not unique to here. Hmmm, it doesn't sit well with me but what can I do? I have a job to do so I'll see how today goes and take it from there.

I quickly rub down the Range Rover with a chamois and admire the shine on the paintwork. My watch shows eleven fifteen a.m. Plenty time to get to the airport.

I change into a dark shirt, black jeans and smart boots. I throw on a casual blazer, and appraise myself in the mirror. This is smart enough.

As I drive towards Edinburgh, my phone rings and Davey's name appears on the display. I can't be arsed talking to him because I'm on a job, so I reject his call. Immediately he sends a text message, 'Fone me.'

I'll call him after I am finished. I don't want any distractions on the first job and he's probably still fucked.

The phone rings again and this time it's Callum.

"Aye, son, how you doing?" he asks.

"I'm fine, how about you?"

"I'm just checking you're sorted for the airport job."

"On my way there now. That guy Joe phoned me this morning, so I have all the instructions."

"That's braw, just remember that these clients are proper big time."

"What do you mean?" I ask

"I mean these cunts are dirty bastards, but they are high profile. We are the facilitators, they need us to keep them safe and most importantly, anonymous."

"What, famous people like?"

"Nah, not so much famous, just high profile, probably respected business men and folk like that. This is their dirty wee secret, so they pay a lot of money to hide it."

"If this has anything to do with kids I'll break your fucking neck, Callum."

"Fuck's sake, Ronin, I'm not a fucking monster. It's basically a knocking shop, you know that, we have done this shit before, just not with these high-profile fuckers!"

"Right, calm down. Was just checking. I've been told not to speak to these wankers anyway."

"Aye, that's probably as much for your safety as theirs."

"Okay, I'm nearly there. Speak to you later."

"Alright bud... you feeling okay now?"

"I'm fine. Listen, I know I've been a fanny and I'm sorry, honest."

"Dinnae be daft, just listen to me more often now."

He hangs up and I'm almost at the airport.

I arrive just before twelve p.m. and find a spot in the arrivals zone fairly easily. There's enough time to check over the car and its interior. It's immaculate, so I relax.

I wait by the car and watch all of the people scurry by, not walking but doing a half walk, half trot while pulling suitcases with damaged wheels behind them. There's a mix of business people and holidaymakers, all shapes and sizes, all with a different story to tell.

My people-watching is interrupted when I see a man approach me. He is short and slightly overweight, wearing an expensive dark grey suit. His receding hairline doesn't do him any favours, particularly as the remaining wisps are forced into a side parting. His round glasses balance precariously on his nose and he licks his thin lips nervously. There's a moment of awkwardness: I'm not sure if he's the guy I'm looking for.

"Mr MacRoy?"

"Yes," he answers abruptly and shoves the handle of his carry-on suitcase into my hand. He approaches the car door and then waits for me to open it for him. Little wanker. But I don't say a word or display the slightest sign of disapproval. I load his suitcase into the boot of the car and get into the driver's seat.

The address is already programmed into the sat nav, so I begin driving towards the destination. I concentrate on the road and don't even glance in the rear-view mirror to look at him. The less I have to do with these people, the better it will be.

As we enter the centre of Edinburgh, he shouts out to me.

"Can you turn down the air conditioning?"

"Of course," I reply.

There is no further conversation.

The sat nav route takes me into an unexpected location. The building is a large block of flats in a fairly affluent area, and it appears to have been renovated recently. When I stop the car, a man in a black suit steps forward from the entrance and opens the door to escort Mr MacRoy into the building. He returns for the suitcase and the small man appears to be writing in some kind of register at the front desk inside the atrium.

Mr Black Suit knocks on my window and I put it down.

"Wan hower," he says with an accent, holding one finger up to me.

I nod in agreement and watch him walk back into the building.

The neighbourhood has a lot of greenery: trees, bushes, lawns. The sterile-looking block of flats stand out. Its windows are tinted in a dark, reflective grey colour and the security entrance is state of the art, with cameras, proximity devices and some very large, serious looking men standing, stony-faced, at the front desk.

I have an hour so I need to go and waste some time. It's not a long time in a busy city like Edinburgh, but I think I have time to go to the Grass Market. The Italian café there sells amazing coffee and has paninis to die for. That should take my mind off this shitty job for a while.

22

By the time I get to the Grassmarket, I have had to negotiate twenty minutes' worth of traffic and find a parking space big enough to handle the Range Rover.

That gives me just enough time to get in the café and nail a mozzarella and chorizo panini before I have to drive back and collect that short-arsed sleazeball. I wonder who he is for a moment but get distracted when I see a dark-haired girl walk into the cafe. She reminds me of Lisa and she's back in my head again when I'm doing all I can to shut her out. That woman is a curse, that's what she is. It must be karma for all the bad shit I've done over the years.

The panini is a big warm mess of melted cheese and spicy meat, but I've lost my appetite. When the dark-haired girl orders a latte and turns to face me, my heart leaps for a split second, but it's not her. Her hair is where the similarities end.

Feeling disheartened, I get up from my table, leaving the partially eaten panini on the plate. I ignore the disapproving looks I get from the server behind the counter, who is clearly miffed at my wastefulness. "Tough shit," I think to myself.

I manage to return within the hour and with only a minute to spare. I turn off the engine then check my phone. Three texts from Davey. As I swipe to read them, the back door opens, and the little tanned man gets into the back seat. I pivot round and watch his chaperone, the prick in the black suit, walk back into the building.

His suitcase is missing. Has he forgotten it or is he expecting someone else to get it for him? I wait for a moment, uneasily glancing quickly into the rear-view mirror, expecting an instruction.

"We need to go now," he says in the same abrupt and arrogant way he spoke to me earlier.

"What about your suitcase?" I ask, feeling that it is my duty to ensure he has all his belongings.

"What about the fucking suitcase? I don't see any suitcase, just drive the fucking car, you cretin," he hisses at me, looking flustered and anxious.

I feel heat rising in my cheeks and blood boiling in my veins. No-one speaks to me like that. It takes all my self-control not drag him from the car and onto the street by his balls. I take a deep breath, keep my mouth shut and start the engine.

The drive back to the airport is in silence and I can't wait to get rid of him. The departures drop-off area is very congested, but I manage to squeeze in behind a black cab. The little man unfastens his seatbelt, opens the door and marches off towards airport departures without speaking or without closing the door behind him.

I sigh and put the car in 'park'.

He did that on purpose, the little fucking wanker.

As I drive home I can't help but wonder what the hell this job is all about. What was in that suitcase? Why did he leave it there? Was there money in it or something more sinister? I don't want to know or to think about it any more, so I turn on the stereo and stream a chill-out playlist from my phone.

As soon as I get home I'm heading to the gym and then I'll pick up my new car. That will take my mind off work for a while.

Back home, I check my phone to read the messages from Davey. They are unusually cryptic.

12.34: 'Ronin, fone me, urgint'

12.57: 'No joken, fone me'

13.28: 'At work, fone ma desk'

I suspect Davey has been offered some dynamite gear and is looking to find others to chip in on the purchase, so he can get a good deal. That can wait; I'm not interested. I need to check in with Callum, so I phone him instead.

"Aye?"

"That's me back."

"Any problems?"

"No, the client was a rude little cunt but with much restraint I behaved myself."

"Good lad. Listen, I need to go, I'll call you later."

He hangs up rather abruptly and I get the impression he has something urgent to attend to.

I didn't like that today, not one bit. It's not in my normal job description but I made a grand and that's good eating. If that's what they are paying me, I wonder what Callum gets. It could be the first gig of many for me but I'm not happy with it and don't think I can do it again without knowing the full story. Why do I get the feeling that knowing the facts will cause its own set of problems?

23

THE GYM IS A GREAT stress reliever and my session there is going well. One of the trainers gave me illegal pre-workout pills from the US, which I took before I came out, so I am buzzing and push myself to do a proper workout. I avoid chat with all the usual guys and concentrate on getting the pulse racing as well as making my muscles hurt.

I do my cardio workout last and although I hate running I'm going great guns on the treadmill. The headphones are in, my dance playlist is on shuffle and I'm in the zone with no interruptions. Seven minutes in to the thirty-minute programme and my phone goes.

Callum.

"Hello?"

"Aye, son, we've just been asked to go to a stag in Brighton this weekend, you up for it?"

"Whose stag is it?"

"Eh, that guy that owns the bookies in Gregg Street, what's his name again? I'm not sure but his brother is a good cunt and he asked us."

"It's a bit last minute is it not?"

"Aye but when has that ever stopped us? Come on, it'll be good craic, just you, me and a couple of others."

"Okay, count me in then. What about flights, hotels etcetera?"

"Nancy will do it all. I'll just put it through the business. I'm getting a suite at the Ramada, you wanting a suite too?"

"Whatever suits, honestly."

The phone goes quiet as Callum gives Nancy muffled instructions.

"Right, cool, cool, Nancy will sort it and we'll just get a minibus ordered to take us to the airport."

"Okay, sounds good," I reply, with fake enthusiasm, and Callum hangs up. I'm really not in the mood for a session in Brighton.

While I have my phone in my hand, I remember I need to phone Davey back.

No answer. I text him, 'Phoned you, give me a shout'

Immediately, I receive a text back from him, 'Stay wr u r, doin a shite, diny wnt 2 answr on bog. 2 mins.'

I smile then put my phone in my bag. I'll catch him later. For now, I just want to finish my run and get to the BMW garage.

At the garage, Dinky is nowhere to be seen. I ask one of the salesmen where he is, and it doesn't get me very far. Blank looks and cheap suits are a prerequisite for this place.

I head to the back of the building to where they keep the stock of trade-ins and new, unregistered cars. Dinky is in the far corner beside a blue X5. I can see his red face and he is clearly trying to hide. He sees me approaching but waves me off, desperately trying to keep me away. As I get closer I can see he's pissing into the petrol tank of the car, using a funnel.

"Fucking hell, Dinky, what are you doing?" I laugh in utter disbelief.

"Fuck off, I'll come and meet you in a minute."

"Whatever, you dirty bastard," I reply as I walk back towards his office to wait for him.

A few minutes later he turns up, out of breath and holding the funnel with a piece of blue paper roll.

"What the fuck was that all about?" I ask him.

"Shhh," he silences me as he looks around him to make sure nobody is listening. "That fuckin' hotshot in Glasgow, the new boy, he wants to get his hands on that car before I can even sell it. So I thought the petrol might need an additive before I send it through to him."

"Why even bother? What if you get caught?"

"He always does this to me, he finds out what good cars are being traded into my branch and then snags them for himself. I'll only get caught if you tell someone."

I raise my eyebrows, jokingly.

He laughs and drops the funnel into a plastic bag then into the bin beside his desk.

"When am I getting my new car?"

"Whenever you like, what about the weekend?"

"I have a stag party this weekend. How about next week?"

"No problem, I'll get it through the workshop and have it ready for you in the showroom."

"Superb, that'll do me."

"You paying cash again?" he asks with a hopeful look.

"Yup."

"Okay, I'll see what I can carve off the price for you... and for myself."

I laugh and shake my head. "I'll give you a call at the beginning of next week, okay?"

"Okay, Ronin, see you later." He's beaming from ear to ear and gives me a jovial thump on the shoulder.

In my car on the way home, I remember Davey was supposed to call me back. Shit, my phone is in my bag, which is in the boot. I'll catch him later. The pre-workout pills are starting to give me a post-workout problem, so I pop into Ash's shop. He is through the back, sipping a drink and texting abuse to one of his relatives in India.

"Ronin, how you doin?" he asks in a broad Fife accent, giving a faint whiff of stale alcohol from his breath.

I shake his hand as he stands up to greet me. His family own a chain of stores across Fife and they are loaded. This store is one of many he had allocated to him by his father. He is more often than not in his office, doing no real work and drinking vodka.

"Have you got any Diazepam left?" I ask him.

"Loads, mate. Here, take a handful."

He opens his drawer and moves various bags of pills around until he finds the ones I need. Without being discreet, he opens the bag and scatters some of the pills onto his desk for me.

I scoop them up then quickly shove them into my pocket.

"Thanks for that. How much?"

"Fuck off, Ronin, your money is no good here," he scoffs and downs the remainder of his drink. "You want one?" he asks, holding up his empty glass.

"I'm fine, mate, kicked the arse out of it at the weekend, so staying off it for a few days."

"Suit yourself." He shrugs, pulls out a bottle from the drawer in his desk and pours himself a large drink, coloured with a few drops of red bull.

"I've got to go but thanks for these," I say politely, keen to get away.

"Nae bother," he says, waving at me.

I've known Ash my entire life. We became friends at school when no-one else would talk to him because he was Indian.

He's a good guy to know; he always has his finger in a pie or two and we have had many great nights out. Let's put it this way: he is no more of a Muslim than I am a Christian.

I pop a couple of the pills into my mouth in the car and wash them down with the bottled water I bought at the gym. Now I can relax, have some dinner, a bath and watch Sopranos before bed.

Not a bad day after all. Yes, the client was a little prick, but I can cope with a few unpleasant words for a thousand pounds.

24

THE JELLIES ARE WORKING, I feel like I am barely awake. Fuck, Davey, he was going to phone me. I skipped dinner and I'm lying in the bath. My bag is so far away. Maybe I'll call him tomorrow, when I feel more with it.

There's my bed. Where the fuck is my phone? Oh, it's in my bag. That's downstairs, can't be fucked.

Bedtime. What time is it? Fuck knows, just want to chill. Where's the remote for the TV? Fuck, I'm lying on it.

What episode was I on? Ah yes, the one that has half a blue line underneath it, that's only half finished.

I'll just close my eyes for a minute. Just a minute and then I'll be right as rain.

25

I WAKE UP TO THE glare of my TV, which has been on all night.

Fuck, those pills from Ash are strong. I'm starving, I didn't even manage dinner, just a bath and then the rest is fuzzy. Richard Ashcroft was right: the drugs don't work, they just make you worse. That's it, no more fucking about, I need to get a grip of myself. Eat properly, exercise properly and have a complete break from dodgy substances.

Where's my phone? Damn, it's still in my bag downstairs. I jump out of bed and stub my toe on the door frame as I leave the room.

"Fuuuuuuuuuuuck," I shout as I collapse to the floor and hold my foot.

After a moment of feeling sorry for myself, I head downstairs and find my bag lying on the floor where I dropped it last night. Davey has phoned four times since yesterday evening.

In my text messages there is one from Callum and one from Davey.

Callum: 'Phone me, need a job done'

Davey: 'U need 2 fone me, cum 2 house tmrw'

I phone Callum as I hobble into my kitchen and turn on the kettle. I'm going to start the day with a green tea.

"Aye, what you got on today?"

"Nothing, why?"

"Need you to see somebody for me."

"Okay, who? Where? And when?"

"Come to the house and I'll tell you."

"Okay, see you in a while"

He hangs up.

Quickly, I drop the green tea bag into the cup and cover it with boiling water. I nip upstairs to the shower knowing that by the time I am out and dressed the tea won't be too hot and I can drink it before I leave.

When my instructions are to 'see somebody'. it usually means paying a visit to issue a warning, and sometimes, I have to be a bit heavier handed.

As I leave the house my cleaner, Agnes, arrives. I smile and wave to her. She can't speak a word of English, but she does a fantastic job.

Just as I am about to get into my car, she comes running over to me, with a mop in one hand and a freshly ironed T-shirt in the other. There's a note pinned to it which reads *Ronin, this is the T-shirt you left at Callum's the other night. I have washed and ironed it and it will be put into your wardrobe by the cleaner. Nancy X.*

It's the T-shirt I took off on Saturday night, just before Lisa came into the room and kissed me. Fuck, why do I keep getting reminders of this girl? I thank Agnes who smiles and lets herself into the house, waving the mop in goodbye at me.

When I arrive at Callum's, he's standing outside his front

door, speaking on his mobile. He holds one finger up to me to indicate he will be with me in a minute. I walk around my car and check out the paintwork; it will need to be tidy if I am going to trade it in to that pirate, Dinky.

Callum finishes his call and invites me inside. He looks serious and I sense he's not in the best of moods.

"We've got another special case," he informs me, as he picks up a notepad from his table in the kitchen.

"What is it?" I ask

"You're not going to like this one, it's fucking tragic and the target needs a sore one."

I sit down at the table and look at the notepad. All I see are scribbled notes that just about make sense. I look at Callum for further information.

"This one has come in from the polis. The boy I know, his wife works in social work and he has given me a heads up. They want this cunt dealt with before they get a hold of him. It's better for them if they pick up the pieces rather than try to hide the kicking they want to give him. It's getting harder for them to get away with that shit, unnecessary force, police brutality etcetera."

"Okay, tell me what needs done."

"A wee boy, always turning up at school dazed, dirty and with bruising. It's always a bike accident or hurt playing with bigger boys according to his mum. The poor wee lad is a wreck, scared to go home and walks the streets, trying to stay away as long as possible each night."

"Is the mum hurting him?"

"Nah, it's the step-father. He's a right cunt too. He's already under surveillance but the wife keeps lying for him. She's scared of him too. He's a right nasty bastard."

"Name and address is all I need," I say as I stand up.

Callum hands me a piece of paper with the details of the target.

"You need to go now. The wee boy hasn't been to school in days, so he is on the Social Work radar. When you're done with the father, phone me and I'll phone my boy at the polis, they'll attend the domestic disturbance and take him in as is."

I turn and leave without speaking. I know what I need to do – it's not the first special case job I've had. They come from Callum's contacts within the police because they know he is a dodgy fucker who can ensure bad people get what they deserve, and it stops them from getting their hands dirty.

When I get into my car, I turn off the music. I need silence when I prepare for these jobs. The postcode goes into the sat nav and I head straight there, wasting no time.

The area is as you would expect. It's a fucking war zone, a combination of good people who have been failed by the system and evil fuckers who take advantage of others. Without knowing their history, it's hard to distinguish between the two.

I scope out the house, looking for signs of life and the best way in. There isn't much to look at. The front garden is over-grown with weeds, the windows are filthy, and the curtains are closed. The street is quiet aside from some shit techno music playing from an upstairs window in the flat across the road.

At the front gate, there are black bags of rubbish on the path and a burst football in the overgrown grass. I can smell dog shit; the whole place is rank. I peer through the front window and see an overweight, scruffy looking man sitting on the couch, smoking and watching porn. That'll be him then. I quickly move round to the side window and can see into the kitchen. There is a woman on chair in the middle of the floor, with a rope tied around her neck, the other end tied to the radiator at the far end of the room. Her head has flopped forward on to her chest and I can't see her face.

I edge my way round the walls to the back garden, which is worse than the front. I look into the window on the back wall.

A small boy stands in his dirty underpants with his forehead pressed against the wall. He doesn't move and I could easily think he was dead until I see his bruised ribs move in and out as he breathes. His bedroom has no furniture or toys, just a stained, bare mattress on the floor. Christ, Social Services can't be aware that it's become this bad.

I've seen all I need to see. I head back round to the front of the house and reach into my pocket. Bill and Ben, my new knuckle dusters, will help me in this job.

The front door is unlocked, and I gently open it, making no sound. I grimace as the overwhelming stench of human excrement from inside attacks my nostrils. I step softly into the hallway and stand outside the front room where the man is sitting. He is watching some seriously fucked-up porn and seems to be just smoking while he does so. I look to my left and the woman has spotted me. Her eyes are wide and terrified. She shakes her head at me, which pulls at the rope around her neck, telling me not to go in. I press a finger to my lips, and she starts crying, making uncontrollable sobs. The man hears her.

"Don't you start the fuckin' crying again, you slut, or I'll be through to sort you out."

I look at her, desperately trying to signal to her that she is safe.

"Nooooo, it won't work, just go!" she screams at me.

Fuck, that's blown it.

"Right, what the fuck are you screeching about?" The man gets up from his seat and starts to head out of the room.

I step back and to the side of the lounge doorway and he walks past me, without seeing I am there. He's a right mess, unshaven, matted hair, awful dirty tracksuit bottoms and a grey T-shirt that's tight around his massive, sweaty gut.

He marches through to the woman and grabs her by the hair.

"Am I going to have to start burning you already? Surely it's too early for that?" he asks her callously.

I move up behind him and tap him on the shoulder. As he spins round I crack him with a right hook, the metallic sound of Bill echoing as he stumbles across the kitchen. I tell the lady to get up and stand out of the way as the man nurses a large cut on his cheekbone.

"What the fuck? Who the fuck are you?"

I don't answer him, I take him down with a rapid succession of hard punches and he collapses to his knees in the corner of the kitchen, knocking down a few dirty cups and plates that were stacked on the counter.

"Please don't hurt him!" the woman screams at me.

I've seen this Stockholm syndrome response before. I can't understand it, especially after what he has done to the wee boy.

A groan comes from the corner, the man spits out a few teeth and stands up, holding onto the kitchen wall for support. He's ready for round two and so am I. He lunges towards me, roaring, and goes to grab my arm. I step aside, and launch blows to his leg, ribs and the side of his head. Again, he drops to the ground, holding his side, spitting blood from his mouth. I give him a final kick in the ribs. He groans loudly and then stops moving. I turn to the lady and reach out to cut the rope around her neck with my knife.

"It's okay, I'm here to help you, don't be frightened," I say in a calm voice, trying to gain her trust.

She lashes out at me, screaming and kicking. It's a combination of terror and confusion. She has no idea of who I am or why I have beaten up her other half.

"Listen, calm down. I'm the good guy, I promise you, I won't hurt you. What's your name?"

She looks at me and her body slumps against the chair in surrender. Her hands are covered in circular red bruises and scars with a fresh cut on the side of her head. There are dirty brown marks on her skirt and she smells of stale piss. God knows how long she was sitting here.

I turn and look at the man. Fucking hell, he's trying to get up again. He puts his hand on the counter and pulls himself up. His face is a right mess, but I feel no pity for him. He feels behind him on the counter and grabs the closest implement to his hand, a corkscrew.

I sigh as I see him adjust it in his grip, trying to find the best way to hold it and attack me.

Before he can move I pick up a chair and throw it at his hand. He drops the corkscrew and I launch a tornado of hard punches to vital points in his body, finishing him off with some disabling kicks to his right knee. He collapses in pain but starts to laugh hysterically.

"You think this is going to stop me? I'll be on my feet in no time and you'll be a dead man. You have no idea who you are messing with, I know people. People that will fuck you up."

I ignore him and inspect Bill and Ben, now stained with his blood. They have served me well on this job and after a clean they will be used again.

Moving towards the lady, I remove the knuckle dusters and try to get her to speak to me.

"Don't touch that fuckin' slag. Her and her son, they are fucking damaged goods, nobody will want you now, do you hear me? You fucking bitch, this is all your fault, you and that evil son of yours, you deserve everything you got, you rancid whore!"

I turn and kick him in the head, which immediately silences his rant. Not once but a few times, then I stamp on his head until I hear bones cracking. His head is sideways, and his eyes half closed. I want to kill the bastard, but he needs to rot in jail. He will get hell in there for what he has done.

I try to remove the rope from the woman's neck. What a mess, she'll be scarred for life; it's infected and she has been battered from head to toe. After some clumsy manoeuvres, trying my best to be gentle, I manage to untie the rope. It falls to the floor and she lets out a massive exhale of breath before crying with her hands up at her face, then hugging her sides.

"My son," she says. "Please help my son. He's been there for days."

I go to his bedroom, stepping over cat shit and other rubbish that litters the hallway.

When I enter the room, the boy doesn't move. He stays absolutely still, apart from his breathing. He breathes faster, clearly scared out of his wits. I look at the state of his back: horrific burns and bruises, fresh scars and welts show the extend of the abuse from that monster of a man.

Gently, I approach the boy and speak softly.

"It's okay. My name is Ronin and I'm here to help," I whisper gently.

The boy doesn't move. He doesn't even look round, just stays in position with his forehead pressed against the wall.

"Come on, your mum is okay, and she's asked me to help you too."

The boy begins to cry and shake. "Can't move," he says in between heart-breaking sobs. "If I move, he hurts me"

I swallow hard. Fuck, this is tough.

"He's not going to hurt you any more, I promise."

I reach over to him and put my hand on his shoulder, gently trying to move him away from the wall. The boy screams at my touch making me stumble back in shock.

"Can't move my head from the wall. He told me to stand here. Not allowed to sleep. Not allowed toilet, have to stand here until he's ready for me."

I can't bear any more of this. The boy is clearly traumatised, and I wonder how long he has been forced to stand like that. I felt how cold the boy was when I touched him, so I undo the zip on my hooded top and quietly take it off.

"Listen to me, we're going to get away from here, you'll be safe but I'm going to have to move you."

The boy cries and shakes even more.

I move ever so slightly, a millimetre at a time and manage to wrap my hoodie round his shoulders. He breathes out a sigh of relief when he feels the soft inside and warmth of the garment.

Without wasting any more time, I scoop him up in my arms and carry him out to the bottom of the stairs. He tries to protest but he's so weak, he just closes his eyes and buries his head into my shoulder, weeping. I sit on the stairs with him and shout on his mother to join us.

"Are you okay?" I whisper gently

He opens his eyes and looks up at me. I inhale sharply, recognising him immediately. It's that boy. The wee shit who was stealing my valve caps outside Jeannie's house; what did she call him again? I wrack my brains, Shaun, that's it. Fuck. I swallow hard feeling bad for chasing him. I had no idea he was going through absolute hell at home. Jeanie thought his mother was an alchie, what a fucking shame, if only we knew.

"Shaun, it's going to be okay, really it is.

I shout to his mother again, "Come here, I have him, you need to come here now."

Eventually I hear her moving, crying loudly and shuffling across the kitchen floor.

She screams, and I realise that something has happened to her.

The boy has passed out, so I gently lay him on the floor in my hoody and rush through to the kitchen. The man has a hold of her foot, biting her heel and pulling at her leg. I kick him in the head again and roll him over. The woman runs into the hall and joins her son.

No way this guy gets to carry on his work, I'm going to make this a long-term hospital stay.

I drag his head over to the back door and open it. I place his mouth on the step and kick his head from behind. There's a crunch and more teeth scatter in all directions. I check his pulse, he's still alive but he's in a bad way.

My phone doesn't have a signal in the house, so I step over the man and go out the back door to phone Callum.

"It's done. You were right, this scumbag was a nasty bastard. It's messy. You better phone the police boy that you know, the woman and the boy are in serious need of some help."

"How messy?" he asks.

"He's fucked up, I lost my temper with him."

"Ooft, I hope you haven't killed the fucker," he says.

"Never mind him, the woman and her boy need attention now. Fuck knows what he's done to them."

"Right son, thanks. The polis are only a couple of miles away, waiting on the call from me."

I look around the house and try not to think about the incomprehensible horrors that must have taken place here. I think about the awful words that came from the boy's mouth. How could someone be so cruel to a child? My childhood was Disneyland compared to the life this wee soul has had. This will haunt me for weeks to come.

"Help me, help me, he's not breathing!" the woman screams.

I rush through to help her cradle the boy. I feel his pulse; he is breathing but he's exhausted. His malnourished, dehydrated body is in desperate need of medical care.

"Look, the police are coming now, they will help you. Just let them help you."

"Who are you? I thought you were the police?" she asks, quivering as she looks at me.

"No, I'm something else," I say vaguely.

She nods uncertainly, not sure whether she trusts me or not.

"Is he dead?" she asks me, looking towards the kitchen.

"No, he's not dead. Don't worry about him, he won't hurt you again. Just concentrate on getting your son some help, he's broken and will need you."

I hear the police sirens in the near distance and stand up to leave.

"Look after him and yourself," I say as I open the front door.

She doesn't look at me but cradles her son in her arms rocking him back and forth.

Several neighbours are standing at their front doors, eager to see what all the commotion is about. Guaranteed, some of them will have known what was going on in that house and did nothing to help.

As I get out of the dreary housing estate, I hit the button on my dashboard to start some music. Redbone by Childish Gambino comes on. It's a psychedelic funk number, so it immediately makes my head nod. I put the window down as I feel the tension ease from my muscles. It's going to take some time before I can erase that job from my head. I don't regret what I did for one minute. But I just want to move on and forget it.

26

I CAN STILL SMELL THE stench from that house on my clothes. As soon as I get home I pull them off and shove them in a black bag. The smell is in my hair too so I jump in the shower then layer on the soap and shampoo in an attempt to wash away the sights and sounds of horrors I was faced with today.

I have a cut on my right hand which stings when the water hits it. I can't complain. I got off lightly compared to the state I left him in.

After my shower, I pull on some loose joggers and a T-shirt. I ask Alexa to play some chill-out music; she complies as I grab the black bag full of clothes and head out to my back garden. I open the lid of a huge firepit and chuck the entire bag into it. A couple of splashes of fire lighter and a match is all it takes for the lot to go up in red, angry flames.

I sit back on a chair at my patio table, watching the black

bag melt away and the flames attack the clothes inside. This is the first time I've burned my clothes after a job and it's surprisingly cathartic. It helps the process of erasing what happened. Staring at the flames, I picture the little boy's back and think about the pain he must have suffered at the hands of that cunt. I shake my head and it dawns on me that I haven't thought about Lisa since this morning.

My phone starts ringing in the kitchen, so I leave the fire to burn and head back inside. It's Davey.

"Davey, sorry I keep missing you, what's happening?"

"Fuckin' hell, Ronin, you are some boy to get a hold of. I need to speak to you, what are you doing now?"

"Just back from a job, Davey. Is it anything urgent?"

"I would say it is, like."

"Just tell me over the phone?"

"Nah, you need to hear this face to face."

I cannot be fucked. I like the guy but the thought of driving back into Kirkcaldy again and all the way down to his house is the last thing I want to do right now.

"Okay, I'll come down later. Will you be there all day?"

"Aye, just come down soon, you're going to want to hear what I have to say."

"Okay, Davey, see you in a while."

Fuck, it's hard to tell whether Davey genuinely has something to tell me or whether he's lined up some gear and is having a party. He has done this before, which is why I need to keep him at arm's length at times: too much of him can be a bad thing.

The phone goes again, and I exhale a loud, "Forfucksake."

"A'right, Ronin?"

"Aye, Jasper, what's new?"

"You going to the gym today?"

"No, I was there yesterday, why?"

"I just hear that there is a new knocking shop in Edinburgh

and I heard you're involved. Just wondered if you could get me mate's rates?"

"Who told you I was involved?"

"Sandy Pratt, saw him at the petrol station, he was driving a new Audi, very nice, like."

"Well, you should know that he talks absolute shite. I'm not involved in any knocking shop, so sorry, can't help you."

"Oh, right, he seemed quite convincing but anyway, I'll let you go."

I hang up and can feel an uncomfortable knot of guilt form in my stomach. This is exactly what I didn't want. I can't be associated with that kind of business; I don't fucking agree with it. Now Sandy has told Jasper and that means every fucker in Fife will know. How did I get myself into this mess?

I dial Callum's number.

"Aye?"

"You tell that fat, sweaty, ugly little bastard that he keeps his mouth shut about me."

"Who, Sandy?"

"Bingo. He is telling folk that I am involved in a knocking shop and I've had a call asking me for mate's rates."

Callum sighs. "Right, I'll tell him. Don't blow a gasket but you are kind of involved, just saying."

"I pick up and drop off people from the airport, that's it."

"Aye, you drop them off at a knocking shop."

I hang up before he can say any more and decide to head down to Davey's anyway, to get away from this shit.

Davey is out in the back garden as usual. Surprisingly, he's not pissed, in fact he is straight as a die and when he sees me he looks concerned. It's unsettling.

"Ronin, son, I've been desperate to speak to you." He isn't smiling and the lines on his brow become more prominent as he approaches me. "You know that lassie you were with at the weekend?"

Here we go.

"It's okay, Davey, I know all about it. Callum and Sandy told me everything. She's fucked off with Pavel and I'm no longer of any interest to her. C'est la vie, I'm a big boy, I can handle it."

"They told you that?"

I sit back for a moment, puzzled by Davey's tone.

"Well, Callum and Sandy told me and her friend Sarah confirmed it. Case closed. Everyone seems to know about it."

"No way, buddy, you need to listen to me. She didn't go home with him. She was dragged out of there unconscious by that wanker."

"What? How do you know?" I demand, leaning towards him.

"Remember my sword from Saturday night? I went to get it back at the club. When I was in, Sandy Pratt was there, asking the security guys to look at CCTV footage from Saturday night. He got shitty when I was around, so he said he would come back later. I wondered why he would want to see the footage, so I asked Mac if he would show me. Then I saw it with my own eyes. That Polish cunt drags her out of the club and shoves her in the back of a van. Not a taxi, a fuckin transit."

"Are you fucking sure, Davey?"

"Honestly, she wasn't in any fit state to know where she was going."

"Why did her friend tell me she was holed up with him somewhere then?"

"I can't answer that one, Ronin, all I can tell you is what I saw."

My face flushes beetroot as the adrenaline starts to pump through my veins. I pace back and forward for a moment, trying to get my head around what I've just been told.

"She sent me a text, Davey, saying she was okay but she wanted me to leave her alone."

"I don't know, mate. Maybe she woke up and fell in love with him, who knows. All I can say is that she didn't leave with him of her own free will. He threw her in the van like a sack of tatties."

"Who else have you told about this?"

"Just you, son. I thought I would tell you first."

"Right, don't tell anyone else for now and don't, whatever you do, tell Callum."

"Okay, Ronin, whatever you like. Listen, I'm not trying to cause bother here, I just thought you two looked good together, like it was going well, you know?"

"Was anyone else there? Did anyone see it when he took her out of the club?"

"Aye, other people are there but I couldn't make out who they were. He just stood out because of his white polo shirt. The others had their back to the camera."

"What about Mac, where was he?"

"He was sorting out the minibuses for Callum and Sandy, getting all the people to stay together. Everyone was smashed, including me."

I run my fingers through my hair, trying to keep it together.

"What you thinking, Ronin?"

"Fuck knows, Davey. I have pissed off a lot of people looking for this girl and everyone swears blind that she went away with this Pavel."

"Well, look, why don't you go and look for yourself? That way you don't have to take my word for it. Ask Mac to see the CCTV footage and then you can decide."

"Aye, I'll do that. Thanks for giving me the heads up, Davey," I say as I shake his hand.

"No problem, son. You're a good lad and you know I'll always help you if I can."

I jump in the car and head straight to Danza to ask for Mac.

"He's not on shift tonight," answers Shona when I get there, the dozy female bouncer at the front door.

"What about John, the gaffer?"

"Aye, he's in, you want to see him?"

"Yeah, tell him Ronin is here and I'll see him at the back door."

I wait for John to open the door at the back entrance. I hear him approaching, as he trips and swears in Italian, "Vafanculo." He appears at the door, rubbing his injured leg but smiling when he sees me.

"Hey, Ronin, how's it agoin'?"

"John, I need five minutes with you."

"That'sa nae problemo, come through the noo."

"I won't keep you long, John, I just wondered if you could let me see the CCTV footage from Saturday night?"

"Aye, Ronin, nae problemo but I've-a nae idea how it-a works. Lemme ask one o' the other folk." He walks off and then turns back to me, looking puzzled. "What's it you're-a lookin' for?"

"I just need to see how some of my friends got home. I have heard that there were a few taxis and buses."

"Aye, they aw gotta the minibuses. I'll ask-a the lassie doonstairs aboot the CCTV, gimme a minute, eh?" He trots off and heads downstairs to his office near the front door. It's mid-afternoon and the club is really quiet: it's bar lunches and nachos at this time.

As I wait on John, I spot cases of drink piled up and carboard boxes filled with various mixers. Almost every crate or every box has been tampered with, which tells me that John has a problem with his staff stealing a sneaky drink. The whole area is filthy – dirty floors, inches of dust and the remains of joints strewn all over the place. This would never be allowed in one of Callum's clubs. He would hit the roof if he saw anything like this.

John comes back with a smartly dressed lady in tow. A member of his office staff, no doubt. I don't recognise her, though.

"You tell-a Ronin what-a you said, I dinnae get it."

"Hi, I'm Rhona. I work in the office downstairs. John said that you wanted to see the CCTV from Saturday night?"

"That's right, I wanted to see footage of how some of my friends left the club."

She looks nervous and struggles to maintain eye contact with me.

"Sorry but we don't have it any more. We only keep it for twenty-four hours because it's an old camera, the hard drive is wonky and doesn't work very well. If there are any incidents, we can copy footage but if not, we delete it."

"Shit."

"I was in on Sunday afternoon and I went over the footage. Is there anything in particular you are after?"

"Okay, someone told me that a lady I know was dragged out of here, completely inebriated and she had no idea who she was with."

"Really?" Rhona smiles. "That could be nearly every girl who leaves this club on a Saturday night, you know. It's a common occurrence in this place." She emits a small, phony laugh. "Can you describe this lady?" she adds.

"She's pretty with dark hair, black dress, was here with our crowd."

"Look there are lots of girls who fit that description, to be honest the only one I can remember was a girl who left with a guy in a white polo shirt and she seemed sober enough to me."

"Well," I lower my tone. "I've been told otherwise"

"If you don't mind me asking, by whom?" she asks, hackles starting to rise.

"Davey, he was in to get his sword and he said he saw the CCTV."

John twitches when he hears the mention of 'Davey' and 'sword' in the same sentence and slaps his hand on his head in despair.

"Davey? That older guy? He is constantly wasted. I would question what he thinks he saw. There's no way that I would have let something like that go."

I'll give it to her, she's good, very convincing. She's right about Davey, he must only be sober one or two days a week, and don't get me started on the volume of drugs he consumes. Nonetheless, I would still trust him over her any day.

"Okay, I'm sorry to have bothered you," I say politely.

I turn to leave and John walks up to my side.

"Sorry aboot that, Ronin. I need-a the new CCTV for this-a place but it's money, money, money all-a the time."

"No worries, John, thanks anyway."

I head back out the rear entrance and slowly walk back to my car. I need to stop all this shit, it's just fucking with my head. But there was something about that Rhonda. I can see a bull-shitter a mile away and she was one of them.

On the drive back home, Callum sends a message to the group chat for the stag do. Leaving his house at five a.m. tomorrow morning, the minibus will pick us up from there. I need to pack and get an early night by the look of it.

I start to think that Davey must have been mistaken. The number of times he has flown off the handle when he gets the wrong end of the stick has taught me he's a liability at the best of times. I'm sure he meant well but it hasn't helped me. There are more people telling me the same story than not which makes me feel like they can't all be wrong. Can they?

27

I HAVE A RESTLESS NIGHT thinking about Lisa and worrying whether she is okay. I see every hour and by the time my alarm goes off in time for our 5 a.m. pick up I'm exhausted.

After I am showered and dressed, I throw all my toiletries into my suitcase. I access my safe and pull out a couple of bundles of cash. It looks to be about two grand, that should do fine. It's my first trip to Brighton and there is no harm in being prepared.

The sun is rising and there is not a cloud in the sky. I throw my suitcase into my car and head to Callum's along the deserted roads. I park up against his garage to leave room for the minibus when it arrives. I'm first there and I walk straight into the house to find Callum totally organised, counting huge amounts of money on his kitchen table. It's all fifty-pound notes and I suspect they have been ironed; there's no way that they could be so pristine otherwise.

"Morning, son, how you doin'?" he asks as I walk into the kitchen and set my suitcase down.

"Good, mate, how about you?"

"Aye, fine, just making sure there's plenty of funds for this weekend. Fancy a line?"

For a moment, I think that it would be ludicrous to snort a line at this time of the morning. It is but I decide to do it anyway. The white powder sits in the usual spot on the island in the kitchen. Callum has been busy cutting out perfect lines, expecting that people will want to have an early morning wake-up.

I take two lines, one for each nostril, and continue to watch Callum finish counting out his money. He rolls the wads and puts rubber bands around them. One by one, he tosses them into his suitcase. I estimate that he must have about ten grand there.

Callum zips up his suitcase then checks the wad of fifties he has in his pocket.

"I think you're going to be alright for cash."

He smiles and heads over beside me, taking a couple of lines for himself. "You a'right now? Got your head straight?" he asks me as he puts his arm round my shoulders.

"I'm cringing, mate, sorry about all of that. I was just caught up in the moment and you know what I'm like, I never back off from anything."

"Tell me about it, I thought you were gonna kill Sandy that night in here."

"I was. He's lucky that someone hit me on the head."

"Oh, that was me. Sorry about that, you were out of control and I didn't know what else to do."

I look at him in astonishment. It was him? Is he fucking having a laugh?

"Are you serious, mate?"

"Yeah, listen, no hard feelings, eh? I did you a favour, you could have got hurt."

Part of me wants to knock him out and part of me wants to ask him how after all these years, and everything I've done for him, he took the coward's way out and hit me from behind. There is so much more I want to say but the sound of the other stag party guests interrupts us.

Three men come into the house: two I know and one I can't place. These guys are friends of the stag but have opted to come here for the obvious reasons – transport and drugs. I exchange some half-hearted pleasantries with them but I'm still seething about Callum's admission. He fuckin' hit me? Again, I am confused. I don't know who this so-called friend is any more.

I keep to myself as Callum does his thing, offering beer and drugs. My two lines have kicked in and the flow of guests increases gradually, until we are all present, including the stag himself, Jordan. He's a younger lad and has done well for himself; he owns a few bookies and knows all the dodgy bets, so he generally makes decent money for his age. His mate, Mark, who is with him, likes to think he is the hard man and regales us with stories before the minibus arrives.

"You'll ken what ah mean, Ronin. That buzz ye get when you've knocked some cunt oot. I did it last weekend, wee body builder boy, he was tryin' tae act hard so ah ripped the T-shirt off his back and leathered him."

I nod disinterestedly, and I'm saved by the minibus which has pulled up outside. We all pile in. The early morning craic is great; the buzz from the cocaine coupled with anticipation for the weekend ahead puts everyone in good spirits.

We descend on the airport, full of confidence and swagger. The EasyJet assistant tries to hide as we bounce up to the desk, fighting over each other to hand over our boarding passes and ID.

On the way to the security, Callum stops and looks around for me. I am a couple of steps behind him and I know why he has stopped: he has cocaine in his pocket. I nod in the direction of the toilets and he follows me. Conveniently, there is a large disabled cubicle in there, so we both go in and finish off the white powder – no sense in wasting it. Lines at six a.m. in an airport toilet, that's a new one for me.

Going through security is painful: shoes off, belt off, watch off, change in a tray, bag on the conveyor belt. All instructions barked at us repeatedly by an overweight security worker who has let the power go to his head. Finally, we get to the airport Wetherspoons where the lads have pints waiting for us. As I drink my beer I think about the weekend ahead and decide that maybe, just maybe, I'll be able to forget about everything and enjoy myself.

The boys are up for it and after four pints in an hour some of the lightweights are already smashed. Jordan and his pal Mark are already pissed, and Callum and I can't resist calling Jordan 'Two Pint Tony', much to the amusement of the rest of the group.

There is a final boarding call and the announcer names us all one by one over the tannoy. We walk casually to the gate, much to the annoyance of the EasyJet boarding staff. Finding seats is a problem, so we end up sitting in between people and generally slotting in where we can. Our inebriated presence causes plenty of tutting and eye-rolling from other passengers along with strained smiles from the hostesses. They reluctantly dish out beers at our request while other passengers order coffee and orange juice. It's only eight a.m. I have bagged a seat against a window at the back of the plane, I lean my head back and close my eyes. Sleep is unlikely but at least I can stay out of trouble.

Halfway through the flight, I hear a commotion further down the aisle and see a few of the boys laughing at Gavin. He is the joker in the group and loves his beer. Back at the airport he was drinking two to everyone else's one and he's well on his way, so much so that he is staggering up the isle of the plane, looking for the toilet. He's singing to himself and already has his zip down.

"The boy stood on the burning deck, I think his name was Jock, the flames shot up around his legs and scorched his hairy... cardigan."

Everyone laughs while the air hostess cringes as he tells her in no uncertain terms that, "Whoever is in the toilet better hurry up or I'll piss against the duty-free trolley."

The boys roar at his outrageousness and the hostess looks relieved when an old lady exits the toilet.

"Fuckin' hell dear, you could have squirted the air freshener."

The old lady blushes as another explosion of laughter echoes from the mid-section of the plane.

By the time we have started our descent to Gatwick airport, the airline staff are desperate to get rid of us.

We disembark and there is a mad rush to the toilets beside the luggage carousel: our bladders fit to burst after our excessive in-flight beer consumption.

Callum had booked a train to get us all to Brighton, primarily because we can continue drinking and it's a direct route, no changes required. The carriage is packed, and our seats taken by a group of girls on a hen do. Rather than move them we spend the entire journey standing by the doors, continuously stepping out of the way to let people on and off the train. We still drink beer and sup on tins until we get to Brighton. I feel slightly jaded now after our early start and I notice the lads are also much more subdued by the time we get off.

It doesn't last though. Jordan, aka Two Pint Tony, leads the group to a hostel at the beach front, where he is staying with most of the group. Callum and I jump in a taxi to head to our hotel, making arrangements to meet the rest later.

As we check in at the front desk, the pretty receptionist informs me her manager wants to speak to me. Callum checked in ahead of me and is already waiting by the lift so I've no idea what's going on when a man in a suit appears at my side then leads me to the corner of the hotel lobby.

"A package has been delivered here for you, sir," the manager whispers mysteriously.

I look puzzled. "For me, are you sure?"

"Yes, sir, the package arrived this morning by special delivery."

He hands me a padded envelope and winks to me.

I give him a blank look as I am clearly not in on the same joke. The package contains something flat and hard. I rip the seal and pull out a DVD case. On the front cover a girl with curly, red hair grins back at me. Annie? I go to open the DVD box and the manager stops me.

"I wouldn't do that here, sir. I'd wait until you get to your room." He winks again.

"Right," I say, still completely confused.

I head over to the lift and Callum is still there waiting for me.

"All checked in and paid for, bud. Here's your key."

"Did you get the DVD I sent you?" he asks, trying not to laugh.

"What the fuck is Annie all about?"

"I'll show you upstairs," he answers, moving into the lift with our bags.

Our rooms are next door to each other, so Callum follows me into mine when I open the door.

"What's going on?" I ask

"Open it," Callum says.

I pop open the plastic case. Inside the case are plastic bags of white powder, flattened to fit snugly into the shallow, rectangular area.

"Fuckin' hell, I thought we would just score some down here. Taking a risk posting it, aren't we?"

"Well, I can't rely on getting good shit down here, at least this way I know it's from my guy," Callum says, clearly proud of himself.

"I notice that you addressed it to me, though? Just in case the police get a hold of it, eh?" I say pointedly.

"Well, you know what you're doing when it comes to all that polis hassle," he says, laughing, slapping me on the back.

I hand him the DVD case and he heads through to his room.

"The hotel manager kept winking at me, he must be used to deliveries appearing for guests at this hotel," I say with a smile.

"It's Brighton, son. Anything goes down here," Callum replies as he opens his door.

"Come through when you're settled," he shouts over his shoulder.

I unpack my suitcase, hang up my clothes and wash my face in the bathroom. I haven't had a drink since the plane and I'm starting to feel tired and thirsty, regretting overindulging so early in the morning.

The bed in the room looks very comfortable so I'm tempted to have a lie down. I fight it though, and instead open the doors out to the balcony to look at the sea view. There's something about the sea that calms my soul: the sound of the waves and smell of salt water reminds me of my cottage. I need to get back there soon, back to my house by the beach; it's my sanctuary. After recent events I don't know why I didn't think about a trip up north sooner.

I hear Callum's balcony door open: he has had the same idea as me.

"A'right, son?" he shouts across, taking a quick look at the view. "You coming in for a line?" he asks enthusiastically.

I jump over the wall that separates the balconies. Twelve bottles of beer have been delivered in a large ice bucket, so he chucks one to me. I'm dehydrated from this morning and the cold liquid quenches my thirst as I sink half the bottle.

Callum nods towards the glass coffee table where he has sliced up rows of white powder into perfect, horizontal lines. I take a moment to finish off the beer before snorting a line and Callum reads out a text from Jordan.

"They're heading to the pub along the road, we've to meet them there."

"Okay, I'm ready when you are."

"I'll just fill this bullet and then we can go," he says, already busy scraping some of the white powder into a piece of paper, planning to funnel it into the metal snorting apparatus.

We head along the beach front and find the boys have invaded a bar called Osiris. It's a funky little place which has welcomed our lot and our potential spending with open arms. Callum and I walk up to the bar to greet the barman and get some drinks in. A name tag on the left side of his pink shirt reads 'Steven': he has to be one of the campest men I have ever seen. Callum hands over an Amex card and instructs Steven to put it behind the bar, telling him to put all drink from our crowd on it.

"Ooh, check you out you big spender, do you need a sex slave?" Steven asks, placing his hand on the hip of his denim shorts.

Callum laughs and politely declines as he orders beers for everyone.

Gavin doesn't seem to have sobered up since the plane and sees the opportunity to get a laugh by tying his T-shirt into a knot at the bottom and flicking a pretend lock of hair from his face.

I chuckle as he approaches the bar with a fruity swagger and leans over it.

"So where do you work out?" Gavin asks deadpan in a faux cockney accent with no trace of his usual Fife twang.

Steven decides to humour him and replies, "I train at the ladies' gym, just across from the station."

"Well, it's working, whatever you are doing," Gavin answers, getting the desired reaction from the crowd, well our crowd anyway.

"Ooh, you are a tease," flirts Steven, playing along.

By the time we leave Osiris, Steven the bar man is best mates with everyone and gets a tip big enough to double his night's earnings, including a little pick me up from Callum's powder stash.

Suitably merry, we move on to the next bar to get food, to soak up the alcohol. An enormous selection of nachos, toasties, chips and burgers keeps up our stamina and prevents us from passing out too early.

It's hitting mid-afternoon now and the majority of the lads are smashed and are well on their way to going to an early night. Callum dishes out a wee 'pick me up' to the guys, in the hope that it will straighten them out. It works well for some and not so good for others. Two Pint Tony and Gavin have lost the power of speech, so we send them back to the hotel in a taxi, where they can sleep it off.

Steven gave us some recommendations on where the hot spots are for a good night out. It becomes a debate and then everyone seems to want to go somewhere different. It appears that drink doesn't agree particularly well with Mark, the hard man, whose default position after fifteen beers is violence.

"If we don't sort this out, I'm goin' to go fuckin' radge, it's just wastin' time and somebody will get a punch in the pus."

Callum decides to offer his solution.

"Right, let's get a taxi back to my hotel and we can kick the arse out of it there for a while?"

"Have you got gear?" one of the stag members asks from within the huddle.

"Does a bear shit in the woods?" Callum responds, raising a few interested smiles among the group.

So that's what we do. The taxi takes us back to the hotel

and we pile into Callum's room. The huge TV on the wall has a music channel and the balcony provides more than enough room for all of us to congregate. A couple of boys nip to the shop and buy a load of beers, so we are sorted for a while.

The cocaine starts to deplete due to the number of people taking a line, so Callum decides to ration it.

"We've got all weekend, let's not burst the whole load on the first day."

Reluctantly, the group agrees. Callum nods to me to follow him out to the balcony, so I do.

"Don't worry, son, I have got more on the way. I just don't want to tell them that."

I smile and nod in approval.

Callum heads back into the room and I decide to head back to my own room for a moment. As before, I swing my leg over the wall between the balconies and go in through the patio doors.

I'm merry but not drunk. I'm intoxicated but not licking windows, so I appear to be keeping myself in a reasonable shape. I head over to the big bed and lie down. Just ten minutes out will do me some good. My phone buzzes in my pocket and I immediately look at it.

Davey again. He has sent me a text: 'Did u c CCTV?'

Fuck, he's not letting up on this. How do I tell him that he's mistaken and not insult him? He's always sound with me but I know his reputation; once you get on his bad side, it's game over.

Shall I just ignore him? Nah, I'll reply later, just not now. I'm trying to have a good time.

The phone gets tossed aside and I jump up from the bed. More beer, more banter, more laughs, that's all I want. I join everyone else in Callum's room with the rest of the guys, listening to the shite that is coming thick and fast out of everyone's intoxicated mouths.

The sun begins to go down and discussions are had around

what to do for the rest of the evening. The best man informs us that he has booked the VIP area in a nightclub, so that's where we will be heading. I suggest to everyone that we all get changed, showered or whatever. It will break up the crowd and hopefully help some people sober up, especially Mark who is becoming more and more annoying.

I hear him arguing with somebody out on the balcony and go to investigate.

"Ah fuckin' ripped the T-shirt off his back and punched him fifteen rapid. Ah handed the ripped T-shirt back to him after he hit the deck."

He's telling the same fuckin' shit story that he told us all this morning. I decide to give him some friendly advice, so I walk over to him and ask him for a word.

"You having a good time Mark?" I ask, easing into the conversation.

"Aye, fuckin' brilliant. Thanks for coming, means a lot to Jordan to have boys like you here, just in case anything kicks off you know?"

"See, you need to ease up on all that shit. Nobody wants to hear somebody talking about fighting and how hard they are all the time, you just sound like a fanny. I know you're a good guy, so just be normal, have fun and relax. Nobody is here to have a fight, we're here for a good time."

His eyes narrow slightly; he's not happy.

"What d'you mean? You saying I can't fight like?"

"Jesus, I said all of that and all you heard was whether I think you can fight or not? That's my point, stop talking about fighting, just enjoy the weekend."

"Fuck off, I'll say what I like. No' having you tell me what I can talk about."

"Calm down, it's just a bit of advice. We are a large group and if we are heard talking like that, then people will think we are looking for trouble."

He goes in the huff and shakes his head.

"Okay, it's up to you, but you are the best man, Mark, so if you fuck it up, it's on your own head, just remember that."

He throws his bottle onto the floor of the balcony and it shatters into a million glass pieces.

"Fuck you, I'll do what I like," he snarls at me.

Callum and a few others hear the stramash and come out to see what's going on.

"Who's smashing bottles?" Callum asks, clearly unimpressed.

"Him," I nod towards Mark.

Callum looks at him disdainfully, provoking Mark.

"What, I'm standing here, doing fuck all and then this cunt starts trying to tell me what I can talk about?"

I interject. "I was just telling him to calm down on all the fighting talk. I don't want people to think that we are here for trouble"

Callum rolls his eyes and walks towards us.

"Listen, Mark, Ronin's right, we are all here for your mate's stag, everyone is sick of hearing your pish fighting stories. If you really want a fight, punch Ronin. He'll fuckin' leather you and then you'll have a proper story to tell."

A few of the boys laugh and this upsets Mark even more, so he pouts like a petulant child.

"I'm going to get a shower, so take the crowd and fuck off back to your hotel," Callum snaps.

Mark walks away in the huff and his friends follow him. Callum and I don't even bother discussing it. We kick the broken glass into the corner of the balcony and head to our rooms to get ready.

The shower is powerful, so the hot water and steam help to freshen me up. I pull on a blue shirt, jeans and a pair of boots. While my hair is drying, I take money from the pocket of the jeans I just took off and transfer it to the fresh pair. I plug my phone in to charge and remember I need to reply to Davey. Fuck, what do I say to him?

I attempt a few messages but they all sound like 'You are talking pish', so I leave it. I'll sort it out with him later.

I join Callum in his room again, via the balcony wall and we drink a couple of beers while coating the inside of our nostrils with disco dust. It's like we never had a problem and we are getting on like we always did. Lisa doesn't even enter my head.

Mark sends Callum a grovelling text asking us to meet him at the club, where he has reserved the VIP area. We decide to join them and jump in a taxi to get there.

We pull up outside a large, renovated building; the original plaque on the wall beside the door tells me it used to be an old library. The eight stone pillars on the outside remind me of the Pantheon in Rome. I took an old girlfriend there once. In between each column are huge marble statues of male and female figures in robes. Searchlights beam out onto the street so that the burly bouncers, dressed in tuxedos, can determine who gets in. I've no doubt the place is filled with posers, gold-diggers and sugar daddies. The name of the club is displayed in bold, gold letters in the centre above the pillars: HADES. Greek God of the underworld. How appropriate: we will fit in perfectly.

Callum and I give the bouncers a nod and we are greeted at the door by a very attractive young brunette, who is the hostess. She escorts us to the VIP area, where most of the stag party has regrouped. A few haven't quite made it – no surprise. They couldn't keep up with the pace.

Before the hostess leaves, Callum catches her attention.

"Here's five hundred quid. Bring us as many half-decent bottles of champagne that you can give us for that."

The hostess agrees and then beams a smile as Callum gives her an extra fifty for her trouble. He's been a prick lately, but I can't argue that the man is generous to a fault.

The night goes quickly as Callum and I watch the lads all get drunk on champagne until eventually they fade out. We leave the club at three a.m., drunkenly congratulating ourselves on completing a twelve-hour drinking session.

Our movements give us away. Not one of us can walk in a straight line and we pile into a kebab shop, slurring our orders then stealing food from people who get served before us.

Navigating the group back to the hotel is painstaking, Callum and I try to master the art of focusing properly, eating kebabs and remembering the exact location of our residence. The others disappear to the hostel and when we eventually get to the doors of our rooms, we don't even say anything to each other. It's game over for the night. Bed is the only option and I'm glad of that. The last thing I do is brush my teeth to avoid waking up with breath smelling like a donkey's arse.

28

THE SOUND OF DANCE MUSIC awakens me, so I look around the room. Fuck, my head is pounding and my nostrils are blocked with crusty cocaine residue. I try my best to lubricate my mouth with saliva but there's nothing there. I'm dry as a cork and feel like absolute shit. I roll off the side of the bed and somehow manage to stagger over to the small fridge to down the bottle of water from the mini bar. Fuck, that probably just cost me a tenner.

The music is coming from next door, Callum's, and by my guess he has already started to drink again. I check my watch and see that it's just after eight thirty a.m. I collapse back onto the bed and shove my head under the pillow, trying to muffle the banging of the repetitive, hard beat, which is like a hammer to my head. It doesn't work and I know there is nothing for it: if I can't beat him, I'll have to join him.

Clumsily, I pull on jeans and a T-shirt, trainers with no

socks then open the curtains. The sun burns my eyes so I quickly grab my sunglasses from my bag. I look and move like an old man with a drink problem who has just shat himself. I shuffle over the balcony wall and into Callum's room, slightly bent over and clutching my middle. I was right, he's up, dressed and looking fresh. I have no idea how he manages it because I literally feel like I am dying.

"Morning, son," Callum says, smirking at the sight of me.

I glare at him and crumple onto the comfy chair next to the table. He hands me an ice-cold beer and a rolled-up fifty-pound note. Here we go again. I think about refusing but I know from experience that it's either kill or cure: if I want to feel better, I'll need to get right back on it.

The beer hits the spot, it's so cold that I shiver as it goes down. I put the note down and grab a tissue from the box on the coffee table then spend a good few minutes attempting to rid my nostrils from day-old coke deposits that have crystallised overnight. I roll the note tight and snort a couple of lines. Callum hands me another beer with one hand and continues to text someone with his other.

I start to feel better already. Looking around the room, I can see that Callum's OCD has kicked in early. He has tidied everything up from yesterday and restocked the ice bucket with beers in preparation for round two.

"We going for some breakfast?" he asks spritely.

I look at him in disbelief.

"Absolutely no fuckin' chance am I having breakfast, unless you want me to throw up all over your toast?"

"I'll ask them to serve us beer," he offers, trying to tempt me.

I raise an eyebrow in interest.

"You go and get a shower, I'll go and speak to the manager and see what can be done."

I don't answer him and force myself out of the chair to head back to my room via the balcony. He leaves his room on a breakfast mission and I'm fairly certain he will manage to sort out something; negotiation skills are his forte, of course. In his line of work they have to be.

Back in my room I start running the shower and go to grab a full fat coke from the fridge. I don't care what it costs, I need something to satisfy this unrelenting thirst.

I step into the shower and close my eyes, tilting my face upwards into the flow of water so that I can feel the full pressure. It's invigorating and helps to relieve my headache. As it disappears the hangover fear seeps in and consumes me like an invisible poison.

I can't keep living like this every weekend. I've had good times, now and again, but the excessive amount of drugs on tap, the drinking all day, the partying all night, it's wearing me out, it's not good for me. I've got to screw the nut, so this is my last blow-out. I've had enough now, I'll enjoy the weekend and then I'm going to get my shit together. I'm done with it all, I really am.

My phone beeps, interrupting my downward spiral into depression. I turn the shower off and grab a towel. It's Callum telling me to get my ass to reception. When I get downstairs he is sitting with the manager, looking very chummy and having a great old chat. The manager has a glint in his eye which immediately tells me one of two things: either he's been paid to comply with Callum's wishes or he's been snorting gear. Maybe it's both; it wouldn't surprise me.

Sure enough, Callum has blagged it. We are escorted into a private dining room, where an impressive selection of breads, pastries, cereals and conserves are arranged nicely on a table set for two. The window looks out over the ocean and beside each placemat there is an ice-cold pint, so cold that I can see the condensation running slowly down the side of the glass.

"That's the stuff," Callum exclaims as he claps his hands together and nods in thanks to the hotel manager.

I sit down and appraise the pint in front of me, remembering the conversation I had with myself in the shower. It took me all of a millisecond to decide that getting stuck in is the best way forward. After sinking half the contents of the glass and loudly exclaiming, "Aaaaah," I check the time to see it's nine thirty a.m. Not quite within the parameters of the legal serving time but thirty minutes off is not bad.

"How did you talk him round?" I ask Callum as he spreads butter onto some toast.

"Money and drugs," he answers nonchalantly.

"Knew it, never fails," I say as I gulp down more of the beer. Despite my earlier resolution, I'm starting to feel better, a little tipsy even. "What's on the plan for today?" I ask Callum as he attacks his pint with similar gusto.

He pauses to catch his breath and he answers, "More pubs, the football's on this afternoon, we can just take it easy while we watch that, then tonight we are going to Revolver."

"What's Revolver?"

"It's a titty bar. The best man, phoned up and booked us into the stag party package, whatever that means."

Standard stag party entertainment it is then.

We down another pint each and head out of the hotel, down to the beach front to the bar we were in yesterday. Steven, the barman, is so happy to see us again, he plants a kiss on our cheeks. He informs us that he wasn't really planning to be open at ten thirty a.m. but that he would open for us. In other words, he's not going to turn down the chance of another good tip.

The other lads wander in slowly, each one looking more wounded than the last. Gavin, on the other hand, immediately gets in on the action again, and makes a beeline for the jukebox selecting She's like the wind by Patrick Swayze. He pirouettes around the pub stroking his backside in a lame attempt to entice Steven.

"Ooh, you're making my mouth water, darling," Steven purrs seductively, playing along and winking at Callum and me as he shimmies over to Gavin before grabbing his hands. The rest of the boys whoop loudly, roaring with laughter as the pair dance to the final verse of the Dirty Dancing classic. Just the pick me up that was needed, and another round of drinks is ordered to get everyone back in the mood for another sesh.

The weather is great, so rather than go hell for leather and kick the arse out of another day we take things easy, drinking at a much slower pace. Steven looks after all of us then at lunch-time some additional bar staff come in to help him.

Callum checks in with Steven to find out about the available stock behind the bar. Steven confirms that there is "Plenty, darling," to which Callum replies, "Make sure you buy a few for yourself, sugar tits."

Feeling hungry, I head up to the bar to order food and find Callum chatting to a guy in red T-shirt with bulging biceps. I am hit instantly with the smell of coconut moisturising cream which seems to have been applied to the very impressive muscles belonging to Callum's new-found friend. I miss the beginning of the conversation and all I hear is this guy telling Callum to "Follow me to the ladies' room, big boy."

On instant alert I frown at Callum who grins at me and shrugs his shoulders. He's up to no good. I spit out my beer as I laugh, watching them stride up the bar towards the toilets at the back. For almost ten minutes, I watch the football and enjoy the banter with the lads. Even the lightweights are having a better time today.

Eventually, Callum comes out of the toilet and sits on a stool next to me at the bar. He picks up his drink and quietly sips away.

"Well? What the fuck was that about?" I ask him.

"What?" he replies, knowing exactly what I mean.

"You and fuckin' Right Said Fred, what was that about?" I ask.

"Just kidding, son. He said he had some fantastic gear, he's a chemist, so he makes all this potent shit in his own lab. Obviously, it would have been rude not to try some."

"What kind of gear is it?" I ask, not sure that I feel comfortable with the fact that Callum has no qualms about accepting home-made drugs from a random in a Brighton bar.

"Fuck knows but it was smooth, one up each nostril and it wasn't like rock salt or anything rough."

I shake my head in disbelief and go back to watching the football.

Twenty minutes later the football is finished, and Callum is absolutely fuckin' wrecked. Whatever he took has taken effect and he's all over the place. With eyes like saucers his jaw slides back and forth, talking at full speed but not making any sense whatsoever. I need to take him back to his room to get his head straight before he gets himself into any trouble. The boys are laughing but look uneasy as I haul Callum to his feet and out of the pub. We agree to meet later at a bar near Revolver.

Trying to get Callum back to the hotel is like trying to steer a supermarket shopping trolley; no matter what way I want him to go, he goes the opposite direction. After a lot of swerving people, avoiding parked cars and strange looks I get him into his room and onto the bed.

His chat is incessant and incomprehensible, he certainly isn't getting tired of talking complete and utter rubbish. I catch the odd word about the club and Nancy but it's all mixed up, not making much sense. I switch off after a while and go to get him some water from the fridge. Just as I do that he says something that stops me in my tracks.

"She had to go with him, we made a deal, sorry, sorry, out of my control, just business."

"What did you just say, Callum?" I say, slowly turning towards him.

"Eh, no, what am I saying like?" He was bleary eyed and clenching his teeth.

"Who are you talking about?"

He repeats something similar to me.

"The deal was done, and she was part of the business, she just went and was gone."

"Who was part of the business? Who, Callum?"

"I thought about getting that dog and then I wanted a cat and that was what my granny said when she said about me having a dog and then a cat and then the fucker ran away, but we were on that boat, mind?"

What the actual fuck? He's off again, ranting more gibberish and not in any state to engage with me or know what the hell I'm asking him. I leave it until he straightens up a bit and my instincts tell me I need to chill for a while. Callum's words reduce to a quiet mumble. He looks like he's about to doze off, so I help myself to a beer and sit outside on the balcony.

As I sip my beer, I feel a cold shiver down my back. Callum's choice of words has really bothered me. There's no chance of getting any sense out of him at the moment, so I finish off the beer and head to the table, intending to recharge with a couple of lines.

I am taken by surprise when Callum sits upright on his bed and turns to me with a smile. "Fuckin' hell, I feel amazing, I'm out my tits but I feel amazing."

"Fuckin' hell, thank fuck you are back in the room, what did that guy give you? I had to take you back here, you were a complete fucking mess."

"I have no idea what it was, but I feel fantastic now. Maybe a line or two will add to it."

I think about stopping him and then decide it isn't worth it. He does what he wants, always has and always will.

"Do you remember anything you were doing or saying?" I ask him as he chops out a few lines.

"Not really, I remember you steering me away from cars though, were they moving or parked?"

"Parked."

"Thank fuck for that."

"You kept repeating some shit about somebody having to go somewhere and you making a business deal, then you kept saying sorry."

Callum pauses for a second but keeps his back to me. He bends over and snorts his lines before turning to me.

"Not a clue what that's about. I was out my face; no shit has ever done that to me in a long time"

"Don't make a habit of it, I barely managed to get you here."

Callum reaches over and gives me a rare hug. "You're a good lad."

"Aye, aye," I say as I reach for another beer.

"Are we eating before the pub?" Callum asks. I give him yet another look of surprise to which he quickly reacts. "On second thoughts, eating's cheating, better just stuck to beer and gear."

After an hour of fucking about in Callum's room, listening to music, drinking beer and indulging in narcotics, we realise that it's time to meet the rest of the stag party.

This new pub is packed with a mixture of both sexes, so shots are ordered to accompany the beers and chat up lines. When we move next door to Revolver, the bouncers lecture us about 'no touching,' 'any nonsense and you'll be out,' 'If you ain't got money, you can't stay.' It falls on deaf ears and none of the crowd really pay any attention.

For a lap dancing bar, this place is actually quite classy. It's trendy, with industrial style décor and could almost pass for an upmarket bar if it wasn't for the discreet little areas for private dances in every corner. The manager greets us and escorts the crowd to the VIP lounge for the stag party package. Before we sit down, Callum has a word in the ear of the manager and hands him a huge wad of cash.

Soon after, staff arrive with bottles of champagne, multi-coloured, sickly sweet shots in tubes and huge ice buckets filled with bottles of beer. They give us a moment to get stuck into the drink and then the ladies start arriving. There is no doubt about it, the women are stunning, absolutely fucking gorgeous and a complete contrast to the kebab-eating mingers working in some of the clubs in Edinburgh. The guys don't know what to do with themselves except gawp.

Jordan, being the stag, gets free lap dances and finds it hard to contain the excitement on his face and in his trousers when they pull his shirt off him to pour chocolate sauce over his chest. Things get a bit Fifty Shades when they tie him up on stage and whip his arse with his own belt, which has the rest of us in hysterics.

Barely able to contain themselves the others disappear to private booths for private dances. I notice Callum handing the dancers fifty-pound notes and pointing to the boys, one at a time. Fuck, he's even paying for all of their dances tonight, which means he is feeling very generous or he is still delirious from the gear he took in the pub earlier.

He leans over to me, money wadded in his hand.

"See anyone you fancy?" he asks, looking around at the selection of dancers who obviously know that there is money being spent in this area.

"Nah, I'm fine just now," I say, laughing at the reaction from some of the boys who are after having their first ever lap dance.

I can't describe it. Despite all the beer, the drugs, the champagne, the laughs, I'm not happy. There's no easy way to describe it, I just don't feel any joy from this kind of thing any more. Maybe I'm too hard to please, maybe I want more or maybe I just need to take a break from this lifestyle for a while. If I knew the immediate solution, I would do it.

Callum senses my mood and suggests that we get out of there.

"Where do you want to go?" I ask him.

"Fuck knows, just have a quiet drink somewhere and let these lads have a good time."

I shrug my shoulders in a way that shows I'm happy to go with the flow.

Callum grabs the attention of Mark.

"Here, take this, there's about a grand there. Don't spend it all on yourself or I'll fucking paste you, dish it out evenly and have a good time, we're fucking off."

Mark, looking grateful, shakes Callum's hand vigorously to show his thanks. Maybe he's not such an annoying cunt after all.

We leave the club and walk down the street towards the beach front. A couple of bars entice us in, but we only stay for one drink. I think we've had it for the weekend. All day drinking, and drugs sessions aren't getting any easier.

It's back to just talking between us. Like what we always used to do in the old days, just openly talk to each other about anything and everything. The kind of thing that friends can do with each other. I think we had forgotten how to do that. We all get so caught up in the money making rat race that we lose track of the fundamentals of life, what's important, what makes us human.

When we get back to the hotel, it's the same. We sit for hours, talking, listening to music, drinking a few beers and snorting some lines. We decide to call it a night at three a.m. As I lie in bed, I replay the weekend in my head, smiling, acknowledging that there were some hilarious moments. I feel myself drifting into unconsciousness but then her face jumps into my mind, jolting me awake; Lisa.

I glance up at the window, which is only partially covered by the curtain, and can see a full moon illuminating the clear night sky. Something catches my eye and I watch as a single, white feather falls gently to the floor. I lean over the edge of the bed to pick it up. I hold it up to the moonlight and run my fingers along the soft edges before putting it on the night table next to me with a heavy sigh. It's late and I have a flight to catch tomorrow.

29

I HAVE BEEN BANGING ON the bedroom door for five minutes but there is no answer. I even jumped over the balcony wall but the patio door is locked and the curtains are drawn. Callum never has a lie-in so I start to feel worried; normally he is up before any of us. Sometimes he doesn't even sleep.

The helpful receptionist offers to come up to Callum's room with me and try to open the door. She has the master key. We have a flight to catch in two hours, so that doesn't leave much time to reach the airport. The door is locked and bolted from the inside and I phone his mobile for the fifteenth time while the receptionist calls the room phone.

Eventually, we hear someone grumbling from inside and the flush of a toilet cistern. The door remains closed as we stand and listen to the slow padding of feet towards the door.

"Come on, dickhead, open up, we can hear you," I shout as I bang my fist on the white wooden panels.

The door opens and two bleary eyed women push past the receptionist and me. We look at each other uncomfortably and then push the door open. Callum is in the shower, groaning and obviously feeling sorry for himself.

"Everything okay now?" the receptionist shouts through the bathroom door, trying to hide her embarrassment at the fact that he is in the shower and two ladies of the night have just exited the room.

"Yes, thank you and sorry for the trouble," he mumbles, barely audible through the noise of the water.

I hand her several banknotes from my pocket – there must be a few hundred pounds in the folded pile. She pauses for a moment, looks around and then snatches the money from my hand before hurrying along the hallway and disappearing downstairs to reception.

"I left you alone and about to go to bed last night, where the fuck did those two tarts come from?" I ask Callum, standing at the doorway of the bathroom.

He doesn't answer.

"You know we only have forty-five minutes to get to the airport now?"

No response.

"Okay, fuck this, I'm leaving now, I'll see you at the airport."

I leave his room and collect my suitcase which I had left sitting on the landing outside his door. He's a big boy, I am sure he can get to the airport by himself. I have done my job by checking that he is alive, and I'll be damned if I end up missing my flight because he can't keep it in his trousers. Striding past the reception, I toss my room key onto the desk and head out onto the main street.

It doesn't take me long to flag down a taxi and the driver grins happily when I ask him to take me to Gatwick airport as quickly as possible. The half-hour journey is tedious with very slow traffic so to pass the time I flick through messages on my phone.

I remember Davey's text and tap out a response to him.

'Sorry Davey, I was at the stag this weekend, shite signal, will call you when I get back up the road. Just heading to the airport now.'

That should keep him happy until I get time to talk to him properly.

I start deleting old messages and eventually get to the text from Lisa. I feel my stomach churn as I read it again, almost deleting it but deciding not to. I can't explain why but I don't want to. I feel like that message is all I have to remind me of the time we spent together. Fuck, I'm pathetic.

Check-in is the usual pain in the arse and when I get to the departure lounge, I see the rest of the stag crew at the bar, all nursing hangovers and stressing about how much money they spent over the weekend.

"Fuck, my wife is going to cut my balls off when she sees how much money I spent in the titty bar," moans Mark mournfully as I approach them.

"What the fuck did you use your card for then? Ya daft cunt!" I ask to annoy him.

"Ronin! Where have you been? Where's Callum? Fuck knows what happened to all his money, or how many lap dances we had!"

"Callum's not the only one who got carried away," I say and the guys laugh.

One of the lads passes me a cold pint and I sink it quickly, feeling better as the liquid disappears from the glass. This weekend wasn't so bad after all: I patched things up with Callum and we had a good laugh. So it's just as well I came. Sometimes a weekend with your mates is all you need.

As we start another round, Callum arrives at the bar, looking like absolute shit. A resounding cheer comes from the lads as he strides into the pub and collapses into a chair at the table.

"Beer me," he utters, wiping sweat from forehead. He looks as grey as a fucking ghost.

"What the fuck happened to you? It was three a.m. when I left you and it looked like you were ready for bed!," I ask him seriously.

"Fuck, I started flicking through the contacts in my phone and realised I have a couple of tarts on the list down here. I text one of them and before I knew it I was snorting lines off their tits."

The younger lads all laugh in admiration and I sit back with a smile, raising one eyebrow.

"And you didn't think to give me a shout?" I joke as I watch him gulp at his beer. His right hand is shaking violently and he can barely hold the glass to his lips. He doesn't even bother to answer me and just drinks as much of his beer as he can, puts his glass down and throws his head into the palms of his hands with a groan.

A call with our flight and gate number sounds over the tannoy, so we all move reluctantly away from our table of beer.

This time there are no lines of gear before the flight meaning I manage to sleep all the way. Callum is in the row behind me and sleeps so deeply that when we land, I ask the lady next to him to make sure he is still breathing.

When the minibus drops us at Callum's house again, he doesn't even speak. He hands the driver a few notes and walks straight into his house, dragging his suitcase the wrong way so that it scrapes along the path. I exchange standard 'great weekend' banter with the lads and then we all go our separate ways.

The need for hangover junk food has kicked in, so I head home via the drive-through. I have most of it finished before I even get home and then finish off my cheeseburger chaser before heading straight upstairs to bed. I need an hour of the Sopranos while my body tries to cope with the belly full of stodgy carbs and shitty meat I have just filled it with as well as the aftermath of a heavy weekend.

The fear is back and I tell myself once again that 'I'm getting too old for this shit', but I bat them away with, 'Fuck it, I'll settle down when I get to forty.'

30

THE PAIN COMES IN WAVES over and over in my stomach and I'm curled up in a ball on the bed, covered in sweat. It is so intense that I can't decide whether I need to be sick or if I need to shit.

Wearily, I stagger downstairs to get a glass of water. I sip it and then pour another which I gulp down. As soon as the second glass hits my stomach I retch and throw it back up into the kitchen sink.

The clock on the wall shows five a.m. and I can see from the kitchen window that the sun is already up. I catch sight of the firepit in the garden, which contains the charred remains of my clothes from last week, remembering that job from hell makes my stomach churn even more. Before I can dwell on it further, I turn on the TV. Jeremy Kyle's confrontational tone bellows out from the screen and three smelly, toothless wonders, wearing scuffed high heels and white socks, complain loudly that the same father of their children won't pay child support. They would have to be Scottish, wouldn't they? I quickly switch to MTV, and Ed Sheeran's voice fills the room: cheesy but it's about as much as I can cope with right now.

I feel a gurgling in my belly and it's the other end this time. I rush to the bathroom, unloading a rear-end explosion that releases all the toxins from the weekend in large quantities with a putrid smell that's enough to make me start retching all over again.

The relief is immense and once I am finished I tidy myself up, wash my hands and stagger through to the lounge. I hardly ever go in here and it's the best room in the house. I save it for when the lads are round and of course Jeannie. The large leather sofa looks inviting so I crawl onto it and lie face down. The soft leather is cool on my forehead and I quickly fall asleep again.

When I wake, it's almost eight a.m. and the sun is beaming in through the window. I expect that I would have slept for longer if the curtains had been closed but I'm awake now and I feel better than I did three hours ago, so I decide to get up.

I empty the contents of my suitcase into the washing basket, fishing out the toiletries as an afterthought. Agnes will take care of this lot.

Surprisingly, the stomach pains have gone and I feel almost good, considering what I'd put my body through, so I drop a couple of pre-workout pills, throw on my running gear and head out along the track next to the house. A decent run and getting a proper sweat on will do me the power of good. My earphones are in and my running dance mix helps me to keep up a decent pace.

Just as I'm getting into my stride, I am interrupted by a call from Callum. Stopping by a field gate I catch my breath and answer through Bluetooth headphones.

"Uuuuuuuuuuuuugh, I am fuckin dying," he moans.

"I'm out for a run," I pant. "Feeling great today. Did you sleep?"

"A wee bit. Maybe four hours but still feeling like shit."

"That's what happens when you get involved with gear and tarts at three a.m.," I laugh as he continues to make groaning sounds down the phone.

"Anyway, just giving you a heads up that the next driving job is tomorrow," he says, quickly changing to business.

"Okay, same setup as before? Will that guy phone with instructions?" I ask.

"Aye, same deal, just pick the cunt up, drop him off and then take him back."

"Okay, I'll wait for the call and I'll deal with it tomorrow."

"Good lad. I'm away to go and die now, so see you later."

He hangs up and I start off on a jog again. Five miles is enough for this morning and I feel better after I've done it. When I get back to the house, I stretch off and mix together spirulina and chlorella powder in water. This stuff tastes like shit but it's great for detoxing. I check my phone: there have been no calls or messages, so I head upstairs for a shower. I ask Alexa to play the radio while I wash and get freshened up.

Right: tasks for today – Jeannie then Dinky, if a new car can't keep me occupied then nothing will. I pull on a T-shirt, jeans and a brand-new pair of white trainers that have appeared in my shoe rack, no doubt courtesy of Nancy.

The sun shines bright, so when I get into the car, I pull on my sunglasses, put the window down and turn on an Apple music shuffle. I arrive at Jeannie's house to find her sitting on a chair in her front garden, or 'wee patch of grass' as she likes to call it.

"Hello, my son, how are you getting on?" she asks with a smile. She is wearing clip-on shades attached to her glasses and flips them up as I close the car door.

I smile as I approach her and plant a kiss on her cheek.

"You're looking happy today, better than last time I saw you," she offers as I pull up a chair and join her in the sun.

"I'm fine, had a run this morning, so feeling good."

"That's good, son, I don't want you wearing yourself out."

I smile and nod as we both sit, enjoying the rays for a couple of minutes. The sounds of birds tweeting and cars accelerating in the distance are the only noises interrupting our comfortable silence.

"What you doing today, son?" Jeannie asks with interest.

"Going to make arrangements for my new car today."

"Another car? What's wrong with that one?" she exclaims rather loudly.

"Just time for a change, you know I like my cars."

"Aye, just be careful in them, there's a lot of idiots on the roads nowadays."

"I know Jeannie, I know.'

"You want a cup of tea, son?" she asks.

"No thanks, I'm fine but I'll make you one if you like?"

"Aye, okay son, plenty milk in it."

I leave her in the garden and head into her house, passing the security door that she has propped open with a chair from her kitchen.

As I make the tea, I watch her through the window for a moment. She lives so simply without a care in the world. Always happy and always making the most of each day. If I make it to her age, I want to be just like her.

Jeannie smiles as I hand her the cup of tea and a Blue Ribband biscuit.

Sometimes this is all I need, just some quiet time with Jeannie. She doesn't want anything from me, neither do I from her but we both need each other; she's my family and I now realise she is all I have.

"How's the love life?" Jeannie asks as if reading my mind and she puts her cup of tea on the table to unwrap the biscuit.

"Not good," I say to her quickly.

"A good-looking lad like you should be able to find a dame, no problem," she says matter-of-factly.

"I just haven't found the right one yet," I tell her, trying my best to put a certain lady out of my mind.

"Well, you just make sure you find somebody nice, none of those punks with the dyed hair and studs in their noses."

I smile. I know Jeannie has the best of intentions but I don't have the heart to argue with her about punk and how it went out of fashion over thirty years ago.

"There's no danger of that," I assure her. I need to get going now but wait for Jeanie to finish her tea. "Do you need anything before I go?" I ask her.

"No, son, just take me for my messages on Saturday."

"That's fine, I'll see you before then though."

I head back to my car and wave to her as she smiles, watching me drive off.

The BMW garage is the next stop and when I arrive in the showroom, Dinky is nowhere to be seen. He's either having a fly cigarette out the back or closing some dodgy deal. Eventually I find him in the back yard, on the phone to someone, slagging off a fellow salesman. He flicks his fag ash and nods in acknowledgement as he sees me coming. Eventually, he hangs up and lights another cigarette.

"A'right, Ronin, when you wanting this car then?"

"When can I have it?" I ask.

"Well, it's been through the workshop, it's just needing a polish and then it's ready to go. You have to pay me first though!" he adds cheekily.

"Okay, give me the bank details and I'll transfer the cash to you," I say.

"We are doing cash, right? Cash instead of electronic cash?" He's pushing it.

"You expect me to hand you tens of thousands of pounds in actual notes?" I ask in disbelief.

"Aye, you've got it." He flashes a wide grin.

"No chance, too risky," I tell him sharply.

"Fuck, I was going to try to skim some off the top for myself," he says, dragging on his fag again.

I shake my head and wait for him to start talking sense.

"Okay, how about tomorrow afternoon then?" he offers, realising I'm not budging.

"That's fine, text me the bank details and I'll send the money this afternoon."

As I walk away, he calls after me.

"Is your car still in good nick? I haven't even looked at it."

"I'm surprised you even have to ask," I tell him and keep walking.

Without looking back, I get back to my car and head home. I like Dinky but he's a sneaky wee bastard at times. I'm not even five minutes on the road and a text appears on my phone from him. He doesn't waste any time when it comes to money; I'll make the bank transfer my priority when I get home. Feeling sentimental about giving my old car back, I decide to give it one last roast along the dual carriageway on my way home.

I accelerate along the road, listening to the deep rasp coming from the exhausts while I concentrate on the traffic in front of me; the drivers who see me coming in their rear-view mirrors are pulling into the inside lane. I watch the speedo creep up to 124mph and I know it can do more. Just as I press my foot on the accelerator again, an old Ford Escort drifts across the road in front of me: no indicators and chugging along at fifty-five mph. I slam on the brakes but there is no time, I'm going too fast and I'm heading for a collision. I desperately pull the steering wheel hard left and swerve into the other lane, skidding to a screeching stop on the hard shoulder.

"Fuck me!" I swear loudly, breathing fast.

I catch sight of the old codger driving the Ford Escort shaking his head at me in his rear-view mirror. Is he having a fucking laugh? I swear and wave my hands at him in protest, resisting the urge to drive up behind him and give him a scare he won't forget. Then the guilt kicks in; I shouldn't have been driving at that speed. It was reckless and irresponsible – I could have killed that old man and myself. Sometimes I don't know when to stop. It's the story of my life. Cars, drugs, women, it's all getting too much. I need to get a grip. I can't go on like this.

I take a few deep breaths and my heart rate begins to slow down. I start the car, gently pull out to join the road again and drive home carefully, sticking to the legal speed limit this time.

When I get out of the car at the house, there is an acrid smell of burning rubber in the air, and chemical fumes from the exhaust. Shit, I hope I haven't done any damage; the car has to go back in the mint condition I'd kept it in. I can't face looking at the tyres. If there is anything wrong, that sneak Dinky can deal with it.

Nancy has been in for a visit and left a bag of goodies for me on the kitchen table. I open the posh, paper bag and see she has been shopping again; expensive hair products, organic body scrub, a new shaving brush with soap and a new razor. I smile to myself as I inspect it all. Life isn't bad sometimes, she's bloody good to me, that woman.

After transferring the money to the BMW bank account using online banking, I text Dinky to let him know, omitting the fact that I'd just had a near miss and the tyres on my old car might be fucked. He replies with a 'thumbs up' emoji, so I assume the money has gone through.

I lay my phone down on the kitchen table, to go and get a drink. Just as I open the fridge I can hear vibrations carry my phone across the wooden surface in the form of a silent ring. I exhale a 'Fuck sake,' and walk back to the table to see that it is a withheld number. Instructions for tomorrow's job, no doubt.

"Hello?"

"Be at Edinburgh airport Arrivals for ten twenty a.m. to-morrow morning. A Mr O'Leary will be waiting for you. He has some mobility issues so will need your assistance, be prepared to help him in any way he requires. Again, he has the number plate of the car, so he will be keeping an eye out for you."

"Fine," I reply and the line goes dead.

The doorbell rings and I let out another 'Fuck sake' as I toss the phone down on the table and head to the front door. As I approach, I see a stocky silhouette through the glass. Getting closer, I can see it's Davey. Shit, what's he doing here? He never comes to the house in daylight, ever.

I open the front door and before I can apologise for taking so long to get back to him, he thrusts a memory stick into my hand.

"Got a computer?" he asks me.

I pause, looking at him then the memory stick, confused. "Yes, through here," I say as he closes the door behind him and follows me to the lounge.

Davey is eerily quiet, which is just not like him.

"You okay, Davey?" I ask him.

"Hurry up, I told you to phone me and you kept ignoring me, daft Davey, nobody believes a word he says, well I'll show you something right now that will change that."

"I wasn't ignoring you, Davey. I was…"

"Don't give me your shit Ronin, I know you went to the club, I know they told you I was talking shit, just look at the file on the memory stick."

Fuck, he's angry. I've never seen him like this before. He actually has me feeling on edge. I know what he's capable of, so I adjust my stance in case he kicks off. He may be my mate but he's a hardy fucker. I know too much about his past too and seeing him angry like this makes me wary of him.

I watch as Davey opens the laptop, plugs in the memory stick and opens up a file. A video screen pops up to reveal a black-and-white picture.

"What's this?" I ask.

"CCTV from the club. Now we will see who is talking shite."

I click on the corner of the video to enlarge the screen size, click 'play' and watch in silence. Davey takes a step back and folds his tattooed arms, leaving me to see the footage with my own eyes.

My heart stops beating for a second, my stomach lurches and I feel sick as I watch grainy footage of a backdoor of a building. For a second nothing happens but then the double fire door opens and a man pops his head out. He looks around, disappears back inside before stepping out again, dragging a girl behind him. A second later a transit van pulls up and the girl is thrown into the back.

I hit rewind and watch the footage again. It's that cunt, Pavel, just like Davey said, wearing the white polo shirt. And the girl, I press pause just before she is thrown into the van. She is unconscious, floppy like a rag doll. It's her.

I feel something inside me that I have never felt before, a fireball of rage so intense that I feel as though I am about to explode. My heart is leaping out of my chest and I grab onto the back of the sofa to steady my shaking hands, digging my nails into the leather and gripping on so tightly that my knuckles go white.

Without watching it again, I turn to Davey. He already knows what I'm going to ask.

"Mac got it for me. That lassie at the club is involved, Ronin. She's been paid off to make this disappear."

"How did Mac get this? They said the CCTV was shit and it deleted footage after twenty-four hours."

"Think about it, Ronin. They give you that half-arsed story about the dodgy system, then blame it on the imagination of old Davey the piss head. I'm surprised you were taken in so easily."

"What about Italian, John. Did he know about this?"

Davey shakes his head with doubt. "John's too daft to know about this kind of thing. It's all going on under his nose."

I stare at the floor, rethinking the events and conversations in my head.

"I need a fucking drink," I say as I push past Davey and stride through to the kitchen. The fireball is still there. I grab a bottle of beer from the fridge and flick off the cap with my teeth, desperate for something ice-cold to soothe it. Davey follows me through.

"I'm sorry, son, but I had to show you this. They are all fuckin' lying to you. All of them."

I splutter as I stop gulping the beer. "Who's they?" I ask, knowing what is coming but not wanting to hear it.

Davey looks at the floor before he answers me. "Everyone, son, everyone… except me."

Slowly I play back everything in my head again. "Callum?" My voice cracks.

Davey nods his head, still looking at the floor.

That's it, the fireball explodes, and I launch the beer bottle at the tiled wall and it bursts into tiny pieces. I grab a kitchen chair and with all my strength I throw it onto the kitchen table: it bounces once, denting the wood before crashing to the floor. I turn to the cupboard doors under the worktop and kick each one with such force that the wood bursts and then turn to grab the kettle, launching it across the room. It catches the stag antler above the stove, knocking it sideways before landing with a clatter on the slate fireplace.

Davey shouts at me to stop but I can't hear him and start punching the top cupboard doors, cracking and splintering the wood, sending tins and burst bags of pasta sprawling onto the worktop and floor. I'm not finished and Davey knows it so he launches himself at me, grabbing me with both arms in a bear hug and wrestling me to the floor. He seizes both my wrists and I try to resist but I can't move: he is a strong fucker, the rage disappears as rapidly as the air out of a burst balloon. We lie in a heap, breathing heavily, saying nothing for a moment.

"Easy, Ronin, easy," Davey says in a calm voice, doing his best to soothe me.

Tears well up in my eyes, a sob escapes before I can stop it. Fuck.

Davey is the first to get up and holds out a hand to me. I grab it, wincing as he pulls me to my feet. He directs me to the table and we both sit down. I look at my swollen, bleeding knuckles, which are starting to throb. That was a sore one, not to mention a fucking waste of time.

For a while, we sit in silence and Davey looks concerned. My heartbeat slows and eventually I feel myself becoming calm and rational. I stare at the aftermath of my explosion in the kitchen, surveying the damage I have caused.

"What now?" I say.

"Let's get some ice on those hands," he says, getting up from the table and going to the freezer, dried pasta and rice crunching under his feet as he does so. He pulls out a bowl from one of the destroyed cupboards and fills it with ice, eventually topping it up with cold water. He places it on the table and holds both of my hands in the freezing cold liquid. It's not pleasant but I know it's the only thing that will reduce the swelling.

I stare at Davey as he focuses on holding my hands in the bowl of water. I'm filled with gratitude towards him, for being there for me, for being someone I can trust. I'm just disappointed in myself for not seeing this in him before now. For a moment, my emotions get the better of me and I wish he was my father.

My focus shifts to Lisa. I feel sick: where is she? What have they done to her? My mind races with a thousand possibilities and I feel the fireball begin to grow again. I'll fucking kill that cunt Pavel. I need to stay calm, think straight and make a plan.

"Where is she, Davey?"

"I don't know, son. I can only tell you what I have heard. Mac spilled his guts to me about everything he has seen and heard. The poor bastard's shitting himself now; he's known Callum for years."

I flinch at the mention of Callum's name and Davey pauses. I nod at him to continue. "I need to know everything, Davey, everything."

"You're not going to like it," he replies, glancing up to meet my eyes.

"I don't doubt that but I can handle it."

"Okay, here's what I can make of everything that I have been told so far. Mac said Sandy Pratt is at Italian John's club all the time, always talking to that snooty office lady behind closed doors. Mac heard them talking when they thought nobody else was there. Sandy is a well-known wanker, right? He's got more fingers in dodgy pies than anyone else I know and the latest is that he is involved with some seriously dodgy fuckers. Not wide boys like we have in our crowd, I'm talking about really bad cunts. Organised crime groups, gangs, you know? The real deal, the ones you read about, the ones they make movies about, for fucks sake. He's pulled Callum in and now he's involved too. Both of them are up to their eyes in fucking shit. It's big jobs ordered by big players who pay a shit-load of money to guys on their payroll, and if they don't keep schtoom? They become a fucking ghost."

I exhale loudly. My head is spinning with all this shit. I feel the need to offload what I know.

"I walked into a meeting the other day at Mirrors. Sandy

and Callum were in the office with some guys. Serious-looking knuckle-heads, with Eastern Europe accents. They both had this tattoo on their necks." I grab a pen and notepad to draw an oval shape with a cross in the centre, just like the one I had seen.

Davey nods to me. "Yup, that's them, they have a name. It's Russian and I can't fucking remember it." He rubs his temple with his thumb and forefinger and then sighs and looks at me. "I'm too old for this carry-on, Ronin."

He looks straight into my eyes with an intensity that makes me want to look away. Usually he's the daft one, the guy having fun and taking the piss out of everyone and everything. Seeing him like this is unnerving.

"You know I come from that world, Ronin. I'm still connected but I left the nasty stuff behind me. I've asked around on the quiet and my people tell me these cunts are no joke. Their business is sex trafficking, kidnapping girls, drugging them, selling them on, using them for brothels, whatever the buyer wants, and they make a fortune!"

I know I don't want to hear what's coming next.

"They will have her, son. That dickhead with the sunglasses, they use him to find girls, pretty girls, he drugs them up and delivers them to secret locations where they keep them whether they like it or not."

"Where? What fucking secret locations?" I ask urgently.

"I don't know, they have multiple locations all over the country. My guys tell me that a new facility has started trading in Edinburgh. It's got the market you see? People have money in the burgh, people prepared to pay a fortune to do whatever they fucking well like to women."

I feel my stomach somersault again as the realisation dawns on me and for the first time in my life, I throw up without warning.

As Davey helps me wipe the watery vomit from my chin, I compose myself.

"I know exactly where it is. I've been taking clients there from the airport. I thought it was just a high-class knocking shop, for fucks sake. I didn't know it was sex traffickers!" I splutter as I try to rinse my mouth with water from the tap. "They lied to me about it. Callum, Sandy, even Lisa's friend. Why the fuck would they lie to me about this?"

"These bastards have the money and the reputation to keep anything quiet, son. I'm sure everyone has been well paid off."

"Why Lisa? Why did they have to take her?"

"I can't answer that, Ronin. She's a beautiful girl, that part is obvious, but who knows what they have her doing."

I don't speak for a moment, piecing together every event, phone call, conversation over the past two weeks. Remembering the last time I saw Lisa, a cold sense of realisation sends a chill down my spine. The club, the lady I had to take home, it was all a set up. Callum's text to Sandy: 'Package delivered'. Lisa was the package. They needed me out of the way so she could be taken.

"Fucking bastards!," I exclaim in an angry growl and boot the cupboard door again at my knees.

I've been so stupid and naïve. I should have trusted my instincts when I knew something wasn't quite right; nothing made sense. And Callum, the closest thing to a brother I'd ever had, is at the very centre of this mess, and he betrayed me.

I look up at Davey, trying to hold in my emotion.

"Why would Callum do this to me? He lied to me...me! After everything that he and I have been through, after the loyalty I've shown him! How could he turn on me like this?"

"Callum loves nothing more than money and status, ken? He loves the rush he gets from shady dealings with folk, makes him feel like the big man. I know how close you guys are, so all I can say is that he must be making a hell of a lot of money to fuck you over, Ronin."

I can feel my blood boil. My heart is pounding and my eyes well up with rage this time. "I'm going to kill them. You do know that, right? I'm going to kill every fuckin' last one of them."

Davey holds his hands up to me, urging me to calm down. "Think about this rationally, Ronin. How are you going to do that? These people are evil, and ruthless. I told you, they are not to be messed with. I'm sorry but you have no fuckin' chance of taking them on by yourself: you wouldn't last five minutes."

"So, what, you think that I should just stand back and do nothing?" I ask incredulously.

Davey shrugs and doesn't reply.

"You know me, Davey, this type of shit goes against everything I believe in. This is not the type of work I do. People have made a fool of me. Callum and that fat little bastard, Sandy Pratt. And the girl, fuck..." I can't bring myself to say any more.

"There's no way you can go charging in and start hurting people, Ronin. You need to think this through. You cause a problem and they will come after you and they won't stop until you are dead."

I stare at the broken pasta on the floor. "What the fuck do you expect me to do?"

"Well, you can't do it on your own. Who's going to be mad enough to help you pull it off though?" Davey states matter-of-factly.

I purposely stare at him until he makes eye contact with me.

"What? Eh.... no chance. No fuckin' way, Ronin. I have done enough, just by telling you this. I'm too old to get involved in any heavy stuff now. I stopped that shit years ago."

I keep staring, using my intimidation techniques. Davey says nothing and I decide to soften my approach. "Davey, I will make this worth your while. Help me and I will give you a lump of cash that will sort you out forever."

Davey's ears perk up, he loves money and I see his eyebrow raise slightly. I have his attention.

"How much are we talking?" His tone has changed, he's interested.

"I have a quarter of a million in cash. Keeping it for a rainy day. A rainy day when I need to get out and disappear, you know?"

"Aye, how much would I get?" Davey asks keenly.

"I'll give you fifty thousand if you help me."

Davey raises his eyebrows again and releases a slow whistle. "Then what?"

"I disappear. I'm going to get Lisa, I'm going to hurt those fuckers and then I'll have no option but to disappear. I'll do it smart though, just like you said."

"Have you got a plan?" Davey asks.

I almost have him. "Not yet but you can help me," I assure him.

Davey pauses for a moment, he exhales as he drums his fingers on the worktop and stares out at the view from my kitchen window.

I shove my hands back in the bowl of water again: they are really throbbing now. Watching him ponder my proposal makes me slightly anxious. I need his help, more than I've ever needed anyone's before. The melting ice clinks against the sides of the glass bowl as I wiggle my fingers. The throbbing is easing but my hands are completely numb in the freezing water.

Davey shifts his gaze from the window to look down at my hands in the bowl. He nods slowly.

"I'll help you but I'm in the background. Nobody can know I have been involved. I'll help out with the in's and oots of your disappearing act but I can't be seen by them. I'm too old to even think about going into hiding. If that's any use to you, I'll help."

A small smile of gratitude creeps across my face and I nod in agreement.

"When do you want to do it?" Davey asks me.

"Tomorrow. I have to do a pick up, so that will get me close. We need a plan to find Lisa and a plan to disappear."

Davey walks into my dining room and opens the drink cabinet. He pulls out a thirty-year-old Balvennie whisky and glances at me for approval. I nod and beckon him to join me as I sit down at the table.

"Get two glasses, I've never needed a drink so badly," I tell him.

Davey collects two crystal glasses and sits opposite me at the table.

"It would be daft of me not to ask you the obvious, Ronin."

"What's that?" I ask him as I tear the foil from the top of the bottle, exposing the cork.

Davey watches me pour the amber nectar into his glass. "Ever thought that you are doing all of this for a girl you barely even know?"

I give him a knowing look as I pour myself a drink. "Yup, it's a thought that has never left my head," I tell him as I take an ample swig of the whisky. "You know what, though? I've never been so sure that I wanted to do something."

Davey takes a drink of his whisky and savours it in his mouth before letting it slide down his throat. "What's the end game for ye then, Ronin? Let's start from the ending and work our way back."

"I get Lisa away from those fuckers. We disappear without a trace. Sounds simple, doesn't it?"

Davey lets out a chuckle as he sips on his whisky again. "What about Callum?" he asks.

I pause to consider his question and take another sip from

my glass. "I'm going to make a mess and leave him to clear it up. Fuck him."

Davey nods and reaches over to the bottle, topping up our drinks.

"Let's get started then, son. Tomorrow will arrive fast."

31

DAVEY AND I SIT AND discuss all options. We end up with an action plan looking something like this:

Task 1 – Jeannie. Get her out of her house and on the train to the Highlands. I'll arrange for a taxi to take her to my cottage when she gets close enough – DAVEY

Task 2 – Collect the new car from Dinky. Nobody knows I am getting it, except Davey, Dinky and Jeannie – RONIN.

Task 3 – Pack two bags. One with cash and the other with basic essentials – RONIN.

Task 4 – Travel to the airport and collect the client as planned – RONIN.

Task 5 – The client has mobility issues, potentially use him to get to the front of the building – RONIN.

Task 6 – Look for Lisa – RONIN.

Task 7 – Get Lisa out – RONIN.

Task 8 – Use the Range Rover to get out of Edinburgh – RONIN.

Task 9 – Meet Davey in a remote spot to switch cars. Get rid of the Range Rover – DAVEY.

Task 10 – Get rid of my mobile phone and head to the Highlands with the new car. Meet Jeannie at my cottage – RONIN.

When we have finished agreeing the actions, I'm impatient to get going. Time is ticking on and my imagination is doing overtime thinking about what could be happening to Lisa, I need to get to her as soon as I can.

I quickly grab some gear from the safe upstairs and chop out eight lines on the breakfast bar. I need to straighten my head out after the whisky.

Davey wastes no time in attacking the lines with a rolled-up fifty note and then hands it to me to take my share. It straightens us up enough to get started on the first part of our mission.

I call Dinky, who answers in his usual smart-arsed manner.

"What the fuck do you want now? Another car?"

I am in no mood to engage in his banter, so I shut him down quickly.

"Listen to me, you fuckwit, I will be at the garage in ten minutes to collect my car. If it's not ready, I am going to back-hand you like a ginger stepchild."

I hang up as Davey cackles at my offensive comments.

Davey smokes cigarettes all the way to the garage, his arm hanging out the window. He's deep in thought and I think he has forgotten I have to hand this car back.

When we arrive, Dinky, sensing my urgency, keeps the facetious comments to himself. I don't have time to make small talk as I sign the appropriate ownership papers, hand over the keys to my old car and shake Dinky's hand with haste. He barely says a word, knowing that Davey and I have reputations for leathering cheeky little shits like him.

I'm stressed out of my mind but can still appreciate a new

BMW which has all the toys. It's an impressive machine to drive. The next stop is Jeannie's house. I tell Davey to wait in the car, so that I can talk to her in private. Davey agrees and starts tinkering with the state-of-the-art controls on the dashboard.

"Fuckin' lovely this, Ronin," he calls to me as I walk towards the entrance to Jeannie's house.

Jeannie sees me coming and the door is already open for me. I kiss her on the cheek and we go through our "Hi Jean," "it's good for the kitchen," routine, before getting down to business.

"Right, Jeannie, you have to listen to me very carefully, okay?" Jeannie looks alarmed at my tone and sits back in her chair. I have her full attention. "You have to leave this place tomorrow, okay?"

"Why, what's the matter?" she asks anxiously.

"I can't go into it right now but you have to trust me."

"Are you in trouble, son? What's happened?"

I feel sick to the pit of my stomach, but I have to tell her that her life is in danger otherwise she will refuse to leave. I can't let anything happen to her.

"I need to get you out of here, send you somewhere so that you are safe. There are people, very dangerous people, who are going to get angry with me and I'm afraid that they will try to hurt you."

Jeannie's eyes widen, and she looks at me horrified.

"What have you done, son? What have you done to make them angry?"

"It's not what I've done, Jeannie, it's what I'm going to do. I have to stop bad people from doing terrible things, which will make them angry enough to want to hurt me. I'm worried they will come for you too, so you need to leave. Don't worry, I'll join you when it's over. I'll come to the place I'm sending you to."

"Where are you sending me, Ronin?" she asks nervously.

"It's a highland cottage. Aunt Vera on Dad's side left it to me years ago. She did nothing with it and gave it to me. It's safe, I promise you. You will catch the train to Inverness tomorrow and I will arrange for someone to take you to the cottage."

"When will you get there?" she whispers as she tries to steady her shaking hands.

"Tomorrow night if I can. I'll need you to light a fire and make the place warm. I'll phone the local grocers and have them deliver some essentials for you, okay?"

A single tear escapes from behind her immaculately polished spectacles and I wrap my arms around her, holding on tightly, trying to reassure her that's it's all going to be okay.

As she quietly sobs into my shoulder, I am racked with guilt for putting Jeannie through this and I almost lose it. I take a deep breath and release my hold on her, trying to regain some composure.

"I'm so worried about you, son, will you be okay?" she cries.

"Don't worry about me, I'll be fine. I just need to do the right thing," I say softly.

She manages a nod and uses a hanky to wipe her eyes.

"Now, be strong for me, don't tell any of your friends, that part is really important, Jeannie. You can't tell anyone. Do you understand?"

Jeannie nods.

"My friend Davey will pick you up at nine a.m. tomorrow and take you to the train station. Pack a small suitcase. Don't worry about any unnecessary clothes, we can get everything we need once we are settled."

"Okay, son," she sniffles, wiping her eyes again.

I kiss her on the head and stand up. Looking out the window, I can see Davey is smoking yet another fag and I am pissed off that he's doing it in my new car.

"Lock your door and don't open it to anyone until nine

tomorrow," I tell her as I leave the house, feeling like the shittiest human being that ever walked the earth. Who does this to an old lady? I've put the fear of God into her, but I have no choice.

I wait until Jeannie locks the door from the inside. Her sobs pierce straight through my heart but I have to do this. These people are dangerous and to get to me they will find her, I can't bear the thought of her getting hurt. I jog up to my new car and see that Davey is watching some random holiday programme on the TV. I get into the car and turn it off.

"Okay, you know what needs to be done?" I ask Davey directly.

Davey blows smoke out of the window and flicks the fag out onto the grass.

"Aye, I'm dropping you off in this car and taking it home. I take Jeannie to the train station tomorrow and give her the address of where she has to go. Then I make my way to the meeting point and wait for you."

"Perfect. Here is five hundred for Jeannie, make sure she gets first class all the way. Call me if there are any problems."

I hand him some folded notes and he takes them with a nod.

"And do me a favour, put that fag out."

The drive back home is silent. We are both on edge, knowing that the job ahead is the biggest we've ever had. Even if I wanted to, it's too late to change my mind: I need to see this through.

We get back to the house and I hop out of the driver's seat, leaving the engine running. The bags I packed earlier are at the bottom of the stairs and I throw them into the boot of the car. Davey holds the boot open for me, fag once again in hand, looking as though he is about to say something I don't want to hear; he's having second thoughts.

Before he gets a chance to speak, I unzip the bag containing the money and pull out fifty grand, rolled up in notes and held together with an elastic band.

"Here, catch this," I say as I toss the roll of notes to Davey.

Davey catches the bundle and looks at me with surprise, clearly not expecting the money upfront.

"I trust you, Davey. I just thought you better have the money now, in case something goes wrong." I close the boot and check it is done properly. "I'm counting on you, Davey. Don't go on a bender tonight, I need you in top form!"

Davey laughs and pulls me into a hug. He kisses the side of my cheek and gives me a manly slap on the other one. "You're fuckin' nuts, Ronin, but I respect what you are doing."

I don't respond, I walk back into the house, hearing him get into the car and drive away.

I go into the kitchen and survey the mess I'd made earlier. What a state: I didn't even realise what I was doing. I use my phone to search for a private taxi firm in Inverness. The use of a private firm is intentional: I want someone independent to greet Jeannie at the train station and take her to the cottage.

I've ticked that off the list and I go through what needs to be done in my head. I can't make anyone suspicious, I need to carry on as normal. It's taking every ounce of willpower I have not to drive to Callum's house and beat him within an inch of his life. I can't quantify how devastated I feel. He completely betrayed me and lied to me again and again, all for money. I was clearly never that important to him, just a guy to do his dirty work. More fool me, eh? Well, not anymore; he's going to get what's coming to him.

Sitting at the breakfast bar, I nurse my hands and knuckles. Applying antiseptic cream and knuckle plasters eases some of the discomfort and I take some anti-inflammatory pills. I attempt to tidy up the mess, trying to keep myself occupied and pass the time.

As the night draws in, I pour myself a large whisky. I need help to get to sleep. I'm exhausted from feeling so angry, worrying about tomorrow, stressing about Lisa. I don't even know if she is still alive. It's fucking with my head.

The excessive lifestyle, the drugs, the money, it's all fake and means nothing. The only two people who have ever really made me feel alive are Jeannie and Lisa. I need to protect them both.

I lie on my bed one last time and watch the Sopranos, a welcome distraction from the whirlwind of thoughts spinning in my head. Tony Soprano's just heard from his daughter that a sleazeball from a rival mob has cracked on to her. He goes fucking nuts and leathers the cunt, breaking his jaw and knocking all his teeth out. I feel a shiver go right through me. If reality could mimic fiction it's right there in that one scene. My life, my fight, my girl. I'll get her out of this, I know I will.

32

AT SIX A.M., I GIVE up on getting any more sleep. I jump in the shower and then go downstairs to soak my still swollen hands in tea tree ointment, cursing my stupidity from the day before. My hands are fucked, which is going to cause me problems later.

I go upstairs and get dressed in a smart polo shirt and jeans – nothing too restricting should things get physical later. I brush my teeth in the bathroom; my stomach clenches as I think about Lisa, alone and scared. She was waiting to see me again that night, then she got taken away by that Polish fucker, Pavel. It's all my fault. If only I hadn't taken the girl home. My rage gets the better of me again and I clear my bathroom shelves in a powerful swipe, knocking aftershave and deodorant bottles to the floor. I stand with my hands on my hips and close my eyes, trying to stay in control. The pressure is getting to me. I need to stay focused.

I check the house for anything I might have forgotten and unplug my phone from its charger. Time to go.

I have wrapped my hands with the minimum amount of protection possible, and I'm wearing leather gloves to hide them. It's tight but I'll get away with it. Bill and Ben, my knuckle dusters, are laid out in front of me but my hands look too swollen to use them. Fuck it, I'll put them in my back pockets, just in case I need them later.

I start the Range Rover and head off towards the dual carriageway that takes me to Edinburgh airport. The phone rings and Davey's name pops up on the dashboard display.

"That's Jeannie on her way."

"Thanks. Davey, was she okay?"

"She was upset, I'm not gonna sugar coat it for you. She's worried about you, Ronin. I assured her you would be alright, so you better not fuck this up otherwise she'll be calling me a lying bastard."

"Okay, thanks Davey. Are you going to the meeting place now?"

"That's me on my way there. Phone me when you get clear of Edinburgh and I'll give you directions on how to find me."

"Superb. Thanks again, Davey, I appreciate everything you have done for me."

"Well, you're a good cunt, Ronin. There's not many of them around nowadays. Good luck pal, I'll see you soon."

I hang up, using the button on the steering wheel. Jeannie is on the train to the Highlands, which is one less thing for me to worry about.

"Stay focused," I say out loud as I accelerate along the road, following signs for the airport.

When I arrive, I follow the same plan as for the previous client. I park in the arrivals section and wait in front of the car for Mr O'Leary. The airport is much quieter this time, and I spot him immediately as he is pushed towards me in a wheelchair by a member of airport staff. No wonder he has mobility issues. He's a fat, ginger-haired fucker dressed in black with a white dog collar. The guy on the phone didn't say he was a fucking priest! I've seen it all now, a fuckin' priest coming here to fulfil his deepest sins, fuck me.

"Mr O'Leary?" I inquire as the porter stops the wheelchair in front of me, next to the car.

"Yes, lad, now help me outta this chair," he says in an accent laced with an Irish lilt.

"I can walk but it takes so feckin' long, I have to ask for a wheelchair whenever I travel."

I'm surprised by his merry demeanour and as I help him move from the wheelchair into the back seat of the car, I almost forget that he is a dirty scumbag priest who is making a mockery of his so-called religion.

We set off from the airport and I keep quiet.

"So, my lad, what's your name then?" the priest asks as he adjusts his collar; he is excessively panting and sweating.

"I'm Ronin, sir," I reply, calmly.

"Ah, a fine Irish name, d'you have family on the green isle?"

"Not that I know of," I reply coldly. I don't particularly want to get friendly with this character or correct him on the origins of my name.

"Well, it's a pleasure to meet you, son. This is certainly a classy service, having a young gent like you picking me up in a car like this."

"You get what you pay for, sir," I reply knowing that his 'trip' would have cost him a substantial sum of money.

"Well, son, between you and me, the collection plate is plentiful in my chapel, so I may as well put it to good use. I can't have too many reasons to earn my hail Mary's," he laughs jovially.

"I'm sure God forgives," I quip, feeling ready to paste this slimy fucker.

The priest chuckles. "That he does, son, that he does. The way I like to look at it is if we don't sin then he has nothing to forgive." He cackles and throws back his head, revealing a mouthful of yellow-stained teeth.

He's good, I'll give him that. I almost like him. He must have his congregation wrapped around his perverted little finger, hanging off every word he says. The thought makes me shudder.

"Do you visit the establishment yourself, son?"

"No, I'm just the driver."

"Ah well, I'm sure it's not for everyone."

"Nope," I reply a little too sharply.

"I like a bit of rough and tumble you know? With the women like," he offers to me, matter-of-factly, like I hear it all the time.

I don't answer him, I just cut him a look in the rear-view mirror. He's talking to the wrong person. He doesn't see me and carries on obliviously.

"The old parts don't work like they used to, but I get a right kick out of a wee slap here and there."

Again, I say nothing; he is really testing my patience.

"I'm not strong by any means, it's mostly slaps and maybe I use my belt now and again, but I get tired now, it's not like the old days." He leans forward and whispers conspiratorially. "You know, the wee sluts really do love it, I know they do, ach sometimes they cry a bit sure but it's all part of the fun."

I am going to blow a fucking gasket. I pull the car to the side of the road and turn around to face the priest.

"Sorry, sir, but I'm not permitted to discuss this type of thing with clients," I tell him in a cold monotone.

The priest looks startled at my reaction and nods, sitting back in his seat, clearing his throat awkwardly. "Right, right you are lad. I'll keep that stuff to myself."

I nod and turn around again, flicking the right indicator and moving out to join the traffic again.

"We will be there in five minutes. I'll assist you into the building when we arrive."

"Good lad, God bless ya."

That was a close one. I nearly pulled the twisted fucker out of the car to smash his head in. I have to stay focused. I can't fuck this up now.

We arrive at the building, I turn the engine off and get out to open Mr O'Leary's door to help him out. This is it, I'm going to get Lisa out of there.

The priest is somewhat restrained now but maintains his jovial manner. I am astounded that he sees no wrongdoing in this whole set-up. I don't know why I'm surprised; his own faith is riddled with repulsive controversy.

He's a heavy fucker who is very unstable on his feet, so I have to support him more than I would like to. Grimacing as I take his weight, I tell myself it's all part of the plan, just go with it.

We shuffle to the front entrance. I can see the reception desk through the glass door and a slim, stone-faced lady presses a button to open it for us. The atrium is a cold and uninviting space with only a reception desk and a dozen leather chairs occupying it. The lady has the audacity to look at me suspiciously as we walk through the doors and before she can say anything, I defend my presence.

"I was told to assist him, he has mobility issues," I explain, waving my hands in the direction of Mr O'Leary's legs.

She stares at me through narrowed eyes. I look right back at her. Her eyes are heavily made up with dark eyeliner and her hair is pure white and poker straight, falling in a long mane over both shoulders.

"Very well," she finally responds tartly, and turns to the priest, welcoming him with a phony, red lipped smile.

"Hello, Mr O'Leary. Welcome, and I hope you had a pleasant journey."

Her accent is foreign, maybe French, I can't quite place it. Abhorrent, whatever it is.

"Yes, I have been well looked after so far," the priest replies in between heaving wheezes and mopping his face with his hanky.

"We have activities to meet your every need here, Mr O'Leary. Tell me what your expectations are and we shall make it so. Once you decide, we will escort you to a suite where you will have exactly one hour to complete your activity."

I shudder at the way she uses the word 'activity'. She makes it sound so clinical, like a business transaction. In fact, I find her whole demeanour so vile that she reminds me of a Disney villain.

"Thank you, Miss," Mr O'Leary says and then lowers his voice.

"I like to... erm," he looks nervously in my direction. "Eh... I would prefer the... the more rough and tumble... eh... activity."

Bitchface, as I will now call her, nods as she listens to him.

"I understand, sir. We have specific ladies who offer a service who can meet your needs. We have strict guidelines for this service. No blows to the face and no permanent scars. Open hand slapping and beatings with smooth objects are permitted to the body only. Strictly no intercourse, this service is to assist our clients in cleansing themselves from violent tendencies."

I nearly choke at the last sentence. What is this fucking place? A therapy centre for deviants? I can't keep my cool much longer.

The priest nods; he is trembling with excitement. "What are the smooth objects?" he asks eagerly.

"Flat leather bats, thick belts, hard back books. That kind of thing. We must ensure there are no scars for other clients."

"Of course, of course, I understand fully," the priest confirms in haste.

I look around the area and beyond the reception is a flight of stairs and two elevators. The décor is minimal yet tasteful. How ironic.

"Do I get to choose which lady I can have?" the priest asks as he signs the register with a flourish, which makes me think O' Leary isn't even his real name.

"Yes, we will take you upstairs to the floor where the suites are. The ladies will be presented to you and you can select the female of your preference."

"Very good, let's get going," the priest slavers as he turns to me for help to the elevator.

Bitchface looks me up and down and addresses the priest. "This man is just a driver. Would you prefer one of our other members of staff to assist you upstairs?"

"No, no, he's a good lad this one, he'll be fine. He can get me upstairs. Don't go to any trouble."

Bitchface purses her lips. "It's no trouble, sir."

I take a deep breath. That cold faced bitch is going to scupper my plans if she doesn't keep quiet.

"No, dear, let's not waste any more time," he answers firmly. Thank fuck.

I grab the spongy flab of his arm and help him walk to the elevator. Bitchface walks with us, speaking on a radio in a language that's definitely not French. I got it wrong, she's Eastern European for sure. A male voice responds in the same style and she nods at us to enter the open door of the elevator.

The elevator is mirrored, with classical music playing from a speaker in the top right-hand corner. There are only three floors and Bitchface pushes the button for the third.

We come to a stop and I help the priest lumber out of the elevator, following Bitchface down the hallway towards several doors at the far end. It is completely silent apart from the soft fall of our footsteps. The décor is still very tasteful, with dark wood, contrasting pale stone vases and ornaments on side tables spaced perfectly along the corridor wall.

I try to scan the area but I can't see anything. If there are women here, they are well hidden.

As we near the end of a corridor, Bitchface produces a key and opens the last door. Inside is a reception room with a large sofa and a jug of iced water placed on a side table beside it. The windows are draped in luxurious cream silk curtains with slim wooden blinds which let enough light in but maintain the privacy of the room.

The priest slumps onto the sofa and pours himself a glass of water. I stand aside, not quite sure what to expect next. Bitchface utters a few words into the radio again and receives a single reply.

A minute later a door at the other side of the room opens and four women enter. My heart jumps but I can see immediately that none of them are Lisa. I watch each one walk in, dressed in red, silky nightwear, and line up in front of the priest. Their heads wobble slightly as they stare at the opposite wall with glazed eyes and vacant expressions. They are all beautiful but I can tell they are completely out of it.

"Fuck," I think to myself. How am I going to get access to where they keep the other girls, wherever they are in this building?

The priest gulps down more water as he looks the women up and down.

"Please choose," Bitchface demands stiffly.

That feeling in the pit of my stomach starts again and I squirm uneasily. Bitchface glances at me, sensing my discomfort.

The priest slurps down the water, barely able to breathe between gulps. He makes noises to himself, as if he is considering the women and which one he would like to abuse.

I think quickly about how I'm going to gain access to other

parts of the building but before I can form a plan, the door is pushed open once again. A tall man in a suit escorts another lady, with curly blonde hair, into the room. He's being heavy handed with her; she has obviously protested to being brought through.

"Ah, another option for you. This one is attractive but has some fight in her," Bitchface informs the priest as the man forces the woman to stand in line with the others. They don't argue with him – he's a giant, sixteen stone of pure muscle and every inch of his body covered in tattoos.

"Don't worry, I gave her more opiates so she will calm down soon," Goliath offers before leaving. As he does I catch sight of the tattoo on the nape of his neck, a half oval peaks out from underneath his shirt.

"Oh yes, I love her spirit." The priest salivates as he loosens his collar and pats his damp handkerchief over his face.

"So, you would like her?" Bitchface asks.

"Yes, yes, she will be perfect. I'm not as strong as I used to be but I'm stronger than her, she's a slender thing."

Do I make my move now? Do I wait? No, be patient, Ronin. I need to keep going with the act.

The only people in the room are the five women, Bitchface, the priest and me.

Think man, think. I've got it, I'll find out where his suite is and decide when to make my move.

"Where is Mr O'Leary's suite?" I ask Bitchface.

She looks at me as if I am shit on her shoe.

"Just over here." She calls out and Goliath appears again, escorting the women back into the room and leaving the curly blonde behind. She is staring at the floor, rocking back and forth on the balls of her feet. Bitchface takes a strap out from her pocket and wraps it tightly around the blonde's throat. She pulls her like a dog through to the suite and orders her to kneel on the floor. She nods to me and I help the priest up from the couch.

It's a nauseating sight and I am filled with a rage that I can barely contain but I can't make a scene just yet. Goliath is close by in the other room and who knows how many other big fuckers are close by.

I escort the priest into his suite and Bitchface leads the girl through, closing the door behind her. She releases the strap from around the girl's throat and roughly removes the red nightwear from her body. The dazed blonde stares down at the floor. She is covered in bruises and marks; the sight of it breaks my heart.

"Help me with my jacket, son," the priest puffs as he starts to unbutton his shirt and throw off his braces, revealing a sweat-drenched vest.

Bitchface looks at me and commands, "We should go now."

I nod and leave the room with her. As we walk along the hallway, towards the elevator, I come up with a plan.

"I have some spare time on my hands now, I have to wait for him to finish his 'activity'." I nod in the direction of the closed door. "I was wondering… would it be possible to arrange some entertainment for me?" I ask, raising an eyebrow.

Bitchface looks me up and down. I can tell she's far from impressed.

"The services here are exceptionally expensive," she sneers.

I smile at her and look downwards as I produce a huge wrap of fifty-pound notes from my pocket.

"How much do you have?" she asks, her tone suddenly changing.

"I reckon five thousand or so," I say, tucking the money back into my jeans.

"What service would be your preference?" she asks me.

"I'm open to options, what do you have available right now?"

"For that kind of money, it's the floor down, the rooms are smaller but the standard of women similar."

"Okay, let's go," I reply breezily.

We enter the elevator and there is silence again as we

descend to the second floor. My heart is pounding and I am sure she can hear it. I don't have a plan B so if this fails, I'm fucked. The elevator stops and I follow Bitchface out into yet another hallway. There are several rooms; the doors are open but I can't see anyone else around. It's eerily quiet.

"You can take a look in here and make your choice," she says as we approach the first doorway.

I glance in to see a beautiful lady, dressed in purple silky lingerie. She has tethers round her arms, keeping her firmly attached to a dark mahogany bed. She's clearly sedated like the others and her head hangs downwards.

"Why are they tied up?" I ask Bitchface.

She raises an eyebrow at my naivety and responds dryly, "We have to keep them under control otherwise they will…"

"Escape?" I offer.

She glares at me and nods. We carry on to the next room and the picture is very much the same, the classy furniture, a drugged woman and painful, barbaric-looking restraints.

We continue further along the corridor, seeing the same scene at least six more times until we reach a closed door.

"What's in here?" I ask.

"This is priced more than what you have in your pocket. This one is new and untouched – she is from what we call our gold standard stock. The door is closed and locked because she is still adapting to the sedation techniques."

Lisa will be behind that door. I can't explain why but I know it. She's in there.

"I have more money. It can be wired to your account. Let me see the goods and maybe I will pay your price." I charm Bitchface with a smile and a wave of my black AMEX.

She nods her head in agreement and inserts a swipe card into the lock.

In what seems like slow motion, the light turns green and the door swings open to reveal a king-size bed. On hearing our entrance, a girl on the bed in restraints begins writhing around angrily, clearly distressed. I can't see her face and walk towards the bed, but Bitchface beats me to it.

"This one is beautiful but is proving difficult to control," Bitchface informs me, as she pulls the leather strap out of her pocket and approaches the girl, whose arms and legs are bound and her mouth gagged.

She ties the strap tightly around the girl's throat and forces her head upwards to look at me.

I'd recognise those eyes anywhere. The blood rushes to my face and I can feel the fireball in my belly erupt. The magnitude of my anger disorientates me and I have to hold onto the edge of the bed to stop myself from stumbling forward. Lisa's pupils are dilated and as the belt tightens on her throat her body drops and the fight disappears. Her eyes begin to focus on me, I see a flicker of recognition and they widen slightly in surprise.

"Let her go," I command Bitchface, glaring into her eyes.

She looks at me, confused. "Why?" she asks, tightening her grip and Lisa struggles to breathe.

That's it, I'm going for it.

I close the door behind me and before Bitchface can say anything, I knock her out with a demonic punch from my right hand. I don't hit women but this isn't a woman, it's a monster. She slumps against the wall and I ease her to the floor to stop her hitting the deck with a thump, attracting any unwanted attention. I pull off my leather gloves and toss them to the floor. Quickly, I loosen the strap from around Lisa's throat and untie the gag to allow her to catch her breath. I am about to speak but before I can say anything Lisa passes out and slumps on the bed. Shit, I don't know whether it's being choked, the drugs or a combination of the two.

I check her pulse. It's weak but she's breathing.

I tie the strap around the mouth of Bitchface and use one of the tethers to tie her up on the floor.

I check Lisa again but she's still out. I think she will be okay for a couple of minutes. I don't want to leave her. I need to get her out but I can't leave the curly blonde with the priest, I need to deal with him first. I quietly leave the room and close the door behind me, checking the corridor for any sign of life.

It's empty and I hurry to the elevator which takes me back up to the third floor.

Sneaking along the corridor with stealth-like precision, I make my way back to the suite where the priest is, as quietly as I can. I reach his room and stand for a moment listening to check he is still in there. I hear his repulsive laugh and open the door quietly, making just enough noise to startle him.

He looks up in surprise and goes to pull up his trousers, which are in a heap around his ankles. He's taken off his black shirt and a white vest is pulled tightly over his bulbous frame. A gold, pectoral cross sits on his protruding stomach attached to a long, rosary bead chain. He hasn't begun his sick routine yet; all he's managed so far is to lay out some leather straps.

"What are you doing?" exclaims the priest. "I'm not finished yet, give me half an hour, will ye?"

I don't answer, he may think he has me on his good side but he's a dirty, woman beater who's going to get what's coming to him.

I walk straight up to him and swing my right boot directly into the centre of his flabby belly: he splutters as his body folds forwards. I rip the cross from his neck, breaking the chain so that the beads scatter across the floor. He puts his arms out to grab me, but with the metal cross still in my hand, I deliver an uppercut to his jaw, producing an unholy crunch, sending him sideways into the corner of the bed frame. I step behind him and boot him in the nuts as hard as I can. He yelps in pain as he falls forward. I try my best to catch him to soften the thud but he's heavy and he hits the carpet with a crash. Blood, as red as his holy communion wine, pours from the sliced flesh underneath his chin, running in rivulets down his neck and soaking into his white cotton vest. I open my fist, looking at the gold cross in surprise: I didn't need Bill and Ben after all.

Worried about the commotion, I pause for a second and wait to hear if the noise has raised the alarm. I can't hear anything and go over to the blonde girl on the bed. Jesus, she can't be more than sixteen years old.

She doesn't flinch and her eyes continue to stare into space, oblivious to what's just happened. She's completely out of it, which is maybe a blessing. What can I do with her? She needs to get away from here but I can't take both her and Lisa, it's too risky. Thinking for a second, I pull back the duvet and help her into the bed. She shivers and closes her eyes immediately. I'll come back for her, and if I can't I'll make sure someone I trust does.

I grab O'Leary's arms and haul him across the room to the radiator on the far side. He weights a ton and I struggle to slide his massive frame across the floor. I take his braces and tie his hands to the radiator. His holiness is going nowhere anytime soon.

I'm going back for Lisa and getting the hell out of here.

33

I CREEP BACK ALONG THE hallway and take the elevator down to the second floor. Lisa is still in the room on the bed; she is awake now, eyes staring listlessly at the ceiling.

I quickly untie the tethers which keep her restrained. Gently, I kneel down in front of her and touch her shoulder.

"Lisa, it's me, Ronin, you're safe."

She doesn't react at first.

I gently shake her and raise her head upwards so that our eyes meet. "Lisa, it's me, darling, it's Ronin. I'm going to get you out of here."

She looks at me, unblinking, eyes still glazed.

"Come on Lisa, come back to me. It's me, I'm really here, let's get out of here."

I almost give up hope but then I see her pupils change shape and her eyes fill with tears.

"Ronin?" she whispers, not sure if she trusts her own eyes.

I smile and wipe tears from her eyes. "Yes, it's me, I'm getting you out of here."

"My Ronin?" she asks in a slurred whisper.

My heart almost bursts, I'm still her Ronin. "Yes darling, come on, I need to get you out of here. Don't be afraid."

She offers a dazed nod and looks down at her silky nightwear.

I gently open my jacket and wrap it around her. Then I help her stand up to sit on the side of the bed.

"Can you walk?" I ask her quietly.

She nods and tries to stand up. I'm not convinced, so I ease her back down onto the side of the bed.

Bitchface stirs, beginning to regain consciousness. We need to get out of here now. I open the door to the suite and peer into the hallway. I can't see or hear anyone, so I take Lisa's wrists and put them around my neck, lifting her gently into my arms, and make my way back as fast as I can along the hallway to the elevators.

As I press the call button, I look at Lisa's face. She is staring at me, still trying to grasp the fact that I've come for her.

"You're here for me?" she asks, confused and groggy.

I kiss her forehead and hold her tighter.

"Yes, I'm really here and I'm going to take you somewhere no-one can hurt you, ever again."

I impatiently watch the digital display above the elevator and finally it arrives. I step backwards, to the side of the doors, just in case it's occupied. It's empty and I carry Lisa in, hitting the ground floor button with the hand that is under her legs.

Lisa stares into my eyes. I think she wants to say more but the effects of the sedatives make it difficult for her.

I kiss her head again. "I fuckin' knew it, I knew you hadn't left me for someone else."

We arrive at the ground floor with a slight bump and step

out cautiously. There's no-one around in the reception area. Gripping Lisa tightly I hurry towards the front entrance. I reach the door and can't open it. Shit, the button is behind the reception desk.

I spin round and I'm nose to nose with Pavel and Goliath from upstairs. Both are breathing heavily with thunderous expressions on their faces.

Wham! The giant punches me in the face and I stumble backwards. I release my grip and Lisa slips to the floor. As I try to straighten up, he hits me again and I go down. The buzzing noise is here again. I try to get up and the last thing I see is the underside of Pavel's boot.

34

I CAN HEAR A SMACKING noise, like the clash of symbols in the distance. It's getting louder and as I come round, I realise it's not symbols but someone slapping me hard on the cheek, repeatedly, trying to wake me up.

My vision is blurry. I see a hand coming towards me as it delivers another slap.

"He's awake," a voice says. I recognise it but I'm too dizzy to focus and can't quite find the name in my woolly head.

As I come to, my vision clears. I'm sitting on a chair in a small room. There are several faces staring at me. I recognise the giant fucker in the suit and there is another man in jeans and a blue T-shirt.

I squint as I move my head to look at the other faces and see Callum and Sandy Pratt. Seeing them enrages me, and I try to get up. The giant pushes me roughly back onto the chair.

"Don't fucking move!" he growls.

"Fuck you, you piece of shit," I bark back at him, putting a hand up to my left eyelid, which has been cut.

"What's going on, Ronin?" Callum asks.

I can't believe the audacity of the man.

"I could ask you the same thing," I reply wiping clotted blood from my eye.

"What do you mean?" he asks.

"What do I mean? Lisa. She was here all along. She didn't go off with anyone. You fuckin' lied to me. Me! Your 'friend'! You fuckin' lied, even when I knew the truth!"

I stand up and quickly I am again pushed back down into the chair by Goliath.

"Look, this is business, nothing more, Ronin. No need to be causing trouble over her." He points to Lisa, hunched over on the floor, still wrapped in my jacket. She lifts her head and gives Callum a look of pure loathing.

"You were like a fucking brother to me, Callum. I would have done anything for you. I did do anything for you. Why did you fuck me over like this?"

"Look, Ronin. You did things for me because I paid you. It was an employer–employee relationship, nothing else."

I look at him in disbelief.

"Are you fucking kidding me? I mean, you really expect me to believe that we were just business associates?"

Callum twitches and briefly breaks eye contact with me. He composes himself and responds with a shrug and a "Yup."

I shake my head and look at the floor. I'm still dizzy but feel like I'm gaining composure.

"So, what now?" I ask Callum.

I feel cold, heavy metal pressed against the back of my head.

"It's simple, Ronin. You walk away from this or I blow your fuckin' head off," says Sandy Pratt's voice, pushing the metal barrel into my skull.

I try to turn to look at him.

"Don't fucking move."

"I have a question," I say to the room.

"Go ahead," Callum replies.

"Why Lisa? Why her? Of all the women, why did you want her?"

Callum glances at Sandy, who sniggers at my question and answers before Callum can say anything.

"Well, Ronin, there were several reasons. Firstly, she took the piss out of me in Mirrors. Her and all her stuck-up friends. I bought them champagne and didn't get so much as a fuck out of it. Secondly, she's a gold-digging bitch but she's fuckin' stunning and I know people who will pay a lot of money for her. It's pretty simple really. As Callum says, it's business."

I spin around on the chair and glare at Sandy.

"You're fuckin' dead, you hear me? DEAD!"

Sandy chuckles, "Ooh, he didn't like that did he? Big, bad Ronin's a sensitive soul after all."

My mind flits to Sun Tzu's *The Art of War*.

'*If your opponent is of choleric temper, irritate him.*'

"So, you need a gun to beat me, do you Sandy, you fat little cunt? I tell you what, this must be your technique with the ladies eh? How else would you get them to fuck you?"

The tattooed men snigger and Sandy marches round the chair to face me.

"Brave words from a brave man, Ronin, eh? All I need to do is pull this trigger and your face turns to mush," Sandy threatens and places the nose of the barrel onto my chin.

"Even then, I'd still be better looking than you," I retort.

Again, the men snigger.

Callum, who has kept quiet throughout this exchange, takes a step towards me. "It's up to you, Ronin. You can't have her, it's not going to happen, so make up your mind. Leave now and we can forget all this happened, otherwise…"

He doesn't have to finish his sentence, I know where he's going with this. I look up at him and scowl. Callum's eye's narrow slightly and he signals downwards with them to two shotgun capsules sticking out the top left-hand pocket of his diesel jeans. The fly bastard has taken the bullets out of Sandy's shotgun. What the fuck is he up to?

I don't know what the hell is happening but I need to keep the momentum going.

"You know what I'm thinking, Callum?" I ask him.

"No, Ronin, what are you thinking?" he replies, still looking at me through narrow eyes and subtly pushing the tops of the cartridges deeper into his pocket.

"I'm thinking there's four of you and one of me. That's not really fair is it?" I offer.

"What would be fair in your opinion?" Callum asks, folding his arms.

"Well, you really need two more to make it fair because I'll kill every one of you before that gun has even gone off."

They all laugh, thinking I'm joking, including Sandy, who is still pointing the gun at my face.

Sun Tzu's instructions go through my mind again. 'He will win who knows when to fight and when not to fight"

I turn to Sandy. "Come on then, pull the fuckin' trigger, you slug. Show me how hard you are, come on!" I shout in his face.

He nervously looks around him then Goliath shrugs and says, "Do it, we have cleaners."

Beads of sweat roll down the side of Sandy's face, he positions himself again. He points the gun at me and I look into his eyes.

"Do it, come on you fuckin' wretch, pull the trigger."

Sandy clenches his teeth.

Click.

"Oh dear," I say as he looks down at his gun in disbelief.

My heart is hammering in my chest, but this is it, I must act now.

It feels like slow motion but in reality I know I'm hitting hard and fast.

I snatch the gun from Sandy's hand and stand up, smashing my forehead onto the bridge of his nose. He's dazed and staggers out of the way, holding his face as blood starts to pour from his wound. I turn the gun around and crack the first tattooed guy in the head with the butt. He goes down easily, then I attempt to follow up with another couple of quick blows to Goliath's head. Nope. He's onto me and grabs the gun, thumping me in the stomach with a massive boot which sends me hurtling backwards, collapsing into the wall. He tosses the empty shotgun to the side as if it was a broken toy.

Shit, I'm going to have to deal with him now and he's a big fucker.

Goliath smirks at me as he removes his jacket, tossing it to Callum, who catches it with a bewildered expression.

"Now we fight," growls Goliath with a broad foreign accent as he rolls up the sleeves of his shirt.

I feel the discomfort of Bill and Ben in my pockets as they press into the base of my back. They are the only hope I have against Goliath; I completely forgot I had them. Quickly, gritting my teeth against the pain, I force the knuckle dusters onto my swollen hands. As I regain my balance, Goliath halts his advance when he sees Bill and Ben. Any trained fighter knows that when you are faced with a giant, you think smart and keep moving. If he grabs a hold of me, I'm fucked. He's much stronger, so I need to be ready to react.

I start moving and the big bastard pursues me around the room, grabbing for me in frustration as I duck under his punches. After two circuits of the room my pace slackens and he catches me by my sleeve with a vice-like grip, pulling me in towards him. I can't reach his face so propel a hard strike onto the joint of his thumb making him call out and release his grip.

As he recoils his hand in pain, I drop to my knees and deliver hard, accurate strikes to his joints. As he buckles and leans downwards, I jump up and deliver an uppercut with the full force of my body. Something cracks loudly, his jaw I hope, but I can't stop, I need to maintain the momentum. Still dazed, Goliath tries to focus as I deliver constant kicks to his knees and shins. He cries out in pain and drops to the floor on his knees.

This is it, I need to finish him. Two round house kicks to his head, almost take him down but he's still swaying and manages to reach out to grab my leg. I awkwardly push him away feeling as though I am about to lose my balance, but can't shake his grip.

His head is within reach and I have no option but to let Bill and Ben do their work. The sound of metal crushing bone makes Callum wince as I punch Goliath hard and fast. Out of breath, I step back to examine the damage. His right eye turns inwards and dark red blood trickles from his mouth. His grip on my leg relaxes before he collapses with a crash onto the floor. I finish him with a final stamp to the back of his head; it cracks, confirming he will no longer be a problem for me, or anyone else.

Callum shudders as he looks down at the mess I have made of Goliath. I look him up and down, not quite sure what to make of him now. He looks scared and vulnerable, a complete contrast to the Callum of old.

Our interaction is interrupted by a crash as Sandy stumbles over a chair. I turn to look at him trying to retreat from me as he edges towards the door of the office.

"No bullets, Sandy?" I mock as I slowly edge towards him.

He's sweating profusely now as I take a few more steps towards him. He grabs a vase and holds it above his head. For a moment, I think he's going to throw it in my direction, then I realise that it's not me he's aiming for.

He's standing over Lisa and holding the vase above her.

"You come near me, I'll drop this over her pretty little face."

I snarl at him, "You drop that on her head and I'll kill you, painfully."

He sneers at me. "You wouldn't want see your precious Lisa get hurt, would you now, Ronin?"

He thinks he's got the upper hand, the fucker.

Just when I think he's got me, Callum comes rushing in from the side and knocks the vase crashing into the wall.

Sandy looks at Callum in surprise and then to me.

I smile and take a couple more steps towards him.

"I've been waiting for this," I sneer at him mercilessly.

I'm calm. Calmer than I think I should be at this moment. I have decided to take my time with him. He's going to hurt everywhere so that when I am finished with him, he will spend the rest of his life sucking food through a straw.

"Come on, Ronin. Let's work something out. I'll pay you whatever you want" he begs backing away from me.

"Nope," I reply.

I grab his shirt and he tries to fight me off, hitting my arm while scratching at my hand.

Bang. Punch number one creates a deep cut on his cheekbone.

"Please," he whines as I let go of his shirt.

I ignore his plea. A front kick to his stomach followed by a round house to his ribs sends him hurtling across the room. He crashes into some stacked chairs and slumps onto the ground.

I'm not finished with him yet and he knows it. I pull him to his feet and he desperately makes a dash for the door. I grab him by the scruff of the neck and push him against the wall, turning him to face me.

"I'd like to introduce you a couple of friends of mine, Bill and Ben."

I hold up my hands and turn them towards him, exposing the brass knuckles.

"They are most effective in certain parts of the body. I am trained to know where those are. Do you know where they are?"

I am patronising and cruel, delighted to be welding such power over the wee cunt.

Sandy shakes his head, holding his hands up to his face.

"The ear," I whisper, smiling.

I strike him several times on both ears with Bill and Ben.

He screams, shifting his hands to cover both ears.

"The nose."

I deliver a bone crushing punch to his nose that causes further trauma to the area where I headbutted him earlier. The skin bursts and the blood starts to flow.

Sandy's hands shift back to his face again.

"The windpipe."

I snap a hard punch to his throat and he splutters, grabbing the area with both hands.

"Oops, I forgot the eyes."

I swing right and left crosses at his eye area, which make deep, painful cuts.

Sandy slides sideways along the white wall smearing blood all over it before slumping to the ground.

Callously, I pull him up to his feet again. I want him to still be able to feel what is to come.

"The solar plexus."

I strike him hard in the middle of his chest and he lets out a wheezy gasp. Before he can collapse again, I grab him and push him hard against the wall.

"Finally, the groin."

I knee him as hard as I can in the nuts and release my grip. He collapses onto the floor next to me, gasping for breath, spluttering blood and writhing in pain. I look straight ahead and lean my hands against the wall. I find my balance and kick him one last time so that he shuts up.

I think about checking his pulse. It's unlikely I have killed him but I don't care if I have. He's a swollen, bleeding heap of sweaty lard on the ground, which is where he can stay, and suffer. I turn to Callum, out of breath, and feel my hands throbbing again.

"I knew he was capable of pulling that trigger. I couldn't let him do it, Ronin, I took the bullets out when they were trying to wake you up," he pants.

I nod: he might have saved my life but I wouldn't be here in the first place if it wasn't for him. "How did they know I was here?" I ask him.

He points to the roof. "CCTV in the atrium of the building. They saw you leaving with her and raised the silent alarm. That's how Pavel got here so quick. He phoned Sandy to tell him what happened. Luckily he was doing lines off the desk in my office at Mirrors, so I knew what was going on. He's in the office along the hall now, so if you are planning on getting out of here with her, you need to take care of him first."

"Get Pavel's attention and I'll take care of him," I say as I drag Sandy away and toss him against the wall behind the door.

Callum heads out the door and I go to Lisa who is still sitting on the floor. She looks petrified and exhausted.

"Ronin, I am scared, you said you wouldn't leave me," she slurs.

"Wait here, I'll be back in a moment. Don't move whatever you do, just stay put. It's going to be okay."

I plant a kiss on her head and wait for Callum to come back with the next instruction. I hear a thump against the door and Callum stumbles in, grasping at a knife in his stomach. He collapses into my arms with a groan and I can see blood seeping through his shirt.

"Fuck, Callum, can you hear me? Can you hear me, bud?" Seeing him hurt like this is devastating, despite everything he has done. His eyes are closed but I can see he is still breathing. Just as I lower him to the floor Pavel enters the room, holding a knife twice the size.

"Ok, fucker, just you and me, I see everything," he hisses, pointing at the camera in the corner of the ceiling.

I don't respond. Instead I put my hands up and try to clench a fist as best as I can. My hands are fucked and blood soaks through the dressings, coating Bill and Ben. He lunges at me and I avoid him, positioning myself to deliver a kick to his hand and then his face. He's stunned but doesn't drop the knife.

"You're going to die now, okay?" he taunts me with a smile, dancing in front of me, waving the blade.

I leap towards him, which takes him by surprise. He swings the knife in an arc so that it catches my arm, slicing my bicep, but I don't flinch. I can handle a couple of minor cuts if it means I can get close enough to grapple with him. I take another step forward and thrust my forearm out to stop his next attempt. With my other hand I grasp the knife and we wrestle for a second before I kick him violently in the nuts. He cries out and releases his grip on the knife. I have it. He tries to snatch it back, but I turn it as he seizes the blade, slashing his palm and producing a deep wound.

He lunges at me furiously so I manoeuvre behind him, slicing the tendons on the backs of his legs. He screams in pain collapsing to the floor. I pin him down to punch him until I can't feel my hands any more. By the time I am finished he has several broken teeth and a face that looks like a bowl of dog food.

I'm exhausted but I help Callum up and with my arm around him we hobble back through to the reception area.

"Callum, have you got Fred the Nurse's number?"

"S'on my phone, bud," Callum mumbles. He's getting weaker by the minute.

I take his phone out of his back pocket and look up Fred. I make the call, asking him to get here sooner rather than later promising a hefty call out fee.

Lisa tries to stand and I wave my hand at her to stop, then lift her up to carry her out to the Range Rover, still parked outside. I open the door and gently put her on the back seat.

"Lisa, I am getting you away from here now, just need one more minute."

Before I close the door I get my phone from my jacket that's still wrapped around her, and phone Davey.

"Jesus fucking Christ, Ronin, where the fuck are you?"

"It's a long story, Davey, I'm really sorry. There's been a whole load of trouble here."

"Okay, son, did you get her?"

"I did, she's in the car."

"There was never a doubt in my mind."

"I wish I could say the same. See you soon."

I close the door of the Range Rover and run back into the building. Callum is bleeding heavily but is still able to talk.

"Ronin, I'm sorry, I totally lost sight of everything. I could never choose them over you. I know it took a while for me to realise that but I came through in the end, eh?"

His near-death experience is making him sentimental, I'm not sure I feel the same.

"You did come through for me, thanks for that. It didn't need to happen in the first place though, Callum."

He nods but doesn't say anything as I apply pressure to his wound.

"Fuck me, that hurts," he moans. "I need to get the pigs involved in this, otherwise I'm dead."

"The police?" I ask him, surprised.

"Aye, the dodgy pigs. The ones that will let me off the hook but crucify these foreign nut jobs."

"What about me?"

Callum looks almost emotional.

"Never heard of you," he says, trying to smile but grimacing instead.

I hug him and help him relax onto a more comfortable chair.

"I'm disappearing, you'll never see me again," I tell him.

"Go on then, don't let me hold you back."

"Do something for me before I go?"

"What's that?"

"Help these girls get to safety."

"Why do you think I'm phoning the pigs?" he says.

There is a lump in my throat as I walk away from him, through the doors out of the building and into the range rover. I don't look back.

"We are leaving," I say to Lisa as I turn on the ignition. I ease the knuckle dusters from my swollen, bloody fingers and toss them onto the passenger seat. My hands are totally fucked; I can barely grip the steering wheel but we need to get away fast so I have to put up with it. I drive as quickly as I can through the streets of Edinburgh and onto the motorway, heading over the bridge towards Perth.

Every now and then I glance in the mirror to check on Lisa who is dozing in the back. I smile to myself with satisfaction. I was right about her. I knew I was.

35

As we head out of Edinburgh I call Davey from the car and he answers immediately.

"Where are you?" he asks.

"I'm just passing the zoo," I tell him.

"Okay, head for the airport and you will see a layby past the BP garage, just before the roundabout. Pull off there and you'll see me in your car. "

"Alright, see you soon."

Lisa makes a noise in her sleep as I negotiate the road. She's still sleeping when I check on her, so I continue until I see Davey in a layby in my new car. He pulls out in front of me, waving his hand out of the window and I follow him for five minutes, down the slip road for the airport and towards the long stay carpark.

We park side by side in a discreet corner of the multi-story car park and I realise his plan. Davey gets out of the car and walks over to us.

"Sorry for the delay, Davey, it got fucking messy in there, messier than I thought."

"I can imagine, Ronin. Knowing you, there would have been casualties."

"That's about the size of it. It was worth it, I got her back." I point to Lisa on the back seat and Davey peeks in.

"Is she okay?" he asks.

"She's drugged up on something, but she's coming round. I need to get her out of here. She needs proper care and attention."

Davey notices the state of my hands and then looks at my eye.

"Jesus, what a mess. Who is going to take care of that for you?" he asks with concern.

"I've probably got a few broken fingers. I can barely move my hands."

"Fuck, that's no good, let me see what I can put on them," he says as he unwraps my bandages and inspects the damage.

"I'd say you have two broken hands there, Ronin. The best I can do is patch you up and give you some painkillers, then you are on your own until you get to where you are headed."

"Thanks, Davey. Let me get organised and I can put Lisa in the car."

Davey cleans my hands with antiseptic wipes from the first aid kit in the Range Rover. He wraps my hands in bandages and gives me a couple of painkillers. It's the best we can do.

I open the door of my new car and recline the seat as far back as possible. Then I pull some tracksuit bottoms from my bag and slide them onto Lisa's legs and gently pull a T-shirt onto her top half. Like a mother cradling a baby, I scoop her up and lay her in the seat of my car, using a rolled-up sweatshirt as a pillow for her head. Davey helps by clicking her seatbelt into place. She complies with all our requests without saying very much. I know she's exhausted.

I close the door as quietly as possible and turn to Davey.

"You need to go, son. Get out of here and look after your woman, both of them."

I squint for a second, wondering who the other one is and I remember Jeannie. Fuck, I hope she is okay.

Davey takes the keys from me, locks the Range Rover and puts them in his pocket.

"Callum is involving the police," I say as we cautiously look around us.

Davey looks surprised.

"Means nothing, son. These crooks will be after your blood, even if Callum does protect himself with the pigs."

"I know. That's why I'm leaving."

Davey smiles at me and whispers, "Give me your phone, watch this."

Quickly I turn the phone off and hand it to him. I watch as he approaches a foreign couple, who seem a bit lost.

"Hello, can I help you find something?" he asks an un-suspecting couple, who are clutching a map and car rental paperwork.

The couple are speaking to Davey. He looks like he is helping them because he is pointing to the map then pointing in the air towards the city. As the couple look at the map, Davey tosses the car keys and my mobile into the ladies handbag, which is on the ground next to him. The fly bastard. I smirk as he bids them "Adieu" in a polite accent and skips back towards us.

"That was too easy," Davey quips as he winks with a smile.

I pat him on the back and tell him he is a genius.

Quickly, Davey jumps into the back seat of my car and I speed out of the carpark, stopping to pay the parking ticket on the way out before heading on to the M90. After twenty minutes, we reach the services at the Forth Road Bridge and I stop at the petrol station to let Davey out.

"Are you sure you want to get the bus?" I ask dubiously.

"Aye, that's fine. I'll get back into Kirkcaldy and head to the pub. I've got a bit of money to blow."

He smiles and winks at me.

I stand in front of him and take a deep breath.

"People rarely surprise me, Davey. I have underestimated you. You are a hero in my eyes and always will be. I will forever be in your debt. Thank you."

Davey smiles and hugs me very tightly.

"It was my pleasure, Ronin. I never had a son but if I could have had one, I would want him to be just like you."

We shake hands gently, careful of my injuries and I get back into the car.

"That's the last part of my disappearing act complete," I say as Davey waves me away.

I get back on the road and head towards Perth, then north through the lower highlands. We get stuck behind lorry after lorry, which tests my patience. I'm not going to relax until I get to the cottage and see Jeannie. When we arrive in Inverness, I stop briefly to pick up supplies, refuel and then get back on the road.

Every now and again, Lisa opens her eyes and stares at me, checking to see if I am still there.

I reach out to her hand and squeeze it. She tries to speak but I press my finger to my lips and tell her to save her energy. There is no rush. We have all the time in the world now.

My new M4 is a dream to drive; the automatic gears make the single-track roads easy to navigate. The road winds through hills, by lochsides and old abandoned bothies, with only a couple of sheep and an occasional tourist for company. Lisa is fully awake now and although she is quiet, I know she is taking everything in, trying to come to terms with the events of the last couple of weeks.

It's late evening and after hours of navigating roads showcasing the most beautiful scenery in the world, we come to the top of a small hill on the road. As we drive over it, we come upon the most spectacular view I have ever seen. Lisa looks at me, smiling in delight as she takes in the scene before her. To our left are the black silhouettes of the Craggan peaks which tower over the glen beneath us, forming a dramatic backdrop against the now crimson sky. Below us to the right is a causeway which crosses a large estuary leading out to the sea. There are cottages dotted at random on the hillside, each with its own croft leading down to the ocean. It's breathtaking.

"My place is over the headland," I say and point to the costal road on the far side of the causeway.

We drive down towards the coast taking the long bridge over the water. The car follows the road round by the sea, through a smattering of croft houses and past an old church. I turn right, away from the main road to follow a stone track which twists its way down to the sea.

"There it is," I say proudly and point to the small cottage at the end of the track, sitting above a small sandy bay over-looking the turquoise, yet freezing waters of the Atlantic. I can see smoke coming from the chimney, Jeannie has made it and the stove is on; she must be keeping herself busy.

I consider how I am going to explain everything to Jeannie. Who is this girl Lisa? Where did I find her? Why are we here? She will understand, though. At least I hope she will.

My priority now is to get Lisa into the cottage, make her comfortable and ensure she recovers properly. Very few people will know who I am in this part of the world. The local nurse, Kate, will remember me as I've had to call on her before after a couple of rough jobs. She thinks I'm a boxer who comes up here to recuperate after a fight: if she only knew. I'll get her to have a look at Lisa and hopefully help my fucked-up hands again too.

This is all I have and this is all I want. No more drugs, no more violence, just me, Jeanie and Lisa. The money should last us a long time, keep us living under the radar.

Maybe we will get a dog and some chickens.

As I arrive at the red front door of the cottage, I see Jeannie looking out of the window, smiling. I wave to her and look over to Lisa. She is staring back at me, with those beautiful eyes. She is weak, but she is also determined; I am confident she will be okay.

I sigh and feel like I'm taking my first breath since leaving Edinburgh.

"Stop sighing," Lisa says, with a cute smile on her face.

I kiss her on the lips and hold her hand again.

"You're safe now, don't worry."

She smiles again.

"I know," she says.

36

I STARE AT THE ROARING fire from my armchair, with my feet on a stool. The weather is dreary, wet and cold but despite that the view from the cottage is still stunning.

I lean forward and grab a lump of peat from the bucket next to the fireplace and place it on top of the dancing flames. Nothing beats the smoky smell of burning peat.

I lean back into my seat and pick up my glass of whisky to take a sip. The wind has picked up now and rain droplets scatter across the window pane as the fire flickers. A single lamp is on, giving the room a cosy glow. We don't have a TV; I find the outside world depressing. The only thing I really miss is the Sopranos.

The door to the lounge creaks open with the draft as I hear footsteps coming down the old, wooden stairs.

Looking every bit as beautiful as the day I met her, Lisa

gently enters the room closing the door behind her. She is just out of the bath, no make-up, no glamour, completely natural, wearing cosy pyjamas with a 'Friends" logo across the front from the TV show.

Her eyes twinkle, her skins glows and she smiles as she climbs onto the chair beside me, cuddling into me affectionately. She's safe, she's happy and we love each other. I feel like the luckiest man alive. I kiss her head and we listen to the sound of the logs crackling and enjoy the comforting heat in silence.

The last three months have not been easy but we are in a good place now.

Lisa's leg drops slightly, so I gently cradle her thigh to hold her in place on my lap. She looks down at my hand and gently runs her fingers over the scars that remain. She inspects them and then raises my hand towards her mouth, kissing it and holding it to her cheek.

The old clock on the mantel piece chimes as the hour reaches nine p.m. Jeannie went to bed an hour ago; she is tucked up in her own wee room on the ground floor. Her strength has been inspirational, just like when she found me and raised me as a child. She jumps into action and knows the right thing to do in any situation. Lisa loves her and the feeling is mutual. Jeanie even calls her 'Hen', a Scottish term of endearment which caused some confusion for Lisa to begin with but they have grown very close. They both mean so much to me.

I've tried my best to keep a low profile up here. The only people who know us is the nurse, Kate, and Bill, the owner of the local shop.

Kate is an amazing lady; she didn't ask any awkward questions and helped us out in a way that we could never thank her enough for. She was able to treat Lisa and get the narcotics out of her system without drawing unnecessary attention to us.

I knew Lisa was strong, but I didn't expect her to bounce back as quickly as she did. Her positivity and lust for life surprises me every day. My hands were broken, as Davey suspected, and they are taking a long time to heal, but they are on the mend.

I struggled to sleep for weeks. I suffered from anxiety, nightmares and paranoia which plagued me for at least the first two months in the cottage. It's eased off this last month because things are starting to feel more normal now. Lisa and I like to take walks along the beach. We go on short road trips to visit local beauty spots and of course we take Jeannie shopping, which is always entertaining for both of us.

I try not to think about Callum and the rest of the crew. I miss Davey because I feel like I didn't find out what kind of person he really was until it was too late. Sometimes I'm tempted to try to get in touch with him, but I know it's too risky. I didn't buy a new mobile phone and I don't have a landline in the cottage either: it's safer that way.

Lisa, as it turns out, is from Hungary. Her parents passed away when she was young, but she has cousins and a couple of close aunts. She sent word that she was okay but kept her location a secret; there is too much at stake to do any more. Maybe in time that will change.

I sip again at my whisky and savour the taste in my mouth before gently swallowing the amber liquid. Lisa reaches over and takes a sip from my glass too; she has learned to appreciate a good quality malt. And I thought it wasn't possible to love her any more!

"What do you want to do tomorrow?" I ask her as she stares, mesmerised, at the fire.

"Hmmm, I want to go to the beach we drove by last week, you know, the one with the campers? They had an orange tent, remember?

"Yes, the big beach with all the rock pools?"

"Yes, let's go there. Even if the weather is shit, I want to write our names in the sand."

I smile and kiss her on the head. She looks up and kisses me on the mouth.

This is fuckin' bliss. I love her. She knows I do and I know she loves me.

We made love for the first time two weeks ago. It was every bit as sensual and wonderful as I imagined it would be. We took time to explore each other, and afterwards fell asleep in each other's arms. I always wanted to feel like this with a girl but my old life couldn't make that possible. That's all behind me now.

The last of the whisky slides down my throat and I lay the empty glass on the side table next to me.

We stand up and Lisa leads me up the stairs by the hand, both of us creeping quietly to avoid waking Jeannie. Going to bed with Lisa is my favourite part of the day. We cuddle up and I listen to Lisa's breath as she falls asleep, I won't let myself go first. I'll then get up and check all the bolts are locked on the doors and windows closed tightly shut. It's neurotic and obsessive but I can't help it: I need to ensure we are all safe from anyone who might find us.

I drift off to sleep, listening to the sound of the rain hitting the window as the wind carries it from the sea to shore.

37

I WAKE IN THE MORNING to the sound of Jeannie singing to herself as she makes her breakfast. I look at the clock on the bedside table: its eight a.m., and she has been up for hours. She makes the cottage cosy and this is the first time, since I was a wee boy living at Jeanie's house, that I feel like I have a real home.

Life is good.

I open the curtains and let the sunshine pour into the room. Lisa is already up and I can hear the shower.

The decision to lie back on the bed is an easy one, I flop onto the mattress and close my eyes, hoping to get another ten minutes.

After wrestling me out of bed and ordering me into the shower, Lisa gets dressed and joins Jeannie downstairs. I catch up with them after getting ready and try to get a word in while I butter my toast.

"What's your plans today, Jeannie?" I ask quickly, grabbing a gap in the conversation.

"Well, now that the rain is off, I'm going to go for a walk to the shop and see Bill. He's got some nice bedding plants in this week. The garden needs a lot of work, Ronin; I'd like to make a start on it, so that when the summer comes it will look lovely."

"Nice, do you want me to take you?" I ask.

"No, no, it's just twenty minutes along the road and the walk does me good," she protests, waving me away with her hands.

"We're going to visit a nice beach we saw on the way back from Thurso last week," Lisa tells Jeannie as she places her used knife on her plate.

"Well, make sure you wrap up, those beaches can be hell of a windy," Jeannie orders as she collects plates from the table and takes them to the sink.

"Okay, we will see you in a while, we won't be long," I say as Lisa hands me my jacket and zips up her own.

The M4 would look out of place up here if it wasn't for the North Coast 500 being a popular route in the Highalnds. There are often impressive-looking vehicles on the road, touring the area, so most folk assume we are tourists and nothing more.

Twenty minutes along the narrow, uneven road, we see a collection of vehicles blocking the way through up ahead. A queue of several cars wait in both directions and as we get closer, I can see a vintage looking car with a slender model type girl draped over its bonnet. A photographer paces around, taking his shots, and a few assistants stand in the background looking on.

"What is this?" Lisa asks with curiosity.

"I'm not entirely sure," I reply as I bring the car to a stop.

Someone who looks like an assistant runs up to the car and I lower the window. He's wearing a black rain jacket and is holding the hood over his head with his hand. Before I can say anything, he begins talking.

"Sorry sir, we are doing a photo shoot for Aston Martin. We will be done in a couple of minutes. Just need to try and get these hills in the background before the mist and rain arrives, forecast is not looking good."

I smile and nod as I raise the window again. I glance up at the sky and although it's cloudy the sun is shining through at regular intervals.

Just as he promised, the photo shoot ends quickly and the model is wrapped up in a blanket and whisked into a van. The assistants in black jackets start waving the traffic past as the green vintage Aston Martin is driven into the next passing place to create space.

As we drive by, I wave to the assistant who spoke to us; he waves back and as he turns his head to go into the van, his hood drops. I stop mid-wave, I can't believe my fucking eyes.

On the base of his neck is a tattoo. An oval shape, with a cross in the centre.

My hand falls and my entire body tenses. I switch my gaze to the road and stare straight ahead, trying to drive away as quickly as possible. He didn't appear to be looking at me but nonetheless, I saw the tattoo, plain as day.

I can't say anything to Lisa and for the remainder of the journey to the beach, I begin to question myself. Did I really see what I thought I saw? Is the paranoia finally getting to me? Am I seeing things now?

Despite my best efforts I can't enjoy the walk along the beach and Lisa is all smiles when she finds a stick and writes our names inside a huge heart on the sand. Jeannie was right, it is windy and the clouds have now covered the sun completely, looking dark and foreboding, just like my mood.

"Are you okay, Ronin?" Lisa asks, looking worried as we get back into the car.

"I'm fine, just tired. I didn't sleep great last night, you know... the usual."

She nods, knowing I've had a rough few months, and leaves it there.

On the return trip we reach the area where the photoshoot was: it's long gone and there is nothing there now but a few sheep.

We arrive back at the cottage and everything seems to be as it should be. Jeannie is busy working away in the garden with her new plants and Lisa goes into the kitchen to make lunch for us all. I nip upstairs to check the rooms and head out into the garden to check the shed behind the house. Nothing out of place. Am I overthinking this?

I go back into the kitchen to fill a glass with cold water from the tap. I can see Jeannie through the window. She is kneeling over the soil, humming a tune to herself.

Fuck it, I was imagining things. There's no way that anyone could find me up here, absolutely no chance. Lunch is ready and Lisa calls out to Jeannie to come in. She bustles through the door and washes her hands in the sink, smiling.

"I'm getting there, son. Bill is selling some lovely pansies; they can handle this cold weather, you see?"

"That's good Jeannie," I say distractedly, taking a sip of my water.

"Oh, before I forget, I meant to show you this. A young foreign lassie was selling them outside the shop." Jeannie reaches into her garden apron to pull out a small bag. She opens the brown paper and removes what looks like a pack of greeting cards. She spreads them out on the table to admire the colourful flower designs on the front.

"She had lots of pretty cards so I thought there would be no harm in buying a pack as I might be able to write to the linoleum ladies again one day. They'll be missing their letters from me." Her voice falters for a second. "Anyway, she said to take this one too, no charge. They are lovely cards but look, this one's plain compared to the others," she tuts holding up a card.

"I only took it because she seemed so keen for me to have it."

I'm only half listening but I lean over the table to see what she is talking about. I feel instantly sick at what I see. Instead of a colourful flower, a black and white oval with a cross in the middle stares boldly back at me.

My glass slips from my hand and smashes on the floor.

"Who gave this to you?" I say, snatching it from her.

"I told you already, you aren't listening. I got it for nothing when I bought the other cards, it's fine, just a lassie trying to make a penny or two'.

I try to stop my hands from shaking as I open the card. It's blank inside. I study the image furiously, trying to make it disappear.

Lisa hears the commotion and appears behind me. She touches my arm as she looks over my shoulder. Breathing in sharply, she takes the card from me then slumps into a chair, looking defeated. Her big beautiful eyes look up at me with such sadness that I can't hold her gaze. Tearfully she whispers four words I hoped I'd never hear her say; "They have found us."

Printed in Great Britain
by Amazon